NO HEART
But Yours

ORLINDA VALLEY

SERIES

BOOK FOUR

Orlinda Valley

DONNA R. MADDEN

Printed in the United States of America

Paperback edition ISBN: 979-8-9939393-0-8

Cover Art by: Small Fry Marketing

Also By Donna R. Madden

More Than Enough series

More Than Enough

Your Love is Enough

You Are Enough

Orlinda Valley series.

No One But You

No Love Like Yours

No Place Like Home

This book is dedicated
to everyone who has been
lucky enough to find love.

NO HEART
But Yours

CHAPTER 1

SUSIE

The Tennessee June morning was not yet stifling with humidity, and the songs of the birds kept me company as I ran to town. I had enjoyed running when I lived in South Dakota, but since I'd been in Orlinda Valley, I hadn't run as much as I wanted to.

I promised my friends Kristy and Lilly that I'd meet them at Orlinda Valley Pharmacy for coffee and breakfast. Running meant I could avoid driving my brother's beat-up truck, and maybe one of them would give me a ride home. *Why run both ways?*

Farmland and scattered houses surrounded me as my shoes slapped the asphalt of Jones Road, the quiet back-country stretch where my brother Kai and his wife, Kora, lived, about three miles from town.

It didn't take long for my legs to feel the burn, and I had to focus on my breathing. I wasn't very athletic, but I'd taken to running in college and fallen in love. But what I called running was really a jog—sometimes fast, sometimes slow, but as long as I kept moving, that was all that mattered. It was the perfect time to leave my troubles behind and not stress over anything, and at six in the morning, it felt like the world belonged to me—the farmers, the cows, and possibly a deer.

That day, though, none of the usual morning peace could shake the uneasiness that crawled up my spine. The previous night, Kai and Kora had left for the airport to spend two weeks with Kora's father at his beach house in Florida, and I'd gotten a text from an unknown number that had my nerves on edge:

Be careful.

Two words—that was all. But as soon as I stepped outside this morning, I couldn't shake the feeling of being watched.

I sucked in a deep breath and cranked up my music. *Focus on the run, Susie.*

Soon, I was on the sidewalk in town. The town was like something in a Hallmark movie. Brick buildings lined the street, which consisted of the typical places in small-town America—a post office, a fire station, a police station, a library I had yet to visit, a small strip mall which was the home of Shear Perfection hair salon, a coffee shop, a clothing boutique, and a realtor's office. I slowed to a walk as I approached Orlinda Valley Pharmacy—a historic building that had been a part of the town since its founding in the early 1900s. Nancy and Pat Johnson owned the pharmacy, serving breakfast and simple lunches.

When I swung open the door, the scent of bacon, the hum of voices, and the clatter of dishes greeted me.

"Good morning, Susie," Mrs. Johnson said.

"Good morning," I answered, smiling warmly.

Kristy and Lilly sat in one of the wooden booths which filled the center of the small building. Thank God they were already there. I needed to talk to them about the text and my insane feelings of being watched. They'd have great advice and help me to avoid overthinking anything.

Well, Lilly would give good advice and lend a useful ear. Kristy, on the other hand, would drop some smart-ass remark about my having a secret admirer. She was tons of fun but not the most helpful.

I started toward their table, but my feet became glued to the ground when I saw who was sitting with them—Lilly's brother, Lance.

Lance Hartley was the biggest egotistical asshat of Orlinda Valley. In high school—decades ago—he'd been the town football star. Now he taught PE at Orlinda Valley High, coached the football team, and was the most wanted man by every twenty- to forty-year-old woman in town.

I puffed out a breath. "Morning." I said to Lilly and Kristy.

"Hey there, Susie," Lance said as he got up from the booth. He stood at least six four and had short brown hair, blue eyes, and a smile that made all the women melt under his gaze. Well, every woman but those of us with a speck of sense and who were not impressed by cocky, self-righteous assholes.

Lance also sported an impossible-to-ignore athletic body that looked damn good in anything he put on. That morning, he wore basketball shorts and a shirt that was cut up the sides. I tried my best to ignore the sculpted muscles that peered out and screamed, *Touch me.*

His eyes gleamed with seduction as they trailed down my body then back up.

My skimpy black running shorts and white tank top seemed a little too revealing.

He gave me what he considered his sexy smirk.

To me, it was stomach-churning. "I wasn't talking to you, but whatever," I said as I slid into the booth.

Kristy and Lilly chuckled.

Lance slid back into the booth with that infuriating grin.

"Wipe that smirk from your face. No one here's impressed by whatever you think of yourself," I said as I opened my menu.

"Are you sure, sweetness?" Lance asked. "I caught you giving me the side-eye when you sat down."

I sighed heavily. Already on edge, I was not in the mood to deal with him.

Lilly shot an apologetic look my way then turned to her brother. "Lance, be nice."

"I'm always nice."

Kristy laughed. "Are you sure you're Lance Hartley? The pain-in-the-ass older brother of my best friend, who always did his best to make sure our lives were a living hell?"

"Y'all were in middle school when I was in high school. And annoying."

The server came to the table.

"Hi, Trena," Lance said.

I could have sworn she blushed. *What the hell? Is there no woman but me who's immune to him?*

Lilly and Kristy placed their orders.

I was still looking at the menu.

"Two stacks of blueberry pancakes, extra butter for the lady," Lance said. "Two coffees, cream, and two waters."

"I can order for myself," I snapped. *How the hell does he know what I like for breakfast?*

"Relax, sunshine. I'm just trying to speed things along. Wouldn't want to keep you from whatever important business you have today."

First, he called me sweetness, then sunshine. I hated nicknames. "The name's Susie, and as a matter of fact, I do have important business."

"Let me guess—reorganizing your sock drawer? Alphabetizing the spice rack?" His eyes sparkled with amusement. "Or maybe planning your next lecture on why I'm such a terrible human being?"

"That one would be popular."

"You know, most women find my charm irresistible."

"Most women have questionable taste," I said and answered Kristy's laughter with my own.

"Ouch." Lance pressed a hand to his chest in mock pain. "And here I thought we were bonding."

"This is being nice, Lance?" Lilly asked. "Just be quiet, please."

"See? This proves my point," Kristy added. "He's still a pain in the ass."

"Change isn't in his wheelhouse," Lilly said as Trena appeared with our orders, her gaze held on Lance's longer than necessary.

I focused on cutting my pancakes into perfect squares, doing anything to avoid looking Lance's way. He didn't need any boosts to his ego.

"Interesting technique," he said, his voice dropping lower. "Very... methodical. I bet you approach everything in life with the same careful attention to detail."

I glared at him and took a huge bite of my pancake. If I didn't chew on something, I'd chew up the inside of my cheek. After swallowing, I said, "Some people appreciate doing things properly."

"Oh, I definitely appreciate it when someone takes pride in what they do. When they complete things slowly and methodically and know exactly what they're doing with their hands."

"God, you're a pig," I said.

Kristy nearly choked on her orange juice.

"Lance, shut up." Lilly tossed a sugar pack at him.

He caught it without missing a beat. "I'm just talking about pancakes. What did y'all think I meant?" His wicked smile completely undermined the innocent expression on his face.

I focused on my food and eating, trying to ignore the frustrating flop of my stomach. *Lance and his attitude. What the hell.*

After we'd finished, Lance stood and tossed his napkin onto his empty plate. "This was a delicious breakfast. Thank you, ladies. Susie, I'll see you later."

"Not if I can help it," I said under my breath.

He tossed money onto the table. "Sis, Kristy, see yas later. Susie, try not to miss me too much." He winked and walked away with the confident swagger that made half the town swoon.

I stared at his retreating form, my pulse racing despite every rational thought in my head. Lance Hartley was trouble wrapped in a devastatingly handsome package.

"It's never boring when he's around," Kristy said, grabbing her purse. "Thanks for breakfast. I gotta run. I'll stop by your house and pick you up later tonight," she said to me.

"And I need to get going also," Lilly added, standing.

"Wait. What? You're both leaving? Would either of you give me a ride home?"

"I will," Lilly said, getting out of the booth. "I've got to make a quick stop to see my mother at Shear Perfection first."

"Perfect." I put money on the table for my part of the bill and hopped up. "I appreciate it."

CHAPTER 2

SUSIE

Lilly dropped me off at the house after a quick trip to the hair salon and a stop at the Dollar General. I watched her drive away then went to take care of the goats.

F-ing, really? I froze. Kora's three goats, Percy, Jackson, and Baby Goat, bounced and twirled like a pack of lunatics around my car—in the driveway, far from their pasture where they belonged.

Kora made taking care of her miniature farm of chickens, ducks, and these crazy goats seem like a simple task, but it was anything but. She must be some kind of goat whisperer.

"Stupid goats. What are you doing?" I groaned as I approached them, my head in my hands.

"Don't. You. Dare!" I hollered at the white goat with brown and black splotches and black ears, who eyed my car suspiciously. "Hell no." I rushed forward, flapping my arms in the air like I was going to take flight. "Don't you dare, Percy... or Jackson. Whoever the hell you are. Stay off my—"

But I wasn't in time. He jumped onto the hood and did a little tap dance in a circle.

"Damn goat!" I spun around at the sound of hooves on gravel. "No!" I pointed at the twin of the one on my car and shooed him away. "Do not follow your brother. That's my car. Not a jungle gym."

He twitched his head and meandered to the grass. *Good.* That was a safer option anyway.

I sighed heavily, crossed my arms, and stared up at the sky. Goat number one was on my car. Goat number two was eating the grass.

Where the hell is goat number three?

Suddenly, a hard head butted my thigh.

I dropped my gaze, and there stood a sweet midnight-black goat staring up at me, a pure, innocent look in his blue eyes. I patted him on the head. "Baby Goat, please be the good one. Don't follow these heathens."

His head cocked to the side as if to say, "I'll be good. I promise."

"See?" I rubbed him behind the ears. "You're a sweet boy. Please go back to the pasture."

He bleated and hopped off after whichever one was eating grass, my car forgotten about for the time being–by those two at least.

My car.

I turned toward it, and the goat was lying on the hood, his attention focused on me.

"Please get down. I'll buy you a snack of animal crackers and carrots if you do."

He baaed as he jumped to the ground and strutted off toward his brothers.

"Thank God." I leaned heavily on the hood and wiped the sweat from my brow. *Now that I've saved my car, how will I corral them back where they belong?*

The crunch of tires on gravel was music to my ears. I crossed my fingers and tilted my head toward the sky. "Please let it be a knight in shining armor to help with this chaos."

I turned as a silver Dodge Ram came to a halt, and my shoulders slumped. Well, it wasn't a knight in shining armor. Instead, it was a silver chariot with my personal headache behind the wheel—Lance, the last person I wanted to see.

I stood tall and crossed my arms. *He will not see how much trouble these goats have been.*

"You look a little worse since I last saw you," he said as he strutted toward me in basketball shorts and an Orlinda Valley football T-shirt, his hair looked slightly damp, like he had showered, and had a wind-blown, disheveled look to it.

Yep, he looked good in anything he put on. That shirt had to be two sizes too small. I could make out every crest and valley of his six-pack.

Stop looking.

"You okay?" he asked. "You look like you've come out on the wrong end of a fight with a wild animal."

I laughed. "You're not far off." So much for seeming to have things under control.

Lance shrugged and pointed toward the goats over in the grass. "Do you know the goats are out?" His Southern drawl was as thick as he was broad.

I forced my eyes to stay on his, which glistened with laughter. I cleared my throat and pushed off my car. "Thank you, Captain Obvious." I was exhausted and frustrated. Even Lance's attitude couldn't make things worse at this point.

I strolled to his truck and sat hard on the oversize bumper, scrubbing my hands over my face. "It's been one day. Well, almost a day. And I can't do this." I waved my hands in the air. "I don't know how Kora deals with them." I pointed at the goats—or where the goats had been a second ago. "Oh my God. Where'd they go now?" I trudged toward the grassy area.

"You don't want to know," Lance answered.

I spun toward him. His beefy arms crossed over his chest.

I followed his gaze. "It can't be." I stooped and leaned my elbows on my knees.

I should run toward them and get them out of Kora's rose garden, but they would just go somewhere else and eat something else. "Those three are devils. Devils in cute little furry bodies."

"You're not wrong," Lance said with a chuckle. "How'd they get out?"

"I fed them, and I guess I didn't close the gate all the way. I really don't have a clue."

"It's all good. Come on. If we work together, we can get them to the gate no problem." He went to his truck, took out a brown bag, and pulled a Ziplock baggie from it. "Apple slices. What goat can resist? We can coax them toward the gate. I'll get their attention. You walk behind them. They'll follow me, and you can corral them and keep them from wandering off. We'll get them in and close the gate. Easy peasy."

"Easy peasy? Is that something you say often?" I raised my eyebrows.

"Got it from Madeline," he said as he walked toward the goats.

Madeline, Lance's niece, was a five-year-old spitfire, just like her friends, Lena, and Darcie.

He threw me a couple of slices of apple. "In case you need to get their attention."

Lance clicked his tongue, and the goats turned toward him. He gave a piece of apple to one of them, and the others instantly became interested, and the journey to the pasture began.

I followed, holding my arms out wide, with the apple slices cupped in my palm, in case they wandered off—like my arms could stop them.

Lance turned around, keeping the apple slices behind him, and the goats got closer and closer. *They're getting close enough to bite his ass. That would be awesome.* I chuckled.

"What's so funny?" he asked, walking backward again. The goats were close enough that they grabbed the apples from his hand. He stopped walking and fed them.

"They were getting close to you, and I could picture them taking a large bite out of your butt."

"Oh, so you were checking out my ass?" he asked with a crooked smile that made my stomach churn.

"God," I huffed and walked ahead of him, waving my apples in the air. "Why did you stop by anyway?"

"Kai asked Jamison to check on you. Jamison and Lilly were busy, so Jamison asked me."

I rolled my eyes and started a slow jog.

"You look—"

"Shut up and occupy those goats!" I hollered as Baby Goat wandered off. Fortunately, he didn't go far, because the leader of the pack was following me. I held my apple slices low. The lead goat picked up his pace, and the other two followed. Soon, we were all moving at a nice jog toward the pasture.

I opened the gate wide and stepped aside. As soon as Lance pushed them through, I closed and latched the gate properly and followed the train to the barn. The twins ate from Lance's hands, and Baby Goat came over to me.

Stooping, I fed him the apple I had and rubbed his head. "Good boy."

He jumped up and caught me off guard when his hooves landed on my thigh. "Shit. Baby goat," I muttered just as the heel of my shoe caught on something behind me, and I stumbled back with a squeal and fell straight into the water trough.

"Susie, holy shit!" Lance laughed. "Are you okay?"

I held up my arms to show him I was good but sank farther into the trough.

He reached out and grabbed my hand, pulling me up.

Flailing, I smacked a hand onto his chest for balance.

Sweet mother of all things—why do his pecs have to be this... substantial? And dear God, he smelled like he'd been crafted by some woodland sex deity. Pine, cedar, and pure masculine perfection wafted off him like nature's own aphrodisiac.

I swallowed as his eyes traveled down my body, hesitated briefly, then finally met mine. They swam with laughter.

Though I leaned away from him, I couldn't quite pull my hand from his warmth as a horrid stench reached my nose.

Is that me? I reeked like I had been wrestling goats in a barnyard sauna. June in Tennessee wasn't far off.

"You okay there?" His voice rumbled through his chest, vibrating against my hand like a tuning fork designed to scramble my remaining brain cells.

Forcing my hand from his chest, I took a step back, looked down at myself, and gasped. Not a patch of my clothes was dry, but my tank top and my thin white running bra were what made my heart stop and my neck warm with embarrassment. Since I was drenched, they were see-through. The thin material did nothing to cover the girls. It was like I had just entered a frat party's wet T-shirt contest.

"I'm good," I said as I crossed my arms and felt warmth crawl up my neck. Maybe he hadn't noticed.

His eyes rose to mine, and his eyebrows shot up.

Great. I'd only been in town a few weeks, and I'd already flashed my girls in front of the town's biggest playboy.

"I need to go shower and change," I muttered, pointing toward the house.

"Totally understand," he said, backing up like a gentleman, but his smirk told a different story. "You go first. I'll lock the gate."

"Thanks," I said and speed-walked away, dripping shame with every step.

Behind me, the fence rattled shut.

"Susie?" Lance called.

I froze yet didn't turn around. I was not going to give him another show. *What more could he have to say?*

"I'll let Kai know you're doing fine."

I squeezed my eyes tight during the long pause. Something else was coming. *I should keep walking. Act as if I hadn't heard him.*

"I'll also tell him you enjoy wet T-shirt contests in secret." The snicker in his voice was impossible to miss.

I huffed, mortified, and stomped off.

Sure, he's damn good looking. But he's also a smug, smirking ass.

CHAPTER 3

SUSIE

"Has Lance ever been a decent human?" I asked Kristy as she lounged on the oversize chair in my bedroom.

Kristy snorted. "How long have you been in Orlinda Valley? Have you not already figured that out for yourself?"

"I've not been here long, yet the Lance I've seen is far from decent," I said as I put simple diamond stud earrings in my ears.

"Yeah, well, that's long enough to figure out that yes, Lance is a total ass, and I say that with love. He's a total ass whose heart is usually in the right place, and he'll stick up for those he's close to."

"Or he'll be a rude shit if he doesn't like you." I thought back to Kora and Kai's wedding and how awful he'd been toward Summer. Thankfully, Rowan had been there to put him in his place.

"True, but he's always been nice to me," Kristy said, rummaging through my jewelry box.

"He's never hit on you?"

"God, no. I'm one of Lilly's best friends. He's like an annoying big brother." She handed me a pair of dangling earrings. "Even though

I'd be blind if I didn't notice how hot he is... and Jamison for that matter. Let's just say Lilly was always the lucky one."

"I don't know," I said as I replaced my stud earrings with the dangles. "Lance's attitude mutes his looks." My gaze met hers, and I shook my head. "I have a hard time believing he's never hit on you or at least flirted. He's such an arrogant ass, and you're... you."

Kristy was drop-dead beautiful with her long blond locks and to-die-for blue eyes—everything that attracted men's attention. She was the complete opposite of me with my stick-straight dark-brown hair and clear silver-blue eyes. While she had all the men in Orlinda Valley lining up, I only seemed to attract the egotistical jerks.

She raised her eyebrows. "Are you ever going to tell me what happened between you two today? There had to be more than him helping you with the goats. You've been fuming since I got here and haven't stopped bringing him up."

I pulled my bottom lip between my teeth as I slid on a white button-up top and stared at my reflection in the mirror. I shook my head. *White. Hell no. Not going to happen.* I shucked it off, tossed it onto the floor, and stalked back to my closet.

"What was wrong with that?" Kristy asked. "You know we're going to Jerry's Pub. Not a parent-teacher conference."

I grabbed a black button-up off its hanger. *Perfect.* I slipped it on.

"You've really got to learn to put on shorts. It's June in Tennessee and hot enough to melt the mascara right off your face."

I gave her a slow sideways glance. "Seriously?"

"Or I could say it's hotter than a witch's titty in a brass bra. Either way, you totally understand what I'm saying."

I burst out laughing. "You're ridiculous. Where the hell do you come up with these things?"

"Doesn't matter," she said, brushing off my laughter. "Anyway, it wouldn't hurt if you dressed a little sexy once in a while. Show off that amazing body of yours."

I glanced at my reflection in the mirror. I had on khaki slacks with the black button-up tucked in. I pulled my hair back in a tight ponytail at the nape of my neck. "This is what I always wear."

"Exactly," Kristy said. "Always dressed nicely, never comfortable."

I snorted at that.

"What?" She turned me toward her.

"I dressed casually today when I met you and Lilly for breakfast."

"See? And you still looked amazing."

"Yeah, well, I still had that on when I went out to take care of the furry devils in the pasture and when Lance got here."

"And it was obvious he couldn't take his eyes off you at breakfast. Did he say something when he was here?"

I ignored her comment and crossed my arms. "It's not what he said. It's what he saw after he pulled me out of the water trough."

"You fell in the water trough?" Her hands flew to her mouth to cover a laugh, but I waited for her to connect the dots and complete the picture.

She sucked in a deep breath, and her jaw dropped. "Oh. My. God. You were still in your white tank top?"

I nodded and stepped out of my pants and into a pair of cut-off shorts.

"You had a bra on, though." Her eyes widened. "How see-through was it?"

"Well, you could say there wasn't much left to the imagination." I unbuttoned the bottom button of my shirt and tied it in a knot.

Kristy wiped the tears that rolled down her cheeks from her laughter.

I huffed and chuckled to myself.

She took a deep breath, and her laughter calmed, but when we made eye contact. She pinched her lips tight and snorted.

"Whatever. I'm glad I can entertain you. Here. Is this better?" I was wearing faded jean shorts with frayed edges, a fitted cami under the black button-up, and white sandals.

"Perfect," Kristy said between breaths. She held up her hand. "There, all better." She focused on me, scrutinized my outfit, and gave me a nod of approval. "Casually sexy and covered up so Lance won't get any more peep shows."

I rubbed my forehead. "Will I ever be able to live this down?"

"Not if I can help it. That is epic."

I rolled my eyes. "No. It was humiliating. Do you think he'll be there tonight?"

Kristy nodded. "Oh, definitely. It's Friday night. Where else would he be?"

"Wonderful. Just what I need. Him and his thoughts all night."

"How bad could it be? Lance is the town's most eligible bachelor."

"Not to mention Orlinda Valley's biggest playboy," I pointed out. The conversation needed to end.

I grabbed my purse, but Kristy stopped me and released the clip from on top of my head, and my hair fell to my shoulders.

She gave it a quick fluff. "There. Lance likes long, flowing hair. Show off those amazing silky locks."

"How do you know what he likes?"

She shrugged. "I don't."

I turned back to the mirror and studied my reflection. I looked good... casual with a touch of sexy.

Kristy met my eyes in the mirror and smiled widely. "Perfect and drop-dead gorgeous." She linked her arm with mine. "Lance will drool in his boots."

"He can drool all he wants, but there's no way in hell he's getting any of this," I said as we walked out the front door and I locked up.

I didn't need any extra attention from Lance, or anyone like him. I had moved here to get away from an overbearing, egotistical asshole, and there was no way in hell would I get involved with another one.

"If not him, maybe Trevor?"

I narrowed my eyes. "Why would you think I'd be interested in Trevor?"

She shrugged. "Don't know. He's good-looking, sweet, hot, and available."

I climbed into the front seat of Kristy's car. She was right. Trevor was all those things and far from an egotistical ass. "Maybe he is, but I'm not interested in getting into a relationship anytime soon."

"I feel like I finally have a kindred spirit," Kristy said as she pulled out of the driveway.

"What do you mean?"

"I need someone not interested in being in a relationship. Lilly and Rose are both married with kids. Don't get me wrong. I love them both, but it's good having someone I can just hang out with. No guys getting in the way. No children to keep us from getting crazy drunk."

"Crazy drunk? I'll have a few drinks, but I don't get drunk."

"Well, then, you can be the DD," Kristy said as she turned onto the road.

I watched the countryside pass out the window. My life had been so different since I'd arrived—quiet, slow, and full of laughter. Getting to know Kora and seeing Kai happy was a breath of fresh air. He'd worked hard to move on from his past, and the life he and Kora had made was exactly what he deserved.

My thoughts drifted back to childhood and our home life, which involved fights between our dad and Kai. Despite this, Kai made sure Sebastian and I stayed in school and did our work.

"Hey," Kristy said. "Where'd you go?"

I sat up and looked around as we pulled into the parking lot at Jerry's Pub. "I keep forgetting everything's so close. Seems like you can get everywhere in town in ten minutes or less."

"That's true," Kristy agreed. "I never thought I'd stay here after high school. I always wanted to get out of this small town and see the world. But as you can tell, that never happened."

The parking lot was full, as it was dinnertime. I waved to a couple who were climbing into their car. It was strange being known, but it felt good. "Lilly and Rose will be here, right?" I asked as we started for the entrance of the pub.

"Lilly is. Rose and Nolan are going to Nolan's parents."

When we entered, the chatter of voices and music greeted us.

The pub, which was owned by a group of firefighters, had a relaxed atmosphere perfect for family dinners and friendly get-togethers. Firefighter paraphernalia, Orlinda Valley High School colors, championship banners, and pictures of Orlinda Valley sport teams decorated the area.

High-top tables sat in the bar, and rectangular tables and booths were in the main dining area. The large patio door was pulled tight to keep the air conditioning in, but plenty of people still enjoyed the outdoor activities—cornhole, dancing, volleyball, and picnic tables.

"Yay, you're here!" A head full of red curls plowed into me. It was Darcie, Jamison's daughter.

Madeline, Lilly's daughter, greeted Kristy with a gentle hug.

"Well, hello, you two," I said, hugging them.

They grabbed our hands and pulled us to a table.

"We got them, everyone," Darcie announced.

"Yep," Madeline said. "We made sure they couldn't miss us."

I chuckled. "Trust me, girls. We could never miss you two."

"No kidding," Lilly said as she gave us both hugs.

Kristy hopped into the seat next to Lilly with a snicker.

I shot her a glare, but she avoided my eyes, and I took the only seat left—by Lance.

As soon as I sat down, I turned my back to him. "How are you feeling, Lill?" She was four months pregnant with twins and was still having bouts of morning sickness.

"Tired, exhausted, starving." She sighed.

"Beautiful," Jamison finished and gave her a kiss.

An exhausted smile filled Lilly's face, and Jamison tucked a strand of hair behind her ear. A private connection flitted between them, then he scooted his chair closer to hers and draped his arm over it.

They were so sweet together. They'd gotten married in January, each their second time, and with the two girls, they had an immediate family. Now, twins were going to be added to it. Excitement bubbled up inside me. "I can't wait to meet the twins," I said. "Sebastian and I had such a unique bond growing up. It will be fun to watch theirs form."

"You hear stories about twins being able to read each other's minds. Were you and Sebastian like that?" Kristy asked.

I shook my head. "No, but it wasn't like he gave me much freedom. He was always in my business. It was a good thing I never really dated anyone in high school. Between him and Kai, it would have been a nightmare."

"Have you heard from Sebastian recently?" Jamison asked.

"No. We try, but with him running on the army's schedule, it's hard to get our times to line up. We text a lot, though."

"Mommy, did you date anyone in high school?" Madeline asked as she climbed onto Lilly's lap.

"Yes, she did," Jamison cut in.

"And we made sure he treated her right," Lance continued. "If he didn't, we promised to take it out on the field."

"Was it you, Jamison?" Madeline asked.

Jamison laughed and brushed Lilly's hair from her shoulders. "Not me, princess. I wasn't that lucky."

"Didn't you think Lilly was beautiful, Daddy?" Darcie asked.

Jamison and Lilly's eyes locked, and more unspoken words passed between them.

"I think you're beautiful, Mommy," Madeline said.

"Thank you, baby," Lilly said as she hugged Madeline close.

"Yep, you're glowing," Darcie added as she squeezed under Lilly's arm. Lilly wrapped them both in a hug with a soft chuckle.

"Glowing? Darcie, where'd you hear that?" Lance asked with a chuckle.

I laughed and glanced at him. When our eyes met, he gave me that crooked half-smile I was sure he thought was sexy. I grabbed a glass of water and gulped it down.

"My grammy," Darcie said.

"Your grammy *is* a fun person," I said.

"She is," Madeline said. "And she teaches us a lot of things."

"Oh, I'm sure she does," Jamison said as food came to the table.

"Here you go, sugars," Barb, the server, said as she placed our order on the table. Chicken tender baskets for Madeline and Darcie, a basket of sliders along with fries, and a large plate of nachos.

"Thanks, Barb," Lilly said as she passed plates around. "I hope y'all are hungry. I couldn't decide what I wanted, so I ordered all of this." She waved her hands over the food. "Eat what you want." She grabbed the sliders from Lance's grasp. "Sorry, Lance. These are mine."

"You can't even share one with your brother?" he asked, sulking.

Lilly glanced at him, shrugged, and offered him one of the five sliders. "Here. This and some fries. The rest are mine."

Jamison chuckled. "I ordered us a pizza. Here it comes."

I glanced up and froze with a fry halfway to my mouth.

"One pizza with everything. Hold the olives," Terry said as he placed it on the table.

I kept my eyes glued to the plate in front of me as my heart fell in my chest.

Terry was my father. Even though I'd been here about a month, I still wasn't used to having him around.

Kai had hoped to be done with our father when he left Atlanta, but it wasn't long after Kai moved here that Terry tracked him down. Even though Terry had started AA and was no longer drinking, I couldn't forget the past. I was proud he'd given up alcohol, and glad Kai was able to forgive him, but I wasn't ready. Nowhere near it.

"Hi, Susie." His voice sounded like he'd spent most of his life smoking and drinking too much, because that was exactly what he'd done. That and forgetting he had children. He was my father in biology only. Kai was the one who had taken care of us and done whatever was necessary to make sure we had what we needed—clothes, electricity, food, water.

I slowly turned to him and nodded. I didn't want to talk to him, but I wouldn't be totally rude.

He smiled awkwardly and walked away.

Tension grew around the table and squeezed the fun out of the room. Between Terry and not wanting to make eye contact with Lance, so far, this Friday night was exactly what Kristy had said it was going to be—epic.

Break the ice, Susie. "Thanks for your help today, Lance."

"No problem. Did those damn goats finally stay in their place, or did they give you another visit?"

"Bad word, Uncle Lance," Darcie said with her hand out.

"Yep, give us money," Madeline added, wiggling her fingers toward him.

Lilly, Kristy, and I laughed. Jamison paid Darcie one dollar every time he said a curse word. From what I'd been told, it was his way of keeping his language in check. Darcie, being the adorable little manipulator she was, had quickly taken advantage of the situation and included every adult close to her in the deal. Since she and Madeline were now sisters, it cost the perpetrator two dollars for not watching their language.

Lance shot a glare at Jamison and Lilly and then gave his attention back to the girls. "What did I say?"

"The D-word," Madeline said.

"Yep, it's a bad word, so you owe us money. You know the rules," Darcie said, her palm up, fingers still wiggling.

"Why would you bring them here?" Lance asked Jamison. "How am I supposed to have fun with these two grammarians at the table?"

"What's a grammarian?" Darcie asked Madeline.

Madeline shrugged. "Don't ask me. I just finished kindergarten like you."

"Mommy, what's a grammarian?" Madeline asked.

"Ask Uncle Lance. I'm sure he knows."

He pointed at Madeline. "Don't ask me anything. I won't answer."

Jamison said, "Sorry if they're keeping you honest. You know they've got to eat, and as we're their parents, it's our job to feed them. Maybe one day, you'll finally find someone and realize there's more to life than having fun."

Darcie stuck out her bottom lip. "We're not fun, Daddy?"

Jamison looked over at Lilly, who rolled her lips over her teeth to hold back a laugh. "Princess, you are the most fun. It's just that—"

"It's just that I want to have a different kind of fun than we can have with you two around," Lance broke in.

"You don't like us, Uncle Lance, do you?" Madeline pouted.

"Yeah, you're hurting our feelings." Darcie looked at Madeline and put her arm over her shoulders as Madeline laid her head on Darcie's. They both pushed out their bottom lips. I could have sworn I saw them quiver.

"Not true." Lance jumped up and wrapped his arms around them both. "Come on. You two know I love you." He kissed their heads and pulled two one-dollar bills from his wallet.

They both gave toothy grins and kissed him on each cheek. All signs of impending tears vanished.

Lance was a difficult guy to understand. When he was around the girls, he was always so softhearted and loving. He never hesitated to play any game they asked or even have a tea party in the backyard. They had him wrapped around their little fingers—hell, their entire hands.

But when it came to women, his conceited, snotty self appeared. He'd been in Orlinda Valley too long and thought every woman wanted to take him to bed. His attitude was annoying, and he'd been hitting on me since I'd been here.

And the show I'd put on earlier sure didn't help.

He was exactly what I needed to avoid. The last thing I wanted was another ego-tripped man to stomp on my heart, but that was always what I seemed to be attracted to.

CHAPTER 4

LANCE

"Mommy," Madeline said as she wiggled in her chair. "We've gotta pee."

Darcie nodded like a bobblehead doll, and they both jumped from their chairs.

"Let's go," Lilly said as she followed. "Be right back."

Susie and Kristy stood.

"Where are you two going?" I asked.

"To the bathroom, of course," Kristy said. "Can't let them go alone."

I watched them walk away and shook my head. "I'll never understand women."

"No shit, but one day, you might realize it's worth trying," Jamison said.

"Meaning?" I asked, then took a sip of my beer.

"Come on. It's so obvious you've got it bad for Susie."

"Bullshit. What the hell are you talking about?"

"You flirt with her like you're a middle school kid. Always pushing her buttons and pissing her off."

What the fuck? I downed my beer. "I don't flirt with her."

"You're right. You just watch her obsessively."

I shook my head and turned away from Jamison. He was so full of shit.

My eyes fell on Susie. She wasn't in the bathroom. Instead, she sat at the bar, talking to Trevor.

I narrowed my eyes as she leaned forward and seemed to hang on to his every word. Trevor was a fireman and one of the co-owners of Jerry's Pub. I knew him well, as he and Rowan, Jamison's youngest brother, were best friends.

Trevor hadn't had an easy early life and had been raised by his grandparents. He still lived on their land, worked on the family farm, and was Orlinda Valley's favorite son. There was no shortage of people who loved the man, and from what I could tell, it seemed like some women did too.

Susie's laugh rang out above the noise of the crowd. *How can he keep her attention and get that kind of response when all she gives me is attitude? What the hell does Trevor have that I don't?*

I downed my beer, my eyes glued to her.

"Hey." Jamison smacked me on the back of the head.

"What the fuck was that for?" I asked, pushing him away and rubbing my head.

"Again, you're watching her like an obsessive creeper. Is there something I need to know?"

I chuckled and shook my head. "Nope, unfortunately, nothing. She hardly gives me the time of day."

"And that's a surprise, why?" Jamison asked as he leaned forward.

I scrunched my face. "What are you insinuating?"

"Well, you've got to admit you made a pretty shitty first impression."

He was talking about how I'd acted at Kora and Kai's wedding last October. Summer, Rowan's girlfriend, and I had never liked each other. I was rude, Rowan and I had words, and Rowan broke my nose. "Rowan and I are over that, and I've apologized to Summer. It's in the past."

"Well, maybe you need to realize that some people have skeletons they're trying to deal with, and forgetting the past is not that simple."

"How does the way I acted back in October have anything to do with Susie?"

"She sees you as selfish and conceited. I'm sure watching you act like an ass paints a grim picture."

"Well, how could I possibly know that? Hell, I haven't even figured out how to deal with my own skeletons."

Jamison took a sip of his beer before he answered. "You're not your father. You know that. You were lucky enough to have role models to look up to. Hell, Charles, who was an amazing role model, basically raised you, not to mention my dad. He took you under his wing even before Charles was ever in the picture. You need to get that chip off your shoulder so you can move on. You're thirty-six, and the longest relationship you've had was what? Six months? And that was here recently."

"Yeah, well, Jayla wasn't the one."

Jamison raised his eyebrows and lowered his chin.

"God, I hate when you do that."

"Whatever. I haven't kept you around as a best friend for nothing. I wish you could show a woman that other side of you. Show someone you aren't a total dick."

I gritted my teeth and pushed away from the table. My gaze traveled to the bar again. Susie was sitting on a stool, and she and Trevor were still deep in conversation.

I turned back to Jamison. "I'm not a total dick. I care about people. My family. Your family. The girls. The football team. My job. This town." I held up my hands. "What else can I do?"

"Just think before you speak and read the room. That's all I ask," Jamison said.

My gaze jumped to the bar where Susie still sat, talking to Trevor. Kristy had joined them. They each had his famous margarita in front of them, and it looked like they weren't coming back anytime soon.

I narrowed my eyes as Susie's laughter floated above the noise of the bar. "What's he got that I don't?"

Jamison followed my gaze. "He's a sweet and genuine guy. Women like that."

Yeah. I rolled my eyes and took a deep swig of my beer. *Sweet and genuine. I could do that—maybe.*

Just then, Madeline came skipping to me and jumped onto my lap.

Thank God for her. I needed the distraction. People said children could sense good people. *If that's true, then what does this say? Madeline and Darcie adore me.* "What's up, stinker?"

Madeline crinkled her eyes, deep in thought. "Uncle Lance, why do you call me stinker but Darcie princess? Stinker isn't as nice. I am also a princess, and you need to call me that."

I smiled as her large brown eyes stared up at me. "I call you stinker out of habit. It's what I used to call your mom. And anyway, you are a princess. Aren't you both *the* princesses of Orlinda Valley?"

She nodded. "Us and Lena," she said with finality and turned to Lilly. "Mommy, did Uncle Lance call you stinker too?"

"Yes, he did," Lilly said with a roll of her eyes.

I cupped my hand around Madeline's ear but whispered loudly enough for the entire table to hear. "The only difference between you and your mommy is that she really stank, but you don't."

Darcie and Madeline roared with laughter.

"What joke did Kaye and I miss out on?" Tonya, Jamison's mother, asked as she and my mom walked up to the table.

"The grandmas are here!" Darcie and Madeline cheered together and hopped up from the table.

I stood to hug Tonya and my mother.

"What did you say that had those two laughing so hard?" my mom asked me.

"He said that Mommy used to stink when she was my age, and that's why he called her stinker," Madeline said.

"Yeah, and the look on Lilly's face was funny," Darcie added.

"Darce," Jamison warned her.

"What, Daddy? Her face did look funny, but her stinking isn't true." Darcie hugged Lilly. "You always smell as pretty as flowers and as sweet as honey, Lilly. You don't stink at all."

"Thank you, sweet girl." Lilly gave her a kiss on the head.

My mother gave me one of her "you've got to be kidding me" looks with her eyebrows raised. I was thirty-six years old and getting the same look from her as I had when I was a teenager.

I shrugged one shoulder. "Sorry?"

She shook her head and gave a tight-lipped smile. "What am I going to do with you, Lance?"

"Love me forever, Momma."

"She has to," Jamison said. "No one else seems to want you."

"Maybe if he wasn't such a turd, he'd be married by now," Lilly said.

I turned toward her. "What is this? Beat up on Lance night?"

Lilly placed her arm over my shoulders. "I think you can handle a little teasing. That skin of yours is pretty thick." She stooped and pulled Madeline and Darcie in for hugs. "Now, you two enjoy your campout with the grandparents, and be nice to James."

"We will," Madeline said, then gave Lilly a kiss on the cheek and skipped away with Darcie, hand in hand.

"As long as he listens to us for once," Darcie hollered over her shoulder.

James was Jamison's nephew. The poor guy would be the only boy at the campout, like it had been his entire life.

My mom and Tonya chuckled and waved. "We'll have them back sometime tomorrow," my mother said.

"Yep, see y'all tomorrow. We've got to go," Tonya said as she pulled my mother away.

Kristy and Susie rejoined us at the table. Susie's face was a little flushed, and her margarita glass was refilled.

Barb dropped off a couple of fresh beers for Jamison and me.

I tipped mine up. "So, did y'all have a good talk with Trevor?" I asked, trying to sound like their time away hadn't bothered me.

"Excuse me?" Susie asked.

"Just asked a question. You looked like you were having a good time over there." My voice came out harsher than I'd meant it to.

What the hell am I doing? I tried to ignore the clenching of my gut by taking another swig of my beer.

"Why do you think I need to tell you anything about what I do or who I talk with?" Irritation clipped the ends of Susie's words.

I turned to face her. *Shut your mouth. Leave it be. She's irritated. But what the hell?* I'd done nothing to make her treat me that way. I'd been helpful and friendly. "That's a little rude after I helped you out today."

"Was that when you helped her with the goats or out of the water trough?" Kristy asked with a teasing grin.

Susie gave her a death stare.

I pushed back my shoulders and sat up straight. *She wants to be rude? Fine.* "Either one. She would have been stuck either way. I came to her rescue, helped her with her problem, and didn't tell a soul about the wet T-shirt contest she seemed to be practicing for."

Susie's face grew red, and her eyes bulged. She pushed away from the table.

Maybe that was a bit much.

"Susie, relax," Kristy said, her hand on Susie's shoulder. "He's teasing."

Susie shrugged off Kristy's hand and spun toward me. "You are such a dick. When are you going to grow up?" she spat as she turned from the table with tears in her eyes.

Damn. I shot to my feet and caught her arm before she could escape.

The moment my fingers touched her skin, a shock of electricity blasted through my chest as if lightning had struck me. *Did she feel that?* My eyes were wide as I stared at her.

If she felt anything, she hid it well. She didn't even glance at me. She stared at my hand on her arm.

She tried to yank away, but I held tight. "Susie, I was just trying to be funny. Make you laugh about what happened today." *Damn. Why can't I figure out how to speak to her?*

Slowly, her eyes rose to meet mine.

Her silver-blue eyes sucked me right in, but the lightning they shot into my gut ignited a fire of unease deep in my core. *That's not the fire I'd like her to ignite.*

"There was nothing funny about today," she said, her words laced with venom. She yanked her arm from my grasp. "I need you to stay away from me and leave me alone." She turned and headed toward the bar. Back to Trevor.

"Let's go see if there's anything going on outside, like a game of cornhole," Jamison said as he pulled me from the table.

"Fine," I agreed in a huff. Maybe throwing bags into a hole would cool me off. I glanced once more at Susie. Trevor's gaze met mine for a second before his hand covered hers.

Fire burned in my gut, and I turned to follow Jamison. No way in hell would I watch whatever was going on at the bar.

We walked onto the patio. Country music played over the outdoor speakers, and people filled the dance floor. As usual, Jamison was right. Concentrating on a competition worked to calm my nerves. We joined a sand volleyball game with a couple of guys we coach with, Alex and Craig. The losing team had to buy a round of drinks.

The air was thick with humidity, and soon, our shirts were off, a crowd had formed, and the competition was as hot as the weather.

After three sets, we came out on top.

"Congratulations," Lilly said as she and Kristy joined us. Lilly hugged Jamison as he put his shirt back on. "God, you're hot and sweaty," she said.

"I like it when you talk to me this way," he said as he leaned in for a kiss.

She giggled as they made out like teenagers.

"God, you two, get a room," I said.

Lilly broke their kiss and pulled on Jamison's hand. "Come dance with me."

"I'd love to, beautiful," he said as he placed his beer on the table and followed her onto the floor.

Kristy watched them. "I still have a hard time believing those two have only been together a year. It seems like it's been forever."

"Yeah, no shit," I said. "It's hard to comprehend. My best friend and my little sister." I studied them on the floor. They fit together perfectly, as if fate had intended them to always be together. After Jamison's first wife had passed away, I never thought I'd see him happy, and with another woman. But there he was, in love with my sister.

My gaze wandered around the floor at all the couples—or those wanting to be couples even for the night. My breath caught. "What the hell?"

"What?" Kristy asked. She followed my gaze and then laughed. "It's called dancing."

I glared at her for a second, then forced my gaze back to the floor.

Susie was in Trevor's arms. He held her close, and she laughed at something he said.

"He should be behind the bar." I said as heat flooded through me.

"You know he gets a break every once in a while." She laughed again and slapped my arm. "Oh my God. Lance, are you jealous?"

I moved my arm off the table we were leaning on and shook my head. Like I'd tell her if I was. I tipped up my beer.

"Holy shit. You are." Kristy's head fell back as she bellowed with laughter. "I've never seen you jealous. This is awesome."

Kristy was a pain in the ass. "Are you done?" I rolled my eyes and turned away. Her laughter grated on my nerves. The song needed to end and put that nightmare to bed.

I watched out of the corner of my eye. When the song finished, Trevor squeezed Susie's hand, and she came toward our table with Lilly and Jamison.

"Have fun?" Kristy asked Susie.

Susie picked up a glass of water and nodded. "Yeah, I did. Trevor's sweet."

My stomach churned with irritation. *Her and Trevor?* "You could do better than him, you know."

She turned toward me and shot a glare into my soul. "Why's it any of your business?"

I shrugged. "It's not."

Her eyes raked over my body but didn't leave any good feelings in their wake. "God, you're a dick."

"You've already made your feelings clear."

"Good. Now shut your mouth for once and listen."

"I said nothing," I answered. *How did this conversation go south so fast?*

She shook her head. "It's not what you say. It's how you say it. You think everyone needs to fall at your feet. *Fall in love with the amazing Lance Hartley.* I see right through you, and I have no time for egotistical pricks."

I was stunned into silence. I tried to think of an amazing comeback that would make her head spin, but I had nothing.

She squeezed Lilly's hand. "I gotta go." She gave her a small smile and walked away.

Kristy didn't hesitate. She said goodnight to Lilly and Jamison, slapped me on the arm, and followed her.

"What the hell?" I whispered as I rubbed my arm.

"Lance, seriously?" Lilly said as she shoved past me and followed her friends.

I fell hard into my seat and drained the rest of my beer in three long gulps. I placed the bottle on the table and combed my fingers through my hair before I linked them behind my neck and stared at the ceiling. "Okay," I said finally, "I'm guessing that was what you meant about thinking before I speak and reading the room." I dropped my eyes to Jamison.

He nodded, his lips pursed. "Basically."

"Fuck," I said under my breath as my arms fell on the table, and I leaned all my weight on them. "Help me understand. What did I say that was so wrong? I was joking with her. She takes everything so seriously."

"It's not what you said, but, like she pointed out—it's how you said it."

I rolled my eyes and sighed.

"Just so you know, she's a lot of fun when you aren't around."

I shot him a narrowed look. "What's that mean?"

"It's simple. She hates you."

I sat up, my eyes widening. "What the fuck?"

Jamison chuckled. "Sorry. That was harsh. Seriously, though." He leaned forward on the table and folded his hands together. "I don't know details, but from what I've pieced together, it seems like she went to South Dakota to teach and ended up in a bad relationship. That's why she's here—to start over. And dealing with you might be a bit much for her."

Jamison held my gaze for a second before I looked away.

I gritted my teeth and let out a heavy breath as a sick feeling wedged itself into the pit of my stomach. *What's going on? When have I ever cared if a woman liked me?* I dated them until I was ready to move on. I used to enjoy fun, women, and drinking. That was until the previous year at Kora and Kai's wedding when I'd first seen Susie. Since then, my focus had shifted. Jayla, the woman I had been dating, even noticed something and ended up breaking up with me. That was a first.

Eventually, life returned to normal, and I could go out without Susie's image in my every thought. But she'd come back to town, and since then, I'd been fucked, and not in my preferred way.

"Why does she hate me so much?" I asked Jamison. "I've done nothing to her." Irritation scratched at my gut like a tiny critter was trying to claw its way out. I raked my fingers through my hair.

"She doesn't hate you," Jamison said. "She hates all guys *like* you."

I jerked my head toward him. "What the hell does that mean? Guys like me? What's wrong with guys like me?"

Jamison chuckled and shook his head. "If you have to ask, there's nothing I can do to help you."

I pinched my lips together. So many retorts sat on the tip of my tongue. I shook my head. "I gotta go."

CHAPTER 5

SUSIE

"Susie, wait!" Kristy hollered across the parking lot.

I stopped and covered my face with my hands and breathed in. *I'm overreacting. Relax.*

"Hey, are you okay?" Lilly asked as she placed her hand lightly on my shoulder. "I know Lance can be a jerk sometimes, but he's really not a bad guy, and I know he didn't mean anything by what he said."

I turned toward her, letting my arms fall to my sides. I was tired and dejected. "I know. It's not that," I said, frustration oozing from my pores. "It's..." I huffed. "Look, you all know about my past, about my childhood, and it's bad enough I'm having to deal with my dad, and I'm really trying. I am, but then Trevor keeps asking me to work at the pub. He's been asking me for a while, and I keep saying no, but I could really use the money. God. I've gotta do something, especially since I'm not going back to teaching." The words tumbled out faster now, one frustration piling onto another. "So, I told him yes. I'm starting tomorrow. I'll be closer to my father than probably ever. Lance is being—Lance. Not to mention I can't take care of those goats. Those damn goats." I covered my face with my hands. "I think I'm losing my mind."

Lilly said, "I think you'll be okay. You've got us." She placed her arms over my shoulders and squeezed.

My hands slowly peeled down my face, and I glanced between my fingers at the two of

them.

Kristy's eyes were wide. "Do you think being around your father is a good idea? Hell, forget that. Have you ever served before?"

I chuckled, and a weight lifted from my shoulders. That was one of the many reasons I loved Kristy. Her straightforward way of dealing with everything was what I needed.

"No, I've never waited tables in my life. I don't know why I said yes, but like I said, I need the money, and now I'm going to be near my dad every day—or at least every day I work."

I combed my fingers through my hair and held it at the back of my head in a ponytail; my eyes turned to the sky. "Working with my dad adds enough stress to my life, but then I saw this." I pulled my phone out of my pocket and showed Lilly and Kristy the text I had received when I walked back to the table after talking with Trevor.

It was another simple text.

Suz. I'm sorry.

"That's it?" Lilly asked.

I nodded.

"Okay, who's it from?" Kristy asked, concern written on her face.

"I can't be certain, as the number's different, but I think it's my ex-boyfriend, Michael. We didn't leave South Dakota on good terms. He didn't think I was actually going to leave him, let alone move and stay away."

"When did you get this one?" Kristy asked and pointed to the text I'd gotten that morning.

"Right before I met you two at the pharmacy for breakfast."

"And you didn't say anything?" Lilly asked as she glanced at my phone and handed it back to me.

"I meant to, but since Lance crashed our breakfast, I forgot. Then with the chaos of the goats, it slipped my mind."

The sound of people leaving the pub attracted my attention. It was Jamison and Lance. Jamison said something, and Lance laughed. He always seemed different when it was just the two of them. He was more relaxed, like he wasn't trying to prove anything. He looked up, and our eyes met.

My heart skipped.

He raised his eyebrows, and I turned away. "Kristy, we've gotta go. I don't want to face him."

They both turned and followed my gaze.

"Not a problem," Lilly said. "I'll head them off. I want to get home, anyway. We have a childless night." Lilly smiled and hugged me. "I'll talk to you tomorrow. Tonight, talk with Kristy. I feel like there's a ton of mess going on inside your head." She backed up. Please know that whatever you have to say, it's all good. We're your friends." She held my gaze, and I smiled.

Friends. It had been a while since I had any genuine friends I could count on and talk to.

"Love you," Lilly said as she hugged Kristy, then she walked toward Jamison.

I watched her, and my eyes connected with Lance. My gut clenched. *Why do all the good-looking guys have to be such jerks?* I sighed heavily. *It doesn't matter.* "Come on, Kristy. Let's go," I said, climbing into her car. "We'll talk more when we get to the house. I'd love for you to spend the night. We'll hang out and stuff our faces with popcorn."

She got in as well. "That sounds great. A girl's night is in the works." She laughed as she turned onto the road.

I kept my eyes straight ahead. I didn't want to catch Lance watching me. *Get him out of your head already.*

It didn't take long before Kristy and I were at the house, comfortable and on the couch, a bowl full of popcorn between us and drinks in our hands.

Kristy crossed her legs under her and turned toward me. "I feel like I'm back in high school. Popcorn, drinks, and two girls shooting the shit. But of course, in high school, we said breeze, not shit. Or maybe I said shit, and Rose and Lilly said breeze. Yeah, that's probably what it was like."

I laughed as she put a handful of popcorn in her mouth, dropping kernels onto the couch and down her front.

A pang of jealousy poked my gut. I knew nothing about what it was like having a best friend in high school—someone to sit around with and talk about boys or about a girl you didn't like. I'd kept to myself. It was easier that way. "You, Lilly, and Rose have been friends for how long?"

Kristy threw more popcorn into her mouth and chewed before answering. "Elementary school. Of course, the two of them have been friends since birth. I forced myself on them in the fourth grade. My family and I had just moved here, and I needed friends. I was never shy and stuck myself into their twosome." More popcorn fell to the floor.

"You know you're going to have to clean up that mess. There's no dog here to eat the popcorn off the floor."

Kristy shrugged. "Bring the goats inside. They'll eat it."

I froze. "You're not serious."

A wicked grin filled her face. "Could be fun. Picture them jumping all over everything. They'd love it. You'd be their new favorite person."

"Yeah, and Kora would kick me out or move me into the barn with them," I said, picking up the popcorn.

"Don't throw that away. I'll eat it," Kristy said.

"It's been on the floor," I said incredulously.

"Right, but as you said, you don't have any animals. The floor's clean. Have you never heard of the ten-second rule?" She grabbed the popcorn from me and popped it into her mouth.

"Don't you mean the five-second rule?" I asked, and chuckled.

She swiped her hand through the air. "Whatever. Tell me about this ex-boyfriend and why his text bothered you."

My mind drifted back to the first day I'd met Michael. The memory was as vivid as if it were yesterday.

I let out a long breath. "We crossed paths at new-teacher orientation," I told Kristy. "He was teaching history. God, he was gorgeous and had this magnetic way about him. We were both fresh college grads, but that's where our similarities ended. He was hometown royalty in that little South Dakota community. His family ties ran deep. He was the kind of guy everyone already knew and adored."

I chuckled. *So much like Lance. Am I always attracted to the hometown-hero?*

Shaking my head, I continued, "It felt like he drew me in the moment we started talking, you know? Those eyes, that charm... I was completely under his spell. Same grade-level team, too, which meant we saw each other constantly. He had me cracking up all the time, always knew how to make things interesting. He became my social connector, introducing me to everyone, and he was incredibly talented at... well..." I was unable to suppress a knowing smile.

Funny how good memories surfaced so easily, like the excitement of starting a new relationship and the fun we'd shared in and out of the bedroom.

"Let's just say he had many gifts."

I had Kristy's full attention. Her eyes fixed on me as I continued.

"Before I knew it, we were an item. Probably the dumbest thing I could've done—getting involved with a coworker—but we tried to keep it under wraps."

I paused and grabbed a drink of water, placed the empty glass on the counter, and stared into it as I continued. "It didn't take long before everything shifted. The easygoing, charming Michael I thought I was head over heels for? He morphed into a possessive, suffocating version of himself. Suddenly, I was walking on eggshells, monitoring every conversation, every glance. Team meetings became minefields."

I glanced up at Kristy. "There was this math teacher. He was young and attractive. I'd be blind if I didn't see it, but he meant nothing to me. He was just a co-worker I could depend on. We talked and collaborated regularly because we taught the same students. Michael absolutely despised it, even though it was completely unavoidable and totally professional. His jealousy started consuming everything. Poisoning what we had. And that's when he began hitting the bottle harder."

As the pieces of my story fell into place, Kristy's forehead creased with worry. The fairy tale beginning morphed into something much darker, and I could see she was bracing herself for what came next as she reached out and gave my hand a squeeze. "You don't have to continue," she said.

"No." I shook my head. "I'm doing this. I need to let someone know what it was like."

I cleared my throat and pressed on. "Michael was always a social drinker—we both were. You know, normal stuff, like we did tonight. But gradually, things changed. I kept trying to convince myself he wasn't turning into my father, but the signs were all there. Drinking until he passed out and not remembering anything in the morning. Yelling obscenities at me while he was trashed. Expecting me to clean up after the mess he always left behind."

A chill went down my spine. The memories were so vivid.

I took a deep breath. "I didn't want to go down that road again. Repeat that nightmare. I thought maybe I was making too much of it because of my childhood. That's exactly what Michael said whenever I mentioned anything about his behavior. To say he didn't appreciate me pointing out his drinking habits was putting it mildly."

"Did he know about your childhood?"

I nodded. "Yeah. I told him about it before we started dating. He seemed concerned then. But later, he always said I was comparing him to my father, and I needed to chill out. The sad thing was—I believed him. I thought I was overreacting.

"I talked to my friend Diana about it, and she told me I needed to break up with him. So of course, that didn't go over well, and before I realized what was happening, instead of breaking up, we were moving in together. According to him, if I didn't, it would prove I didn't love him. Diana tried to talk me out of it, but that wasn't going to happen. According to Michael, I needed to choose. Diana or him. So, I packed up, moved out of the apartment I shared with her, and moved in with Michael." I took a sip of my drink and ate a handful of popcorn. "And there was one less friend in my universe."

"Susie, I'm so sorry." Her jaw tightened slightly.

I shook my head and continued, "He made it sound like this big romantic step, you know? Like we were taking our relationship to the next level. But really, it was just another way to cut me off from anyone who might point out what was actually happening. Diana tried to talk to me afterward, but Michael had already started his campaign about how she was jealous of our happiness and wanted to break us up." I shook my head at my naivety. "And I bought it. Hook, line, and sinker."

I stood and took the popcorn bowls and the cups to the kitchen.

Kristy followed. "Why did you finally decide to leave South Dakota and move here?"

"Simple—Kai. I talked to him about my situation when I was here for the wedding. I didn't mean to. I didn't want to burden him with my drama when he was about to get married, but he's always had this ability to see right through me, and that didn't disappear because we were on opposite sides of the country."

I loaded the dishwasher and became thoughtful. Kai had been my savior—again. "Kai made me promise I'd leave Michael. He called in January, and when Michael answered my phone, Kai became livid and said if I didn't take care of the situation, he'd come out and pack my things himself. He ended up buying me a plane ticket and brought me home at the end of the school year, and here I am."

"Michael called you Suz," Kristy said. "Is that why you don't like anyone else to call you that except Kai?"

I shrugged. "I'd never thought about it before. Probably. Hearing it makes my stomach curdle."

"I'm so sorry things were so shitty, and he was a dick."

I threw the dishwasher door closed hard enough to cause the plates to clatter and held my hand up to stop her words. "Look, yes, it was a crappy relationship. Yes, he drank too much. Yes, he was a controlling ass, but I'm not with him anymore. I've moved on, and I'm here now. It's all good. He's over a thousand miles away in South Dakota. So what if he misses the thought of me? I'm not going back there. I'm *going* to make it here, near Kai and our new family. I'm hoping Sebastian comes to visit at some point. Heck, maybe if Kora ever has a baby, that'll get his butt here. But right now, though, I'm glad to have you and this town. I need a friend. I need a community. And I want to be part of this awesome extended family Kai found, because I've never had that in my life. If I have to learn to deal with Lance and his egotistical attitude, so be it. He may be a jerk, but at least he's not overbearing, overprotective, and emotionally abusive. I know his father was, and sometimes, the apple doesn't fall far from the tree, but in his case, I'm sure that's not true."

"Trust me. He's not that bad," Kristy said. "I know we all joke that Lilly got all of Kaye's good traits, but Lance fiercely protects those he loves, and his family—blood and extended—are very important to him."

I nodded. "Good to know. This has been fun, but I'm tired and have to work tomorrow. Let's get to bed, then tomorrow morning, you can help me with those monsters out in the pasture."

"Sounds like a blast," Kristy said as she locked up the patio door. "I think it would still be easier if we let them free—free to do whatever they wished."

I rolled my eyes. "Kora would love that."

CHAPTER 6

LANCE

I parked in front of my townhome, slammed the car into park, and stared ahead, gripping the steering wheel so tight that my knuckles were white. Susie's face invaded my mind. Her disdainful look when our eyes met across the parking lot remained seared in my memory.

I pinched the bridge of my nose and took a deep breath. "Lance, why do you care so much?" I asked myself as exhaustion took over my body. *Fuck, I wish I knew the answer to that.*

I climbed out of the car, took the short walk to my front door, and let myself into the house. After throwing my keys onto the small kitchen counter, I grabbed a beer from the fridge and went into the living room.

Falling onto the couch, I checked the time. It was only ten o'clock, yet I was exhausted. I should go to bed but was too amped up. There was no way I'd fall asleep. *Hell, when did ten o'clock become late, anyway?*

I laughed. Damn, I was getting old.

Was it really just a few months ago that Jayla would be here and we'd be getting ready to have fun at ten o'clock at night, either going out or up in bed?

I took a sip of my beer. *Jayla.* I'd thought maybe she and I could become something, but then my mind became occupied with Susie, and Jayla couldn't compete, and she knew it.

The first time I laid eyes on Susie, that was it. She was only around for a few days, yet she spun my world upside down. I sure as hell hadn't made a good impression, talking shit about Summer and getting into a fight with Rowan the day of the wedding.

Yeah, not my best moment. But she took control of the situation, put me in my place, kicked me out of the wedding party, replaced me with Rowan, and ruined my love life ever since.

Ever since then, I've only seen Susie. No other woman comes close. There was something about her, and it wasn't just her beauty. She was confident, with a quiet, controlled demeanor, and the way she carried herself—I wasn't sure I could put my finger on it, but it commanded my attention.

It seemed almost as if she was inspecting everyone, seeing right through us all and trying to figure out if we could be trusted. With her shitty home life, who could blame her for having trust issues? No mother around and a father who was an alcoholic.

I sighed heavily. I could relate to having a shitty father. Mine was anything but loving to my mother, and she kicked him out when I was young. Even Jamison's father, Carl, and Charles couldn't fill the void that his absence caused, so my mother let me see him occasionally.

He and I would go out to eat, or to a game. He got so much attention from women and flirted shamelessly.

When I was old enough to realize that the women weren't just friends, he taught me his motto: "Life is too short for only one woman."

I am thirty-six, and until recently, that had been my motto as well. I scrubbed my hands over my face and took a swig of my beer. *Shit.* I pulled the bottle away and looked at it—really took a good look.

Terry was an alcoholic. My father was a womanizing jackass. And here I was with a beer in my hand, always having to have the last word, and be the life of every party. "Shit, Lance, you are an immature asshole. No wonder she can't stand you."

I pushed off the couch, went into the kitchen, and poured the beer down the drain. "Lance, you're single, and you've never even considered marriage. Maybe everyone is right. Maybe it is time to grow up."

I climbed the stairs and got ready for bed. As I lay in the dark, my thoughts kept racing. My life flashed through my mind—school, football, Jamison, Kai, my family. *What else do I have?*

"Damn, I'm pitiful. My life hasn't changed since childhood. I'm lucky I still have my family. Well, except my father, but he hasn't been around for so long that I don't even remember the last time I saw him."

I turned over and threw my arm across my eyes. *Tomorrow, it will be time to change and show Susie what kind of man I can really be.*

I woke at the crack of dawn the next morning. *Damn, I slept like shit.*

I dreamt of Susie dancing with Trevor. Her laughter haunted me and jerked me awake, and the joy in the tone gripped my heart. I wanted her to laugh with me like that and see me as something more than the jackass who saw her half naked. The image of her perky tits in that wet T-shirt made me hard in a flash.

Fuck this. I pulled myself out of bed. I needed a run to clear my head, so I threw on a pair of shorts and grabbed the first shirt I could get my hands on and sniffed it. It wasn't the cleanest, but I was only going to sweat anyway. No need to smell good. I tied my sneakers and was out the door.

My apartment was close enough to town to run to the coffee shop, Cafe Mocha, get a coffee and a muffin, and run back. Jamison was always on me about running after the muffin and coffee, but I'd done it so often that my body was used to it. It wasn't like I was running a marathon.

It was early enough that the humidity wasn't oppressive like it would be later in the day, and not much was open yet. I always loved the town in the early mornings. It was quiet and empty, almost as if it were all mine. I slowed to a walk as I reached the parking lot. Shear Perfection hair salon, a small white house, was at one end, with the strip mall next door. The strip mall contained Cafe Mocha, Everything 'U' Need Boutique, and OV Gym. A couple of cars were parked in front of the gym but none in front of the cafe. *Good. No lines.*

I strolled through the door of Café Mocha and ordered a coffee with cream and sugar and a banana nut muffin—made in-house and the best.

I sat at a table in the corner and scrolled through a social media app while I sipped my coffee and ate the muffin.

Susie's face popped into my head, and my heart beat faster. It was time to figure out how to get her to see me as more than a jackass. But God, she despised me. She could hardly look at me without disdain in her eyes, not to mention her lack of desire to talk with me. I puffed out a breath. This would be almost impossible.

It's a damn good thing I don't do impossible. Susie doesn't stand a chance.

CHAPTER 7

SUSIE

"God, my feet are killing me." I huffed as I fell onto the bar stool next to Shannon, one of my coworkers at Jerry's Pub.

My first weekend shift was finally over, and I was exhausted. Serving turned out to be much more difficult than I thought. Then and there I decided that being a teacher was so much easier.

"You look rough," Trevor said as he stood behind the bar, washing glasses.

"Gee, thanks." I glared at him with a smile as I helped Shannon wrap silverware.

Trevor chuckled and slid me a glass of Diet Coke. "It's not a simple job."

"I see that. Free drinks, though, are a plus," I said, then took a sip of my drink. The caffeine worked its magic.

"You hanging in there, sugar?" Barb asked with her elbows on the bar.

Barb had to be in her mid-forties. She was pretty, about five foot six, a little chunky but not overweight, and hid any gray hairs well in what had to be a bleach job, since she had dark roots. She was single and an insatiable flirt with the men—all men, especially my brother.

The term *sugar*, though, was annoying. She used it for everyone—men, women, teenagers, kids, and coworkers. "Do you think you could use my name?" I asked her.

She chuckled. It sounded deep and raspy, like she'd smoked at least a pack of cigarettes for most of her life. "Sorry, sugar—Susie. It's a Southern habit."

I smiled widely. "I know, and I don't mean to be rude, but I have issues with pet names. But yes, I'm hanging in there. It's my feet that are suffering."

Shannon chuckled. "No kidding. The secret to serving is comfortable shoes."

"I'll have to go shopping then, I guess," I said, looking down. My sneakers were anything but comfortable. They were old and worn.

"You want me to order y'all anything from the kitchen before they close up?" Trevor asked.

"A plain burger would be great for me," Barb answered.

"Grilled cheese and fries, please," Shannon said and turned to me. "Nico makes the best grilled cheese. I love it."

I glanced at the kitchen. My father had been working all weekend, and I'd done a pretty decent job of avoiding him. But if I ordered something, he would deliver it. I could go without and wait until I get home.

"Susie?" Trevor asked.

My stomach rumbled, like it didn't enjoy my thought process, and I loved a good grilled cheese. That and fries sounded amazing.

It wasn't worth it, though. "Nope. I'm good."

Trevor tapped in the order while Shannon pulled a vape from her pocket and put it to her lips.

"Nope, Shannon. Not in here, even after hours," Trevor said. "I've told you that." He pointed toward the door.

"Fine," she huffed and strutted off, releasing her blond hair from its clip as she walked. "Don't eat my food before I get back!"

"I'm confused about why young people think vaping is safer than smoking. Who knows what that shit is doing to their lungs?" Barb took a deep drink of her beer.

"This from a thirty-year smoker?" Trevor asked with a smile.

"Thirty? What do you think? I started smoking when I was fifteen? I wish I had been that old. It was more like twelve."

My eyes widened. "You were smoking at twelve?" That shouldn't surprise me. When I was twelve, I could have been smoking, drinking, and doing drugs. Hell, I could have done anything I wanted with the company my father kept and how much he gave a shit.

Barb shrugged. "Cigarettes were everywhere, and one day, my mom left a lit one in the ashtray, and I took a hit and passed it to my friend. After that, it was fun. You know, sneaking cigarettes when adults weren't looking. It was a thrill, I guess."

I pursed my lips. "My brother Sebastian and his friends snuck cigarettes and beer from our dad's friends whenever they could. Of course, with random men passing out all over our house all the time, it wasn't too much of a challenge."

"So, you don't smoke, you did well in school, and you never got into any trouble. How did you manage that, growing up like you did?" Barb asked.

I shrugged. "I had two brothers who were always in my business and made sure I never did anything stupid, even though both of them did."

"I had sisters," said Barb, "so we weren't lucky enough to have someone look out for us."

"I was an only child," Trevor said. "But I had Rowan, Bryson, and Jamison, so it was like I had brothers. Rowan and I were mischievous but did nothing terrible. His father would have killed us."

I continued wrapping silverware and listened as Trevor and Barb talked about their childhoods. Barb was originally from West Tennessee, but Trevor was from Orlinda Valley, born and bred. His stories of the things he and Rowan had done when they were young were hilarious.

Movement from the kitchen caught my attention, and my father exited with his arms filled with plates. "Here you go," he said and held up the burger plate.

Barb tapped the table.

He placed her food in front of her.

Then she said, "And the grilled cheese is for Shannon." She tapped the seat next to her, where Shannon had been sitting, and he sat her plate down.

There was one left in his hand, and he placed it on the bar in front of me. The plate was filled with grilled cheese on sourdough bread along with french fries and a small bowl of mayonnaise with Tabasco squirted in it.

"I know you didn't order, but this is your favorite, right down to the mayo and Tabasco." Terry's tired eyes shone with what I could only describe as hope, and his lips pinched together in a tight grin.

Part of me wanted to be rude—slide it back to him and say no thank you—and hurt him like he did to me so many times all those years ago, but the mature, adult in me won out. "Thank you," I said and returned his small smile but didn't hold his gaze. I'd promised Kai I'd try to forgive him, but damn, it was difficult.

He left, and I took a french fry and mixed the mayo and Tabasco.

"I've only seen one other person do that," Barb said. "Is it a family thing?"

I chuckled. She was talking about Kai. He was the one who started all three of us eating this mayonnaise and Tabasco concoction. It had become a habit, and my dad remembered. A rock lodged in my gut. "Kai did it once when Sebastian and I were young, and it became our thing."

"Kai made me try it," Trevor said. "It's pretty good." He reached over and took one of my fries and dipped it.

"Hey!" I chuckled. "Get your own."

"You weren't hungry anyway," he said.

"Just because I didn't order anything to eat doesn't mean I'm not hungry." I looked away. "Honestly, I wanted to avoid my dad."

"He's come a long way since he's been here," Barb said.

"I know. I can tell, but I can't forgive and forget as easily as Kai."

"Maybe with time?" Trevor asked.

I shrugged and put a fry in my mouth. "Maybe."

Memories flooded back, filled with things I wished I could forget, such as Terry and his friends acting up while drunk at our house, and Kai making me and Sebastian promise to lock our bedroom door. Sebastian and I had shared a bed. When we became too old to do that, he moved into Kai's room, but most nights I didn't want to be alone, so he slept on my floor. He'd always been my protector. When

I left for South Dakota, it was hard for me to be so far from him and Kai, but I was determined to make it.

"Hey, look what was outside," Shannon said as she rushed into the pub with a bouquet in her arms.

"Who gave you those?" Trevor asked.

"They aren't for me," Shannon said as she placed them on the bar and pushed them in my direction. "The card has Susie's name on it."

I glanced wide-eyed at the bouquet, which consisted of fresh-cut wildflowers in blues, whites, and pinks, my favorites. "It's beautiful. I've always loved wildflowers the best. I think fresh-cut bouquets are prettier than roses. But who knew that?"

I thought hard. No one but Kai, Kora, and my tiny friend group knew much about me. No one in town knew my favorite flower.

Barb said, "Already got someone's eye. At least the men of Orlinda Valley aren't blind when a beautiful woman comes into town."

I gave Barb a small smile. *This is weird. Who would send me flowers? Who knows me?*

I glanced toward Trevor. He was putting away glasses and didn't see me watching him. It could be him. We talked a lot, and I caught him watching me across the pub occasionally.

Then Lance popped into my mind. He was always so focused on me, and I couldn't miss the flirting, but I didn't think he would send something anonymously. He was more of a "Hey, it's me" kind of person.

I pulled the card from the holder and read: *As beautiful as you.* My heart thumped hard, and my gaze met Trevor's.

He raised his eyebrow. "Are you okay? Who are they from?" He gestured to the bouquet.

I shrugged and slid the card across the bar. He picked it up and read it, his face expressionless. *Do I expect him to admit they're from him? Do I want them to be from him?*

"Oh, I bet they're from Lance," Shannon said, bouncing out of her seat. "He's always flirting with you, and didn't he call you beautiful the other night?"

Before I could speak, Trevor said, "Lance does flirt with her, but he's not the type of guy to give a girl flowers, let alone drop them off without taking credit."

"So true. That Lance is a ladies' man," Barb said. "Hot, sexy, and not one to hide his feelings." She wiggled her eyebrows.

I cringed. "Look," I said, interrupting the crazy discussion as I wrapped the last set of silverware. "If someone wanted to give me flowers, they should have signed their name. I have no desire to keep something without knowing who it's from. I've gotta go." I headed for the door. "See you tomorrow."

"You don't want the flowers?" Shannon asked.

"Nope," I said without turning around. "You can take them home. Throw them away. I don't care."

Butterflies fluttered in my gut, but heat crawled up the back of my neck. *Why does Trevor's nonchalant attitude bother me?* I wondered as I climbed into Kai's truck. *Do I want the flowers to be from him?*

I started the truck, waited the prescribed two minutes for the engine revving to die down, then pulled out of the lot. Trevor's face flashed in my mind—his wavy light-brown hair, hazel-green eyes, and that smile that was almost a permanent fixture on his face.

Or maybe they were from Lance. He was as handsome as the day was long and had a smirk that made my insides twitch. The gleam of mischief seemed to be a permanent fixture in his eyes. He had a tall body and was built for days. "Yeah, and his ego to match. Dammit, Susie. Get Lance out of your mind. Hell, get all men out of your mind. You don't have time for dating or the desire to deal with men."

But I loved wildflowers, and only one person knew that.

My stomach plummeted as if I were going down a steep hill on a rollercoaster.

It was impossible. It couldn't be him. He didn't know where I was. It had to be a complete coincidence. You could get those flowers at any grocery store. They could be from anyone.

I turned left and glanced in my rearview mirror as the car behind me followed suit.

My gut reacted with a violent flip. It seemed to be closing in on my tail. I was being followed. The headlights blinded me. I sped up, and so did the car.

Shit. What should I do?

My heart raced. I was never one for scary movies for this very reason—my overactive imagination. "Relax. There's more than just Kai's place down this road."

I passed the turn before Kora and Kai's and released a pent-up breath when the dark SUV took it.

I pulled into Kora and Kai's driveway, my heart pounding and my senses on high alert. *Now would be a perfect time to have a dog. My personal alarm system.*

I entered the house, locked the door behind me, and got ready for bed.

My plan for the next day was to sleep in, take care of the animals, and get to Jerry's Pub in time for my shift. At least I didn't have to close.

I'd get off in time to enjoy my night. Maybe I'd ask Kristy to stay over again. We could hang out and watch a movie.

CHAPTER 8

SUSIE

Annoying! That's all he is. I tapped in my customer's food order and cursed under my breath.

"Hey, what did the computer do to you?" Trevor chuckled beside me as he rinsed glasses.

I shook my head and could have sworn steam was jetting out of my ears. "Lance is such a—"

I paused. Two men were sitting close by at the bar, sipping their beers. I caught their eyes and held their gazes, raising my eyebrows. It didn't take long before they turned away and continued their conversation.

I had to watch what I said about Lance. Calling everyone's favorite football coach derogatory names wouldn't go over well, so I turned to Trevor and whispered, "He's a dick."

There. No one else heard.

Trevor chuckled. "He's mastered that art for sure. What did he do this time?"

"He didn't *do* anything. It's just his attitude. He's showing out over there in front of his coaching buddies and calls me sweetheart or Suz, and he knows I can't stand nicknames."

"If he bothers you too much, I can swap Shannon to their table. She loves flirting with the coaches, and between you and me, I think she's crushing on Lance."

I rolled my eyes. "Just what he needs. More of a fan club and someone encouraging his behavior."

Trevor filled their drink order. "You got this?"

I met his gaze, and the sparkle in his eyes gave me the encouragement I needed.

I smiled. "Yep. Don't fire me if one of these beers accidentally finds its way into Lance's lap."

"Won't see a thing or hear the cursing. My ears are immune to his complaints." The crooked smile he gave me was adorable.

My frustration was gone by the time I filled my tray and left the bar. It was as if Trevor could zap all irritation out of the air. He had a knack for honing situations and helping people relax.

As I approached Lance's table, I squared my shoulders and stood straight. No way in hell would he get to me.

I placed a beer each in front of Jamison, Craig, and Trig. Then the fourth I placed near Jamison. "Here, Jamison. Please give this to the asshole across the table. I've decided not to serve jackasses like him today."

Jamison laughed. "You got it, Susie. Don't worry. I've got your back. I've known him since diapers, and trust me—he can be a lot to deal with."

I glanced at Lance, and our eyes met. I shot him a glare and shook my head.

He smirked and wiggled his eyebrows.

My heart skipped a beat. Damn, even my body was a traitor.

I bit my tongue to stop myself from getting angry. "Your food will be out soon." I narrowed my eyes and walked away fuming.

What the hell is going on with me? I promised myself I'd focus on me, and I sure as hell would not fall for another asshole. Being in Orlinda Valley was about straightening out my life and learning how to be on my own.

I glanced at my watch.

Almost four. Thank God. My shift was almost over, and then I was off to the hair salon for pampering. And Lord knew I needed it.

I spent the last thirty minutes of my shift avoiding Lance. Finally, it was four. I clocked out and walked across the street to Shear Perfection. The humidity was still high, but after the freezing air conditioning of the pub, I appreciated it.

The bell over the door announced my arrival at Shear Perfection. The hum of hairdryers, the smell of chemicals, and the low whisper of voices reached me.

"Hello, Susie," Kaye—Lance and Lilly's mother and a co-owner of the salon—greeted me. She, Tonya, Diane, and Ruth had been friends forever, had never met a stranger. They called themselves the Orlinda Valley book club, even though I didn't think I'd ever seen them with a book.

When Kai had come into town, they had given him a place to stay, a part-time job, and an instant found family. They were the reason he'd adjusted so well to his new life, and I couldn't be more thankful for them.

"Hello, Kaye. How's your day been?"

"It's been great," she said, sweeping up her station. "Just another day in paradise."

"Are you ready to go yet?" Tonya asked as she and Ruth came out of the kitchen. "Diane's waiting for us."

"Y'all have big plans?" I asked as I gave Tonya then Ruth a hug.

"Book club night at Diane's," Ruth answered. Ruth's daughter, Rose, had an adorable five-year-old daughter, a teenage son, an amazing husband, and was best friends with Lilly and Kristy, so I'd gotten to know her well.

"So once Kaye's ready, we're off. This body needs wine," Tonya said.

"Maybe you should slow down on your alcohol consumption, lady," Summer said, emerging from the shampoo station with Kristy in tow. "I have no desire for you to move in with me and your son in your old age because you've killed your liver."

"Summer, it's a good thing I love you. Or else I'd find something for my baby to dislike about you."

"Like that's even possible." Summer removed the towel from Kristy's head. "Your baby loves everything about me. And by that, I mean ab-so-lute-ly everything." Summer tilted her head and held Tonya's gaze. The banter they threw back and forth was always entertaining.

"Okay, you two," Kaye interrupted. "Enough. Summer, you and Rowan are perfect together, and Tonya loves you, but we don't need to know details of what he loves most about you." She put the broom back in the corner.

"Now I'm finished, and we need to get going. Ladies," she said, addressing us. "Enjoy your night." She tucked her arm in Ruth's. "And let's go. Ruthie, you're driving, right?"

"Of course, and if I need to be y'all's Uber driver to get you home safe, I'll do that also."

I laughed as I watched them leave. Friendships could last a lifetime. Those women proved it.

CHAPTER 9

SUSIE

"Lock the door and turn the sign, please." Summer gestured toward the door once the ladies had left. "Then there's a bottle of wine in the fridge and plastic cups. Grab those."

I did as she asked, poured each of us half a cup, and relaxed in the chair by her station as she brushed out Kristy's hair.

"How was the pub today?" Kristy asked. "Are things getting easier?"

"Yes," I answered, as I took a big sip of the wine and instantly felt my body relax.

"But something's bothering you." Summer took a quick break to sip her wine then got back to Kristy's hair.

"Lance."

Summer nodded. "Makes sense. Rowan told me he seems to have his eyes on you."

Kristy wiggled her eyebrows.

I swatted her. "How can such a sweet lady like Kaye have a daughter as perfect as Lilly and a son as big of an ass as Lance?"

"If you ever met their father, you'd know," Kristy said. "He hasn't been around in a long while, but he's a jerk. The best thing Kaye ever did for her and her family was chuck him to the curb."

"True, but Lance got his DNA. Just think how much worse he'd be if he didn't have Kaye mixed in with him," Summer added.

"You make him sound like a baked good." I chuckled.

Summer thought about it. "Well, if he is, someone slipped in cayenne pepper instead of salt. He's a bit overwhelming and doesn't sit well with most people."

"Good analogy," Kristy said.

"Yeah, it is a good one. He gives me heartburn," I said.

Kristy and Summer chuckled.

"In all honesty, he may be a lot to handle, but he's gotten better since the wedding, thanks to Jamison being the peacemaker, as always." Summer fluffed up Kristy's hair. "What do you think? I took a little off the ends and touched up your layers."

"Amazing, as always, Summer," Kristy said, glancing in the mirror.

I chewed my bottom lip, deep in thought. If Summer could forgive him after how he'd treated her at Kora and Kai's wedding and the issues that occurred between him and Rowan, maybe there was hope for him.

"Earth to Susie. It's your turn," Kristy said as she got out of the chair.

I took Kristy's place, and Summer placed the cape around me.

"So, why all the questions about Lance?" she asked, meeting my gaze in the mirror.

I pursed my lips and shook my head. "No reason. He's just irritating. I strongly considered accidentally dropping a beer on him today but thought better of it. Trevor didn't even try to talk me out of it."

Kristy and Summer exchanged glances.

"What?" I asked.

Summer shook her head and held up a bit of my hair. "This much? Or do you want to try something drastically different?"

"I'm not brave when it comes to my hair. Keep it the same."

Summer nodded with a smirk on her face.

I glanced between Summer and Kristy. *What are they thinking?* "What's going on?" I asked.

"The fact that you have no clue is adorable," Kristy said.

"True. It is," Summer added. "Look, I have it from a very reliable source Trevor has it bad for you."

My eyes widened. "What? How does Rowan know that?" Rowan and Trevor were best friends. I had no doubt that was who Summer's "reliable source" was.

"Please, even if he didn't talk about you all the time, it's obvious by the way he watches you. I've seen that look before. It's the same look he had for Kora."

"Whatever." I stared forward. *Trevor likes me? Lance flirts with me? What the hell?* Trevor was the sweetest man in Orlinda Valley—heck, probably the world. He'd had the patience of a saint when I screwed up orders on my first day of work, his smile lit up a room, and I knew he'd be someone who wouldn't think twice about lending anyone a hand. Trevor was everything a woman should want. If a sweeter man in Orlinda Valley—heck, anywhere—existed, I had yet to meet him.

Then there was Lance. The way he had leaned back in his chair with laughter earlier and flashed me his crooked grin filled with arrogance and confidence, invaded my thoughts. The way he'd looked at me when I told Jamison to give him his beer, like he could read my mind—the man was infuriating. Yet, I couldn't ignore the way he made my pulse quicken and my heart race, even though I wished it wouldn't.

God, what is wrong with me? I had a mental checklist growing before I could stop myself. Trevor was dependable, reliable, sweet, kind to everyone, hardworking, and handsome. He would make a perfect husband someday—not that I was looking.

But that damn smirk of Lance's wouldn't leave my mind along with his insufferable confidence that I wanted to knock down a peg, even though it drew me to him like a moth to a flame.

Trevor made me laugh and feel comfortable in my own skin, something I couldn't remember ever feeling before. Meanwhile, everything about Lance set my nerves on edge and sent an electrical pulse through my veins, which made me feel alive.

No two men could be more different. They were total opposites, yet I had a pattern.

My attraction to toxic men, the ones who never promised a future, was my drug of choice. Lance seemed to fit that bill perfectly.

Trevor was everything sensible. Lance was everything dangerous. *Damn, why am I even having this debate?*

"Hey, earth to Susie," Summer said. "Again, I don't know where you went, but I'm done. What do you think?"

My hair was long and straight. Summer had cut it so that the sides framed my face and it fell below my shoulders, just like usual. "Looks great. Thank you."

"No problem. Now, let's go out back and finish the wine."

I followed Summer and Kristy. *Get your head on straight and stop thinking.*

Out the back door of the salon, what used to be a dirt area with patchy bits of grass had become a patio area with stone pavers, a large round table, and a couple of benches. Flowers in large planters added color and made the space inviting. It was perfect for customers waiting for their appointments or who needed fresh air while they waited for their color to set.

We'd just gotten comfortable around the table when my phone announced a text.

I glanced down.

You can't hide. I'll find you.

My blood ran cold, and my eyes widened. It had to be Michael. He always said I'd never get away or find anyone better than him. But I'd thought Orlinda Valley would be the perfect place. I never told him where Kai lived or gave him my new number.

"You okay? You look like you've seen a ghost," Summer said.

Kristy leaned over and grabbed my phone. She read the screen, and her eyes bulged. "Shit, Susie. It's that creeper again."

"What creeper?" Summer asked as she took the phone from Kristy. Her eyes matched Kristy's. "Susie?" She held the phone out, her eyebrows raised.

I shook my head and took a deep breath then puffed it out. "It's my ex, Michael."

"Umm, if this is your ex, he sounds a bit unraveled," Summer said. "It needs to be reported to the police. Patrick will want to know about this."

I jumped up and yanked my phone from her hands. "I think it's Michael, but I can't be one hundred percent sure. I've never seen this number before."

I couldn't involve the police. That was crazy, and if it was Michael, he would flip if he knew I'd gotten the authorities involved.

"He could have changed his number or gotten a new phone," Summer said, sitting up straight. "This isn't something to ignore."

"See? It's not just me," Kristy said. "Good thing I'm staying with you tonight."

"I didn't ask you because I'm scared of a text. I asked you because I wanted to hang out. I'm not a child and don't need a babysitter."

"I didn't say you're a child. We'll have fun. It's what friends do, so no arguing." Kristy finished her wine and sat back, her arms crossed.

I bit my bottom lip.

I wasn't used to people caring and had no idea what friends really did. My one true friend had had no problem leaving when Michael became overbearing. Not that I'd had a choice. He insisted on it. Cutting ties and burning bridges was his way of controlling me. I finally knew that. I had wanted to be loved by a man so badly that I was blind to his controlling ways.

"Fine," I said, standing with my hands on my hips. "Do what you want. I'm getting out of here. I need to check on the goats."

"Fine," Kristy mocked me. She stood, putting her shoulders back and her hands on her hips as well. "I will. I'll go home, pack, and then head to your house."

A smile broke across my face, and she smiled back before she walked toward her car. "See you soon, and thank you, Summer. As usual, you do amazing things with scissors and a comb."

"You know it," Summer said.

I waited until Kristy pulled away then said, "Don't tell Rowan any of this. Please, Summer."

She chuckled. "You don't understand that man. I've known him forever, and he can read me like a book. Once he thinks I'm keeping something from him, he'll keep something from me, and that ain't happening."

I deflated a bit. "Seriously, Summer? All he has to do is keep sex from you, and you fold?"

"Like an old newspaper." She winked. "Be careful and call if you need anything. I'm going to lock up."

Every noise I heard as I was taking care of the goats made chills run up my spine. I couldn't shake the feeling that I was being watched, which was ridiculous.

I threw a handful of scratch on the ground, and the chickens all scattered after it except for one fluffy yellow chicken. She stood staring at me. "Chicken, stop looking at me with your little eyes. You're creeping me out."

I sat on a log Kora had for the goats to climb on, and the chicken jumped onto my lap, chirping and talking. I petted its feathers. They were as soft as silk. "Hey there, chicken. You have it easy. All you need to worry about is someone feeding you, a soft place to lay your eggs, and a place to perch at night. You don't even need that. Bugs, a hidden spot, and somewhere high would suffice."

She cocked her head to the side and continued her little chirping sounds. I could see why Kora loved her animals and the farm life.

Being in the barn with the chickens and the goats outside the door was relaxing.

The chicken jumped down and began pecking the ground with her sisters. I picked up the basket Kora used for gathering eggs and went to the chicken boxes. Six eggs were in one box, and a black chicken was laying in another.

"Hi there, pretty girl," I cooed. "I'm just going to check under you for eggs." I'd seen Kora do it a couple of times. She slid her hand under the chicken and came out with a few eggs.

I tried it, but the chicken fluffed up its feathers, made a strange, almost growling sound, then pecked my hand. "Ouch." I jerked my hand away. "That wasn't nice, chicken."

She clucked at me and jumped out of the box. Three eggs lay there. *Good. Exactly what I needed.* I put those in the basket.

The goats, which had been lying in the sun right outside the large door, started running and talking. Something had gotten their attention. My pulse raced, then I heard tires crunching gravel.

I jogged to the edge of the barn door and peeked out. *Why the hell am I being a chicken?* I chuckled, since I was surrounded by them, then Kristy's car came into view.

Thank God she was there. I was too jumpy to be alone any longer.

CHAPTER 10

LANCE

We'd just finished evening football practice, and the last guy had gone home.

"You ready to head to the park?" Jamison, who coached the offensive line, asked.

"Yep," I answered. We were meeting Rowan and Trevor for an impromptu game of basketball, two on two. "You better bring your A-game. I'm not losing to them again. It's about damn time they pay for a round of our drinks."

"No shit. So, this time, don't be a dick. Pass it when I'm open. You know the saying. 'There's no *I* in team.'"

I narrowed my eyes and shook my head. "Unless the other teammate is named Jamison and couldn't get the ball through the hoop to save his life."

"That's bullshit. I can out-shoot you any day of the week."

"Oh my God." I chuckled. "That's a crock of shit."

We continued our trash talk as we crossed the street and reached the park. Rowan and Trevor were already there, shooting.

"Here come the old men," Rowan said as we approached.

"Might be older, but we're smarter," Jamison said as he caught the ball and bounced it back to Rowan.

Rowan and Trevor looked at each other and laughed. "I'd agree with *you* being smarter, Jamison, but him?" Trevor nodded in my direction. "There's not much more than air taking up space inside that thick skull of his."

I ground my teeth together. Rowan and Trevor always started this way, trying to get a rise out of me, and unfortunately, it usually worked.

"Don't let them get to you," Jamison said as he smacked me on the shoulder. "Ignore them." He grabbed the ball from Rowan and the game got started.

We always played to twenty, best of three, and the first set ended the same as usual, with Rowan and Trevor winning.

We won the second, but they pulled out the third by heckling me and getting in my head.

"That's game," Trevor said, letting out an annoying "Yeehaw."

His country-ways grated on my nerves and always had.

"So, when are you two going to stop torturing yourselves like this?" Rowan asked, patting us on the back.

Jamison, always the good sport, smiled and patted him back. "One day when we're only able to walk with a walker. Maybe."

"We have to keep you young ones feeling good about yourselves. Some of you are still single," I said.

"What? And you aren't?" Trevor replied. "Last I heard, Jayla dumped your ass and left you with your favorite date."

"Your left hand," Rowan finished and roared with laughter. He and Trevor high-fived.

I stared at my hand and clenched my fist. *I really want to punch his smug ass.* I glanced at Jamison.

He arched an eyebrow and shook his head.

His ability to be calm in all situations irritated me but was one thing that made us such good friends. We canceled each other out. God forbid if we were both like me. We'd be in jail.

"What do you two jackasses say we get together Wednesday night at Jerry's Pub and cash in on that drink?" Trevor asked.

"Works for me," Jamison said. "I'll let Lilly know I won't be home for dinner and make sure she doesn't have any plans." He glanced at me.

"I got nothing but a morning practice," I said as we all gathered our stuff. I took a seat on the bench and drank deeply from my water bottle. "How was Susie's weekend at work?"

Trevor glared at me for a beat.

"What?" I asked.

He continued to stare, then finally shook his head. "I guess you don't know about the flowers Shannon found outside the pub."

"Flowers?" Jamison asked.

"Yeah. Sunday night after closing, Shannon stepped outside to vape and found a bouquet left at the door, addressed to Susie." Trevor's eyes found mine. "I thought maybe you left them."

A muscle in my cheek twitched. "Why the hell would you think that?"

"You've been flirting with her since she got here," Rowan said.

"Why the fuck are y'all up in my business?"

"Just stating facts." Rowan shrugged.

Jamison stepped in before I could snap back. "What happened to the flowers?"

"Not sure," Trevor answered. "Susie had this strange look when she read the card, but when I asked her if anything was wrong, she said no. But she left them behind when she went home. She didn't want them."

I stared at the ground. That seemed odd. Most women loved flowers, especially anonymous ones. Suddenly, I didn't want to go home. "Anyone up for another game?"

"Nope, I've got to be at the firehouse early tomorrow," Trevor said.

"I have work in the morning, and a beautiful woman waiting for me," Jamison answered, picking up his bag.

"Me too," Rowan added. "Work in the morning and fun to get to tonight. I lost a bet to Summer, and I promised her I'd pay up. That's one bet I don't mind losing. I'll see y'all later."

Jamison and I walked back across the street. Orlinda Valley was deserted. It seemed like everyone had someone to go home to. Well, almost everyone. Sure as hell not me.

"Any big plans after practice tomorrow?" Jamison asked.

I shook my head. "Just visiting my mother at Shear Perfection so she can cut my hair. After that, you know, the same thing, different day. Go to the gym, then maybe my mother's to swim and catch some rays, then to your house to mooch dinner off Lilly."

Jamison laughed as he climbed into his car. "Great. I'll see you tomorrow night." He waved and pulled away.

I was alone in the high school parking lot and leaned against my car, staring at the school. My mind wandered back twenty years ago when Jamison and I roamed those halls as students.

I loved high school. Okay, maybe not the classes, or most of my teachers, or the learning, but I loved the fun—pep rallies, football games, the girls. Orlinda Valley might be a small town, but it never struggled in the women department. We used to joke that the water must make them perfect.

I sighed heavily. I'd never imagined I'd be single when I was thirty-six. Shit, when you were eighteen, thirty-six seemed like a lifetime away. But reality was different. *Here I am, and that lifetime is now.* The only things I had to look forward to were football practice and, when the summer was over, work.

No one was waiting for me at home, not even a pet. If it weren't for Jamison and the few guys from high school who were still around, I'd be alone, and I didn't even have Jamison that often anymore, since he was with Lilly.

Susie's crystal eyes crossed my mind. The glare that often greeted me turned me on more than was probably healthy. I didn't know what it was about her, but I couldn't get her out of my mind. She appeared in my thoughts at the most random times, and earlier, when she'd been pissed at me at the pub, copped an attitude, and placed my beer in front of Jamison, damn, that was hot.

I got into my car and drove out of the vacant parking lot.

I'm obsessing over a woman who hates me. Hell, she can't even look at me without shooting daggers in my direction.

But something about her shot an arrow straight into my heart and kept it beating with anticipation of seeing her again, even though I knew she'd hate everything I said to her.

How do I get her to see I'm not always an ass? Grow up, read the room, think of others. I shook my head and rolled the tension from my shoulders.

I'd learned my life's motto from someone who was alone and selfish. I didn't want to be anything like him. I really didn't. *And*

I'm not going to be. I can't change who I am, but I can change how I treat people and react to situations.

But shit. Who bought Susie flowers and left them outside the pub? It hadn't been me or Trevor.

Someone else in Orlinda Valley had their eyes on her.

CHAPTER 11

LANCE

"Hey, you," Diane said when I walked into Shear Perfection.

My mother and Diane had owned the salon for as long as I could remember. Everyone went there, and as usual, it was busy. Diane's client, Mrs. Carlisle, was having her hair wrapped in foil, and she smiled when I sat at my mother's station.

"Hello, Lance. How's your summer going?" Mrs. Carlisle asked.

"Hello, Mrs. Carlisle. It's going well, thank you. I'm staying busy." It wasn't a total lie. I had football.

"Good to hear it. How's the team looking so far?"

Mrs. Carlisle's grandson was a freshman and on the junior varsity team. "It's looking good. You know, with all the seniors who graduated last year, this is a growth year, and I think Jackson is going to be an asset to the team."

She grinned. "Well, he's absolutely loving it. He says the practice is difficult, but it's worth it."

"I'm glad he's enjoying it," I answered as my mother and Summer walked out from the back room. "Hi, Summer."

"Good morning, old man. I hear Rowan and Trevor made you look like a fool on the basketball court again last night. When you make good on your bet, don't keep him out too late or let him drink too much. I need him home in tip-top shape."

"You know…" I snapped my mouth closed. *Now would be the perfect time to practice biting my tongue. Let her comment pass.* I shook my head and hugged my mother instead. "Hey, Mom."

"Hi there, buddy," she said as she hugged me tight. "How do you want me to cut your hair today?"

I looked at her in the mirror as I sat in her chair. "I was thinking I'd go short on the side, keep the top long, and bleach the tips. I'm up for a change."

She raised an eyebrow. "Yeah, I don't think so. How about I do the usual?"

I laughed. "Why do you even ask? You know what I like and how you're going to cut it. You've been doing the same thing since high school."

She passed a comb through my hair. "I know, but it's a habit."

"Did y'all hear we're getting bad weather tonight?" Mrs. Carlisle asked.

"I thought it was just rain tonight. A storm tomorrow," my mother said.

"That's what I heard," Diane chimed in.

"I don't know. I heard a storm tonight. But you know how this weather is. It might storm in Nashville, but here, we could get nothing," Mrs. Carlisle added.

"That's so true," Diane answered. "I guess we'll all have to be careful either way. You know how quickly storms pop up."

"Do you ever wonder why all the worst storms seem to hit at night?" my mom asked.

I listened to the women talk about the weather. Storms never bothered me. I enjoyed the heavy rain. Thunder always seemed to relax me, and it was part of living in Tennessee. One minute, it could be sunny, and the next, the sky could turn black, especially when there was so much humidity.

The chime on the door rang, and I glanced over. My pulse picked up as Susie entered.

"Good morning, Susie," Diane called.

She smiled at Diane, but it didn't quite meet her eyes. "Good morning." Her eyes met mine for a second— sent my pulse racing—then darted away. *The effect she has on me.* I shook my head.

"Have you heard from Kora and your brother?" my mother asked.

"I did. They're having so much fun that they're planning on staying another week. I told them everything at the house was fine and to take their time."

While she talked, I took in her features. I'd seen her Friday night, and I knew she'd worked all weekend, but she looked exhausted. She had circles under her eyes, and the glow that usually lit up her face was nonexistent.

"Is everything okay, Susie?" I asked. "You look rough, like you haven't slept in a while."

She turned toward me, and her eyes narrowed. "Wow, thanks." Her words were short and dripped with irritation, which I was beginning to recognize as her preferred method of communication when it came to me.

Okay, my words had come out wrong—again. I held up my hands to ward off her wrath. "I didn't mean anything rude by it. Just being a concerned friend. I know you worked a lot this weekend, and I was wondering if the goats were treating you well. Have they gotten out anymore?"

Her shoulders relaxed. "No, they haven't. I think they're getting used to me. Gotta admit I woke up earlier to spend extra time with them this morning. It was nice. They really are sweet. Good thing I had a chance to enjoy a small part of my day, because work was busy."

"Trevor's not working you too hard, is he?" Diane asked.

Susie laughed. "No, he's been helpful and accommodating. I usually work the opening shift, as Barb enjoys working late. She says the tips are better. The early afternoon is a great time for me to get broken into serving without being totally exhausted. I work two nights a week, though."

Her laughter sounded like wind chimes blowing in a light summer breeze and stirred heat deep in my gut.

"Well, I'm glad you're enjoying it," my mother said.

"Weren't you a teacher?" Mrs. Carlisle asked.

Susie nodded. "I was."

"Have you thought of applying at Orlinda Valley Elementary or High?"

Susie breathed deeply and stared toward the back of the salon, where Summer was waiting. "I think I need a break, Mrs. Carlisle."

She nodded. "Totally understandable. But the preschool at the Methodist Church needs a teacher. Maybe you'd like that. I could put in a good word."

Susie's face lit up just a pinch. If you didn't know her, you probably would have missed it, but with how I'd been obsessing over her, I already seemed to understand her moods.

Damn, could I be any more desperate?

"Thank you. I'll think about it." She nodded and walked past us.

I watched her in the mirror. She went to Summer, who set her up at a pedicure station.

I wished I could have heard what they were saying, as they were deep in conversation. Susie's arms flailed in dramatic form. Summer commented, glanced up at her, then looked back down at her toes.

Something was wrong. I could sense it in her attitude, in the way she carried herself, and in how little she'd talked to me. I chuckled.

"What's so funny?" my mom asked, hesitating in her cut.

"Nothing, Mom."

I couldn't say I knew Susie was upset because her typical irritation with me sounded even more irritated. In the short time she'd been in town, we had yet to have a decent conversation. No one would see that as anything strange.

I stared blankly into the mirror. Every time I opened my mouth when she was around, I sounded like a total ass and pissed her off. If we were with a group, I said something rude and pissed her off. If I helped her with the goats, I cracked a joke and pissed her off.

It didn't matter what I did. The outcome was always the same.

"You seem like you're in another world," my mom said as she ran her fingers through my hair. Her eyes met mine in the mirror, then glanced over my shoulder at Susie and leaned in toward my ear. "Susie seemed a little uptight when she came in. Anything I should know?" Her gaze met mine again, and she raised her eyebrows.

I swear *mothers have special powers.* "Don't know what you're talking about, Mom," I said.

She turned on a hair dryer and blew all the loose hair away, took off the cape, and hugged my shoulders. "I love you, buddy."

I smiled. "Love you back, Momma."

She kissed my cheek. "Stay out of trouble," she said as I stood.

"Always try to." She started sweeping, and I took one last glance back at Susie. I should go. That was the smart thing to do. I turned on my heels. I wasn't known for doing smart things. I tended to gamble with my options.

Susie was there, and walking away would be simple and not very risky. *Where's the fun in that?* Summer and Susie were probably the only two women in Orlinda Valley who weren't a part of the Lance Hartley fan club. I walked toward them. *Yep, I'm a glutton for punishment.*

"I didn't realize we asked for you to bless us with your presence," Summer said as she carefully slipped Susie's flip-flops onto her feet then stood with her hands on her hips. "What do you want? We're busy."

"Your positive attitude never ceases to amaze me, Summer. But I'm not here to talk to you. I came to check on Susie."

Susie crossed her arms. "Thanks, but I don't need you checking up on me. I'm sure it won't be hard for you to find a woman who will love your attention." She walked to the manicure station and sat across from Summer. "I'd prefer to be left alone."

These women are two peas in a pod. If only I could take the hint, but I must like abuse, because I took the seat next to Susie.

Summer placed a bowl of solution that looked like dish soap and lots of water in front of her.

"Well, we don't always get what we want," I said.

Susie gave me a sideways glance and placed her fingers in the bowl.

"So, you're going to stay and watch?" Summer asked.

"Nope," I answered, not taking my eyes off Susie. "I heard you got flowers from someone at Jerry's Pub on Sunday night."

Summer's eyes jumped to Susie, but Susie didn't make eye contact with her either. She kept her eyes down. "Yeah, I did. So?"

"Who were they from?" A bad feeling crawled its way into my gut.

"Don't know. There was no name." Again, she didn't meet my gaze. She glued her eyes to the counter. Summer looked at me and tilted her head.

I shrugged. I should probably drop it. Susie didn't seem like she wanted to talk about it at all, but something scratched at me to keep asking. "Then why'd you leave them on the bar and not take them?"

She didn't answer.

I waited.

Still, she said nothing, so I continued. "It's just a little strange. If you didn't know who it was, I'd think you'd take them home out of curiosity if nothing else. Are you sure everything's okay?"

A hiss of breath escaped her, and she turned toward me. "Lance, I appreciate your concern. I really do, but I can take care of myself. Drop it. I don't need your cocky ass in my business. If I wanted to tell you, I would." Her jaw twitched.

I leaned back. "So, there is something."

Our eyes met, and I held her gaze.

She huffed and turned away.

"I'm sure it sucks to have someone care," I said as I stood and walked away. I had a churning feeling in my gut. Something felt off. I was sure she was hiding something.

"Hey, ladies," I said to my mother, Diane, and Mrs. Carlisle. "Would y'all like something to drink?"

"Yes, that would be sweet," Mrs. Carlisle said. "Diet Coke would be wonderful."

I nodded and went into the kitchen. I grabbed Mrs. Carlisle's Diet Coke and two bottles of water. One for my mother and the other for Diane.

"Thank you, Lance, honey," Mrs. Carlisle said when I passed drinks to the women. "I can't believe you're still single. A handsome and sweet boy like you." She *tsk*ed.

"Mrs. Carlisle, I promise you it isn't for a lack of trying."

"Well, I believe there's someone for each of us," she said. "You just need to be willing to work for something if you want it badly enough. Love isn't easy."

"I second that," Diane said. "There's someone out there for everyone."

"I third it," my mother said. "I haven't lost hope that you'll find the perfect person and get married one day."

"Marriage? That's a bit much," I said.

"One day, Lance. It will happen," Mrs. Carlisle replied.

The women continued their discussion of fate and love, but I wasn't sure I agreed with them. Their discussion became more annoying than entertaining. I heard all about how they each met their significant others. Of course, I knew all about my mom and Charles, but I did forget that Diane and Tom weren't each other's first marriage since they've been married for as long as I could remember.

"Hey," Susie said as she walked toward us. Her smile was bright and genuine, not the polite mask she usually wore around me. It transformed her entire face, like all the stress she usually carried around had disappeared. It made her more beautiful than ever. I stared longer than I should have but couldn't help myself.

Her dark hair caught the salon lights, and when her eyes swept the room, they seemed lighter somehow—less guarded. For just a moment, when her gaze met mine, I thought I saw something different there, not the usual wariness, but curiosity maybe.

But it was gone so fast that I might have imagined it.

"That color looks great on you," my mom said, holding up Susie's hands and admiring Summer's work.

"Thank you, I like it too." Susie's voice was warm. "I need to get some shopping done before the rain moves in. I'll see y'all later."

I watched her leave, the moment when our eyes met still replaying in my mind. Something had shifted, even if I couldn't put my finger on it.

I stayed frozen against my mom's station, phone in my hand. Maybe I should text Jamison—see if he and Lilly had room for one more for dinner. Lilly could ask Susie, and if we both showed up, it wouldn't be a date.

I hadn't gotten up the nerve to send the text to Jamison when Susie walked back in the salon and directly to me.

I pushed off Mom's station and stood tall. *This is a first. Act cool.* I cocked an eyebrow. "Hey, what's up?"

"My brother's truck won't turn over. Do you think you could look at it?"

I struggled to keep the smile off my face. I'd do anything for this woman, and now I had an excuse to spend time with her. "Sure. I'm not doing anything else."

CHAPTER 12

LANCE

I followed Susie from the salon to the parking lot, where she had parked Kai's truck. I popped the hood as she turned the key. The engine gave a rapid clicking sound but wouldn't turn over. "It might be the starter. The lights are on, so it's not the battery."

"What am I going to do? I broke Kai's pride and joy." Her voice was a concerned whisper.

I closed the hood, pulled my phone from my pocket, and dialed the number for Bubba's Towing. "Yeah, well, it's amazing this hunk of junk hasn't caused Kai problems before this."

Bubba, who always answered his business phone, promised to pick up the truck within the hour. "There. Taken care of. Bubba's Towing will pick it up and take it to the garage. He knows Kai, so he'll call him and see what he wants to do."

Susie leaned heavily against the truck. "Guess I should call Kai first and give him a heads-up." She pulled her bottom lip between her teeth, rubbed her hands over her face, and massaged her temples.

"You okay?" I asked.

She sighed. "I planned on going to the store on my way home. I need to pick up milk, eggs, and bread."

I chuckled at her shopping list. "You know we're not having a winter storm. It's just going to rain a little."

She scrunched her forehead, then let out a small laugh, and her face lit up.

"You should laugh more often. You're beautiful when you laugh."

"So, you're saying I'm not beautiful at any other time?" She asked with a teasing tone.

I held her gaze. "Trust me. That's not what I meant at all."

She blinked but didn't look away.

Those crystal eyes of hers sucked me right in. I lost my breath as we gazed at each other.

Suddenly, she broke the spell. "I laugh a lot," she said, looking down the road.

I shook my head. "Not in front of me."

"Well, then, what's that tell you about the current company?" Her smile touched her eyes. It was the most beautiful smile I had ever seen.

I chuckled and smirked at her snarkiness. "I was going to be helpful and offer to take you to the store then home; but I don't know if you deserve my gentlemanness after that remark."

"Gentlemanness? Is that a thing?"

I shrugged. "Don't know, but it could be. What do you think? Would you let me help you out?"

Her gaze wandered around my face before she spoke. "Do we need to wait for the tow truck?"

"Nope. We can throw the keys onto the seat, and they'll come pick it up."

"Okay, then. I guess it would be worth it to see if the self-absorbed football hero of Orlinda Valley could actually be a gentleman."

I placed my hand over my gut as if she had punched me. "Ouch. That was harsh. I'm not self-absorbed."

She raised her eyebrows and tilted her head.

"Okay, I'm not *that* self-absorbed."

She laughed.

I shook my head, walked toward my car, and opened the door for her.

"Wow, thank you," she said, as she pressed one hand to her chest like she had witnessed something scandalous. "Look at you being all chivalrous."

"You've met my mother and Charles," I said as I hopped in on my side and started the engine. "My dad might not have taught me anything decent, but Charles is nothing but a gentleman." I turned the air on cold. "I'll run into the hair salon and let my mom and Diane know someone from the garage will stop by for the truck. Be right back."

Her surprised, wide-eyed expression remained etched in my memory all because I had opened her door. She was going to see me differently. From that point on, I'd make sure she understood the man I really was, and that chivalry wasn't dead.

Once I was back in the truck, I drove two blocks to Food Land. "Look, I get it." I said as I pulled into a parking space. "You think I'm a jackass." I put up my hands, surrendering. "I understand. What do you say I prove to you I've changed or at least I'm trying?" I turned off the truck and turned toward her. "No, I'm not perfect, but I think I've shown you I care. Have I ever been disrespectful toward you?"

She pursed her lips and stared at the roof of the truck. "Well…"

I chuckled. "Okay, don't answer that." I hopped out and ran to her side to open her door, and she hopped out. The air was thick with humidity, and the temperature was soaring. The Frosty Freeze was just a couple of doors down. "I know I told you we could go shopping, and we will, but why don't we grab ice cream first?" I said with a gesture down the street to the walk-up ice cream shop.

Susie nodded. "I've been here since May, and I have yet to eat there, even though it's all anyone talks about." She shrugged. "Sure. Why not? It's hot, and ice cream would taste good."

It was late enough in the afternoon that downtown was bustling. I said hi to a couple as we passed them on the sidewalk.

"Hey, Dan!" I hollered to one of my fellow teachers, who was pumping gas at the station across the street.

Susie glanced at me and smirked.

"What?" I asked, nudging her with my shoulder.

"Nothing," she answered and nudged me back.

We reached the Frosty Freeze. There was a couple on the bench swing under the shade trees, and two middle school boys ate ice cream and fries at one of the circular picnic tables. I knew the boys from working with the middle school football team occasionally.

"Hey, guys," I said with a nod.

"Hi, Mr. Hartley." They sat up tall when I approached.

"Chuck and Bryan, right?"

They nodded.

"Are you both having a good summer?"

"Yes, sir."

"Great to hear. Make sure you keep working out. Only be a couple more years till you're on the high school football team. I want you in top shape."

Their faces lit up.

"Absolutely," Chuck said.

"Yes, sir," Bryan answered.

I led Susie to the shorter line so we could place our order. She was watching me with a thoughtful expression. I raised my eyebrows and considered commenting but thought better of it. If she knew I'd caught her admiring me, she'd deny it. "What will it be, Susie? The ice cream is homemade, and the milkshakes are amazing."

"I'll take one scoop of cookie dough and one scoop of chocolate peanut butter cup," Susie said.

I placed our order and paid before she could complain, turned, and collided directly with her. My hands shot out, gripping her arms, and the contact ignited something fierce that shot straight from my fingertips to my already-racing heart.

We stood frozen, our faces inches apart, her eyes locked on mine. When her lips ticked up in that barely there smile, my heart slammed against my chest.

CHAPTER 13

SUSIE

I jerked away from Lance as electricity shot through my body at his touch. *What the hell was that? I need some space.* "Should we go grab a table?"

"Sure. We'll hear our names."

I walked quickly toward a table and took a seat.

A man in an Orlinda Valley baseball hat stopped Lance. They shook hands, and Lance's face lit up like a kid's on Christmas morning as they talked about the upcoming football season.

He was definitely in his element and totally comfortable in his own skin. The residents adored him. The boys' eyes had lit up when he said hi to them. This was a side of Lance I'd not seen yet. The self-absorbed ass I knew was not the same person the town adored.

His eyes met mine, and the grin that filled his face—sincere, polite, and sexy—sent my stomach fluttering, and I bit on my bottom lip.

His name was called, and he went to grab our order.

"Here you go, ma'am," Lance said as he passed my ice cream to me. "Cookie dough and chocolate peanut butter cup." He swung his leg over the bench seat and sat straddling it, facing me, casual and confident.

"Ma'am? Suddenly, you're getting all mannerly."

"Whatever," he said. "You see only what you want to see."

My gaze shot to his. *What does he mean by that?*

I took a bite of my ice cream as I churned his words around in my head. *What have I seen? Who is Lance really?* I took another bite of the chocolate peanut butter cup ice cream. The richness of the chocolate mixed with the deliciousness of the peanut butter filled my taste buds. It was yummy. I focused on the ice cream and not on Lance.

The boys yelled his name and waved as they left. Lance waved back.

"Everyone seems to like you."

"Is that surprising?"

I shrugged. Maybe I had been mistaken.

"Well, you know I grew up here and played football. I was one of the town favorites then. Now I'm back and coaching the team. This is home. And just like high school, I'm loved by everyone." A corner of his mouth ticked up.

There was that cockiness and the damn sexy grin to go with it. The town might love him, but that was where the admiration would end. "From what I heard, Jamison was the actual star during your high school glory days, then you followed him to college, right?"

"It was something like that." He nodded.

"I also heard that Jamison could've gone pro."

He let out a soft chuckle. "Yeah. He could have. We were an amazing team, but Jamison was a natural on the field. He made me a better player. A knee injury put him on the bench his sophomore year of college, in one of the first games he actually got to start, and he never regained his traction. But in typical Jamison fashion, he took it in stride. He found himself something else to occupy his time, left the team, and focused on his fraternity, his girlfriend—and future wife—Carley, and his career. I stuck with the team and rode the bench with pride throughout senior year."

"Was that tough for him, seeing you still on the team?"

"Not that I ever noticed. Even though Jamison wanted to play, he moved on. I wanted the prestige of saying I played on a college team. I knew I wanted to coach high school football, so I majored in health and PE and figured I'd come back here to coach and teach one day. I'm living my dream."

I licked ice cream off my lips and studied him. "For someone who's living their dream, why don't you seem happy?"

Lance's smile met his eyes. There was a gleam there that again sent those butterflies fluttering in my stomach.

He shook his head but said nothing and went right back to his ice cream, though he kept glancing at me from time to time. I felt his gaze burn into my skin.

Ignore him.

I took a deep breath and finished my ice cream, then pushed the Styrofoam cup away. "You know you ignored my question," I said.

He glanced over. "What question?"

"The one where I asked why you don't seem happy if you're living your dream."

He chuckled and shook his head slightly. "You don't miss much, do you?"

I shrugged. "You don't say much."

"Agreed. Well, you know I teach PE. I get to focus most of my time on the football team, and I've been teaching for twelve years. I've helped shape some amazing football players over the years. Some incredible young men. I love being part of this town and living in this community." He pursed his lips, then one side ticked up, and he shrugged.

He wasn't finished. I could tell there were things left unsaid. The moment between us stretched on, and the air got thick with thought.

"Finished?" Lance asked as he gestured toward my empty cup on the table.

I nodded.

He took my trash and his and threw them into the garbage. "Let's get going. You have groceries to purchase." He placed his hand lightly on my back as he led me to the sidewalk.

It was a slight gesture, nothing serious, but the heat from his hand lingered on the small of my back long after he removed it, though I noticed he'd still avoided my question. He was good at that.

We walked to Food Land, and he grabbed a shopping cart, then we wandered up and down the aisles, made small talk, and cut up as we filled the cart with food.

"What do you say I buy steaks and impress you with my famous grilling skills tonight?" Lance asked as we stopped in front of the beef section. "Or do you have something else planned?"

"I was just going to have a turkey sandwich and chips and find a movie to watch."

He grinned and picked up two steaks. "Perfect. I'll cook steak and potatoes, and you make a salad."

He grabbed two steaks, then we backtracked to the produce section to get potatoes and fixings for a Caesar salad, and we picked up a loaf of Italian bread.

Finally, we were walking toward his truck with the groceries.

"I've never had such a good time grocery shopping," I said as Lance and I loaded the bags into the back seat.

"See? I have talents outside of football, drinking, and being a jackass," he said as he closed the door.

"I never said you were a jackass."

He chuckled. "Yeah, I call bullshit."

"Seriously. I've called you an asshat, an asshole, and a dick. But I don't think I've called you a jackass—not to your face, anyway."

He laughed as he walked me around the truck and opened my door.

"Wow," I said.

"See? Not a jackass move, was it?"

"Nope," I replied as I climbed in. "Seems as if you have some gentlemanness in you after all."

He winked, closed the door, and walked around to the driver's side.

That wink made my pulse race. *Lord, what the hell is my brain thinking? I need to knock the temperature down a few notches. Say something rude.* "You know, Lance," I said as he sat behind the wheel. "You surprised me."

He glanced over as he pulled out of the space and onto the road. "I surprised you? How? That I can be fun and a gentleman? I told you I was raised by Charles." His eyes danced with humor.

A blush crept onto my cheeks. "I can see that," I said with a smile.

"Good. Now I hope I can prove myself even more to you. As soon as we get to the house, I'll start the grill and season the steaks. You prepare the salad. You'll see that I'm also an amazing cook, especially when I'm starving."

I faced the window. *So much for saying something rude and lowering the temperature between us.*

It seemed the temperature had ticked up instead.

I wiped the counter, hung the kitchen towel over the handle of the stove, and grabbed two bottles of beer from the fridge. Lance was out on the patio. He had just finished cleaning the grill and wiping down the table.

His cooking skills were top-notch. He'd cooked the steaks to medium perfection and microwaved the potatoes. Then he wrapped them in tinfoil and placed them on the grill to finish. It had all turned out perfectly, even the Caesar salad.

He looked up when I approached, and I handed him a beer. "Thought you might want one."

"Thanks," he said. "Want to walk down to the river? It's a nice night."

I nodded, and we walked side by side on the trail leading from Kora and Kai's backyard to the riverbank. It was a perfect June night, less humid than usual, and a slight breeze was blowing.

We sat in the Adirondack chairs around the firepit. It was quiet and serene by the river. The only sounds were the rustling of the leaves in the trees, the flowing of the water, and the singing of birds.

The sun sat low on the horizon, but there was still enough daylight that we could stay out here a couple more hours.

"Dinner was delicious, and you proved yourself right," I said.

"I did? About what?"

"You are a good cook. Thank you."

He nodded once. "You're welcome." He smiled into his beer. His eyes stayed on mine as he took a drink.

I looked away as a blush crept up my cheeks. It had been a good day, and I might have to admit to myself that I'd totally misjudged Lance. He wasn't as much of an ass as I wanted him to be.

"What are you thinking?" he asked quietly.

"Nothing."

His eyes questioned me.

"I swear. Nothing at least worth talking about."

"Fine. Then tell me something about yourself. What's it like being a twin?"

"Do you know how many people ask me that?" I leaned back in the chair and laid my head back.

He did the same. "Never thought about it. I know I always wanted to have a twin. Someone my age. We would be close. Best friends, all that."

"Yeah. I was never alone, that's for sure. But it was a bit different for me, with being a girl and all. It wasn't like Sebastian and I could share clothes. Though I wore his shirts as nightshirts. What fit him perfectly went down to almost my knees."

Lance turned his head toward me. "When was the last time you saw him?"

God, it had been a while. "About two years ago. He left for basic training right before I went out west. We Facetime when we can."

Lance shook his head. "Not the same."

"True, but it's all I have for now, so it's better than nothing. It's been almost a month since I've even talked to him on the phone. He's overseas for a few more months, so with the time difference and all, it's been difficult." I smacked my arm. The mosquitoes were getting awful.

"You know, you just killed our state bug. They're a protected species."

I jerked my head toward him and smacked at another one. "Well, then, call the authorities. I plan on killing as many as I can before they suck me dry."

Our gazes locked. His throat constricted as if he had swallowed a large lump of food. I turned away and took a sip of my beer.

He cleared his throat and stood. "Okay, the mosquitoes are pretty bad. Let's head back to the house."

"It's getting late anyway. I have to go to work tomorrow."

We stood and walked back to the house and around to the front toward his truck in comfortable silence.

"It was a fun afternoon. I hope you've seen a different side of me," Lance said. His blue eyes searched my face.

A pull held my eyes on his. I sucked in my bottom lip, and his eyes darted there.

I let out a nervous laugh and stepped back, breaking whatever that was between us. "It was fun. Thank you for stepping up and taking me shopping, bringing me home, and cooking. All of it."

He stepped closer, and my pulse raced. My eyes widened.

What was he doing?

He raised his hand and slapped his fingers lightly across my temple.

I flinched.

"A mosquito," he whispered. His fingers lingered on my cheek and brushed lightly against my skin, causing my gut to flutter and my heart to race.

My gaze froze on his. His eyes sparkled with gold flecks, and his eyelashes were long.

He was so close, and the breeze was just light enough that I could smell his cologne—woodsy and masculine—and my pulse picked up.

He grazed his fingers down my arm and squeezed my hand. A tingle passed slowly through my body.

Then his hand fell to his side as he stepped away. The spell was broken.

"I'll check on Kai's truck tomorrow and let you know what Bubba says."

"Thank you." My voice was a whisper.

He smiled and walked around the truck to climb in on the driver's side. The engine revved, and he rolled down the passenger window. "Lock up. I'll talk to you tomorrow." He smiled and winked. "Night, Susie."

"Good night." I waved as he pulled away. That smile turned my insides to mush.

What the hell happened today? Where did the egotistical jackass go?

I puffed out a breath and walked around to the back of the house.

CHAPTER 14

SUSIE

"Yes, everything here is going fine. You two enjoy Florida," I said to Kora and Kai on the FaceTime call as I sat on the steps of the front porch.

The morning was beautiful. It seemed hard to believe there was a storm coming. I nodded as Kai and Kora went on and on, concerned about the weather.

"I know. It's been raining on and off since late last night, but right now, we have sunshine."

"Still, they're saying it should be bad by noon," Kai insisted.

"I know. I promise. I'll keep my eye on the weather. Love you. Now go back to the beach."

I disconnected the call. *Good lord. Like I've never been through a storm before.* I stepped off the front step as I heard a vehicle pull up the driveway.

Lance. My pulse raced. He'd sent me a text that morning and insisted on helping me lock up the animals before the storm hit. I could have taken care of things on my own, but I didn't have it in me to say no.

"Heading out to the goats?" he asked as he climbed out of the truck.

I looked up at the sky. Large gray clouds raced across it and blocked the sun. The rain would move in soon. "Yeah. It looks like the storm's not going around us."

"I agree. Let's get this done. I don't think we have much time."

We walked side by side toward the pasture. His six-foot-four broad frame towered over me. His now-familiar scent blew off him in a soft breeze, and my pulse matched my heartbeat. "You didn't have to help. I could have handled it on my own."

"I know," he said as we reached the gate, and he opened it. "You've been handling it on your own all week, but sometimes, the goats don't fully cooperate, and I told you I'd help." He closed the gate and met my stride. "I stand by my word." He glanced at the sky, and my gaze followed his.

The gray clouds morphed into enormous black bits of swirling cotton as they hovered over the house. "I just told Kora and Kai it was sunny, but it looks like we may need to hurry. I guess your help is better than nothing."

"Thanks," Lance said.

I chuckled as the goats poked their heads out from the door of the barn and welcomed us. "There must be bad weather coming for them not to greet us at the gate. They hate getting wet."

"Without them fighting us to go outside, our job shouldn't be too difficult. I'll get the door. You check their food."

We entered the large interior of the barn, and the goats were more than happy to get attention. The air was thick with humidity and the smell of straw and goats. "Secure the windows, also. I want nothing to be left open. Just in case it gets bad."

Lance did as I asked as I gave the animals fresh water and the goats hay. While they ate, I petted them and gave them the attention they desired.

"Look what I found huddled in one of the chicken boxes."

I turned toward Lance, and my mouth dropped. He was holding a tiny brown tabby kitten. The soft mew he gave stole my heart. "Oh, let me hold him."

Lance held him out to me.

I took the kitten and cuddled him. His coloring was rich brown with swirls and lines of black. His fur was soft, with tufts coming out of his ears. The *M* on his head was typical of a tabby. "He's adorable." I held him up and looked into his yellow eyes. "How did you get into the chicken box, little one?"

He answered with a soft meow.

"He was probably looking for shade and somewhere cooler than outside in the direct sun," Lance said.

I glanced at him. His face held the same soft grin I'd noticed the previous day, and his new attitude—friendly, sweet, and fun—was so different from the Lance I thought I knew.

I turned my attention back to the kitten as a rumble of thunder shook the barn. "I think we'd better get the doors closed." I held the kitten in one hand and scratched each goat on the head as Lance closed the large garage-like door. Then we slipped out the side exit.

We raced across the pasture but didn't get far before rain started falling in large, fat drops. We picked up our pace, and Lance closed the gate behind us as I cuddled the kitten close to my body in a vain attempt to keep him dry.

The rain soon became a torrential downpour.

"Shit," Lance said with a chuckle. "Come on."

We sprinted to the porch and ran up the steps.

I struggled to catch my breath and wiped water from my face.

"We almost made it," he said.

"In what universe? We're soaked." I laughed, looking down at my feet. My socks squished in my shoes. I looked up, and Lance's hair was stuck to his head, and his shirt dripped with water.

"It could always be worse," he said.

I wiped my wet hair from my face and shrugged. "That's true. I could be wearing white."

His eyes met mine, and a smile filled his face. "Sense of humor now?"

I shrugged. "Before, you were an ass. I don't think you're a total ass anymore."

His eyes raked over my face, and the air between us became electric, but it had nothing to do with the storm raging around us.

A crash of thunder pulled me from the trance Lance had placed on me, and the kitten meowed. I shushed the kitten with a kiss to the top of his head and turned the doorknob. But it wouldn't budge. "Shoot." I scrunched up my face. "The door's locked. I guess I didn't unlock the knob when I came onto the porch."

The rain fell in sheets. We could hardly see Lance's truck in front of the house.

"The back door's unlocked. I went out it a few times today. I guess we can run for it," I said.

Lance looked out at the rain. "Okay. I'll run around to the back. You stay here."

"Lance, not by yourself. We can both go."

"Absolutely not. You stand here, and I'll run around to the back, go through the house, and let you in."

A sudden flash of lightning split the sky, and I nearly leaped out of my skin. My heart thumped hard at the crack of thunder that followed. It sounded as if two massive trees had splintered and crashed to the ground. God, I hated storms.

Lance squeezed my arm. That slight touch calmed my racing heart. "I'll be quick," he said in a soft voice, then took off into the rain.

I huddled with the kitten, trying to keep the rain that was blowing onto the porch from getting him wet.

Luckily, it didn't take long for a dripping Lance to open the front door. I stepped into the house and over a puddle on the floor, where Lance stood.

He looked as if he had climbed out of a pool. His shirt stuck to him like glue. His hair stuck to his head even worse than before, and drops of water ran down his face. His lips parted just slightly, and his warm breath radiated over my damp skin. I tore my eyes from his body and tried to close the door, but Lance stopped me and stepped onto the porch.

I stared in awe as he shucked off his shirt and squeezed the water out onto the porch. Heat bloomed across my cheeks as the muscles in his arms and back rippled with the effort, and my mouth went dry.

His skin was dark from all the time he spent out in the sun, working around his mother's house or swimming, and it was obvious he loved spending time at the gym. When he turned around, the most perfect six-pack and set of pecs I'd ever seen greeted me.

"There. That might help keep some water out of the house," he said as he stepped back inside.

I swallowed hard and forced my eyes to stay off his chest and on his eyes.

"I need to mop up the floor," he said.

I followed his gaze along the water path that went around the corner to the kitchen. "We need dry clothes first, then we can deal with that. I'll grab you one of Kai's T-shirts. He has some down here." I spun quickly and walked to my room. Thoughts of things I could do with Lance and that hot body flew through my mind. *Enough.* I blew out a heavy breath. I'd promised myself I wouldn't get attached to another man. And Lance was one hundred percent a bad idea.

I made it to the safety of my bedroom just as another flash of lightning lit up the sky. I jumped and cuddled the kitten close. "It's okay, kitty. That thunder can't hurt you here."

"Are you telling him that to help him feel better or yourself?"

"Shit." My heart hadn't calmed from the fright of the thunder, and Lance hadn't helped. "What the hell? Don't sneak up on me." I hoped my words came out sounding irritated. I was. *Irritated at him being so damn—* "Shit," I said under my breath as I placed the kitten on my bed and turned toward the dresser.

Breathe. Calm down.

"Sorry, I thought you knew I was behind you. I didn't mean to startle you."

I grabbed a shirt and a pair of basketball shorts from the drawer and tossed them in his direction. "Here. Get out of those wet clothes."

He raised his eyebrows, and that smirk—that damn sexy smirk—ticked up his face.

"I meant. Get. Dressed," I said through clenched teeth.

He stepped closer. "I *am* dressed." His eyes held mine.

My chest heaved as my heart raced. I tried to pull my eyes from his, but they were superglued in place. His eyes held mine, and the specks of gold sprinkled in them danced with something I'd rather not name.

"I'm only shirtless," he said as he took another step. "I'm not naked. You're acting like you've never seen a man shirtless before. Does this bother you?"

"No, of course not." *Not that I'd tell you if it did.* I could feel the heat of his skin radiating off him, and a shiver raced through my body.

He glanced down at my body, and his smirk ticked up. "You're cold. Maybe you should get out of your wet clothes."

"Excuse me?" Damn him and his irritating attitude. I stepped back and knocked into my dresser. My shirt was tight across my breasts. My face heated, and I crossed my arms.

"I'll change in there." He gestured toward the bathroom and stepped away.

I let out a heavy breath.

"Why do you have men's clothes down here anyway?" he asked before he stepped into the bathroom.

I cleared my throat. "Kai used this bathroom when he was finishing upstairs. I have more than enough space, so I never emptied the drawer."

"Good to know."

"Wait," I said before he closed the door. "I need you to change down the hall. I've also got to get out of my wet clothes."

"Trust me," he said. "I won't come out until you tell me to. Anyway..." His smirk changed to a smile that filled his face. "It's not like I haven't seen you basically naked."

Heat raced up my neck. *My damn dip in the goat trough again.* "You're such a dick."

"Maybe," he said with a wiggle of his eyebrows. "But you don't dislike me as much as you used to." He closed the bathroom door behind him.

I stared at the closed door and shook my head. "God, I hate that he's right." I combed my fingers through my wet hair, and changed faster than a racer on pit row, then froze. *What is that noise?* "I can't believe it, Kitty," I said, picking him up. "He's taking a shower."

His shirtless body in my room flashed through my mind, and my brain undressed him and manufactured a picture of a naked Lance in my shower. I shook my head and headed for the kitchen. I needed a cup of coffee immediately.

I set a full pot to brew, though I had no idea if Lance even drank the stuff. Not that it mattered—it was for me.

While the rich scent filled the room, I opened the pantry and sighed. "What am I going to feed you, kitty?" He tucked his little head under my chin and purred himself to sleep. "Well, I guess it doesn't matter anymore."

Another flash of lightning lit up the kitchen, followed by a crash of thunder. That time, it was close enough that the lights flickered and went out.

"Shit." I held on to the kitten and looked into his little eyes, which I could see in the dim light through the window. He blinked sleepily. "Maybe they'll come back on in a second, Kitty."

I waited, but no luck.

Now, where would Kai keep candles and flashlights? I dug into the cabinets. It wouldn't be long until the natural light disappeared, and who knew how long the lights would be out.

"I just talked with Patrick," Lance said as he entered the kitchen.

I jumped at the sound of his voice. "Didn't I tell you not to sneak up on me?"

"Sorry."

I leaned against the counter and kissed the top of the kitten's head. "And?" I asked.

He leaned on the counter across from me and pulled his lips between his teeth, his eyes wide.

I don't think I want to hear this.

"The storm did damage in town. The lights are out everywhere, and there's been some flooding. Jones Road is impassable at the south end. The river has flooded it, and trees are down on the north end, which is why we have no electricity."

Jones Road is this road. And it's blocked. "So, what chance do you have of getting home tonight?"

"Looks like you and the kitty are having company."

That's what I was afraid of. "Wonderful. Good thing this is a big house."

"Yep, but now what are we going to do about food? I'm starving," Lance said as he opened the pantry.

I sat at the counter, teasing the kitten with a pen as it batted and pounced after it. My gaze drifted upward, against my will, to Lance. "What are you doing?" I asked as he took peanut butter, bread, and an unopened jar of jelly from the pantry.

"Making dinner."

"We have jelly in the refrigerator."

"I'm sure you do, but I don't want to open the fridge door. The electricity could be off for a while." He grabbed two apples from the bowl on the table and started cutting them.

I went into the garage to look for something for a litter box and a bed for the kitten and found a bag of wood shavings that hadn't been taken to the barn yet. Wood shavings weren't the best for litter, but they were better than the floor. I turned an old container into a makeshift litter box and found another that would be perfect for a bed. I set the kitten up in my bedroom and left it there to rest.

When I came back into the kitchen, food filled the table.

"Dinner's served. Is the kitten comfortable?" Lance asked. He gestured for me to join him at the table.

I chuckled. A plate filled with peanut butter and jelly sandwiches, a bowl of potato chips, and sliced apples were in the center of the table. The place I sat in front of had a paper plate, a napkin, and a bottle of water.

"I know you made coffee, but it never finished. Hell, it barely started." He took two sandwiches from the plate and then passed it to me.

I took a sandwich, chips, and a handful of apple slices. "Thank you. This is nice. Now, I'd prefer a ribeye and salad like last night, but under the circumstances, this is perfect."

"I agree. Maybe I could take you to dinner another time, like when the town has electricity and we don't drown getting to the car."

Did Lance just ask me on a date?

My stomach fluttered as I studied his face in the wavering light.

Should I say yes? Do I want to say yes? I bit into my sandwich, trying to appear casual while my heart raced. "We'll see," I said and focused on my apples and peanut butter.

The light from the candles painted everything in warmth and intimate shadows. Each flash of lightning through the kitchen window felt like the storm was echoing the electricity crackling between us.

CHAPTER 15

LANCE

I wasn't surprised that Susie had brushed off my date proposal. She still saw me like everyone else—an egotistical asshole who only cared about himself.

We ate in silence as the storm raged, much like the one that wreaked havoc in my chest. Getting to know Susie had churned up feelings I don't think I'd ever experienced before. I found myself canceling any plans just to spend more time with her. I would do anything to see her smile. I'd walk over burning coals if it would make her happy. Those feelings used to terrify me, so I avoided any woman who could evoke them. But since Susie had been back, I'd done just that—multiple times. I'd frequented Jerry's Pub more than usual. I'd offered to check on her and changed my plans to do so. Hell, I helped with the goats just because I wanted to be near her.

A soft meow pulled us from our meals.

"Kitty, how'd you get out of the bedroom?" Susie said as she stooped over to pick up the ball of fur. He reached for her plate with his tiny paw. She broke off a piece of bread, which the kitten ate. "Can kittens have bread?" she asked.

I stared into her eyes for a beat, mesmerized by their caring and gentleness, then shrugged. "I have no clue. I saw a can of tuna in the pantry. At least it will be something soft and something cats are able to eat. That's all we can do until we get to a store." I found the can, opened it, mashed the tuna up with a fork in a small bowl, and placed it on the table.

The kitten ate as if he hadn't eaten in days, and for all we knew, he hadn't.

I filled a second bowl with water. We laughed as he stuck his face in it and shook, sending water droplets flying.

I turned my eyes from the kitten to Susie. A sense of peace and relaxation covered her expression as she watched him. Her eyes shone with laughter, making her even more stunning. My gaze fixed on her. Her perfect Roman nose, pouty lips, and those crystal eyes pulled me into their depths.

I've got to stop looking at her before I do something stupid. I turned away and cleaned up our dinner, which didn't take long. The plates went into the trash, and I washed the two knives I'd used to prepare our sandwiches and cut the apples.

After putting them in the drawer, I joined Susie and the kitten in the living room.

We sat on the floor as the kitten inspected the room. I crumpled a scrap of paper into a ball, and before long we were laughing as the kitten chased it across the floor.

He slid and tumbled after it with wild determination. Susie's laughter filled the room as the kitten entertained us with the ridiculous game.

I leaned against the couch, mesmerized by Susie and the relaxed way she played with the kitten. She was naturally loving, as if a maternal instinct had risen to the surface. I'd seen it when she talked and played with Madeline, Darcie, and now with the kitten.

Spending time with her was something I could get used to. She made the simplest tasks so much more enjoyable. She enjoyed life—when she wasn't getting pissed at me.

I tried to look away and get my mind on something else but failed miserably.

"What are you looking at?" Susie asked when she caught me watching her.

Do I tell her the truth—that she's rendered me speechless? That the simplest task—like playing with a kitten—has made me see a whole new side of her? I'm infatuated, stuck, and can't get away. Like a fish on the hook, I'm at her mercy.

Yeah, that wouldn't work. I'd either scare her off or piss her off worse than if I were my typical smart-ass self.

Her phone vibrated against the floor.

Saved by text.

I tapped my fingers on the floor, gaining the kitten's attention, and laughed as it attacked my fingers.

But when I glanced at Susie, the expression of fear and trepidation that crossed her face made my blood turn to ice.

Again, her phone went off, and her eyes became large. She looked ashen, like she had seen a ghost.

That was the look I'd been seeing all week, and I didn't like it. I sat up straight. "Susie, what's wrong? Who was that?"

She forced a smile and put her phone back in her pocket. "No one."

I narrowed my eyes and studied her. *Is she telling the truth?* "You sure?"

She nodded. "Yep. It's no one. Wrong number." She tried to continue playing with the cat, but her body language wasn't the same. The laughter in her eyes had been extinguished, and her movements were robotic.

I touched her arm. "Susie, what's going on? You look surprised or even worse, fearful."

"I said it was a wrong number." The cat curled up in her lap, and all her attention went into petting it. The discussion was over.

I'd never been good with feelings—Lilly had told me that my entire life. When things got dramatic or emotional, my instinct was to bolt. I'd heard more times than I could count that I needed to be more understanding. And that was exactly what I wanted to do. The expression that filled Susie's face lit an instinct I couldn't ignore—a fierce need to protect her.

Another text buzzed on her phone, and she froze.

Whoever was messaging her was insistent, and it frightened her. I wasn't imagining it. My chest tightened. "Hey," I said gently. "I need to know what's going on."

"Stop." She stood with the cat in her arms. "You don't *need* to know anything. It's none of your damn business." Her voice was stern as she stalked from the room and slammed her door.

"Shit." I leaned heavily against the couch and stared at the ceiling. *What the hell did I do wrong now? When did being concerned about someone become a crime?* I rubbed the stress out of the back of my neck. *Should I go after her?*

Between Susie's negative attitude and the fact that the air conditioning was off, the house was becoming stuffy. I went around and opened windows to let air circulate.

The house was eerily quiet without the air conditioner and appliances running. The only sounds were my footsteps on the floor, the rain on the roof, the wind against the walls, and the thunder crashing in the sky.

After I'd sat back down, my phone rang with a call from Jamison. "Hey," I answered. "Y'all good? How're the girls?"

"We're okay. No electricity, but everything is still in one piece. Lilly's worried about Susie. We heard her road is impassable, and she won't answer her texts. I know you took her home. Have you checked on her?"

I laughed and glanced toward the hall. It had been about thirty minutes since she stalked off, and I hadn't heard a word, so it depended on what he meant by checking on her. "Yeah, you could say that. I never had a chance to leave. The storm hit so fast, and now I'm stuck here."

"Really? And how's that going?"

"Well, we got the goats and chickens put away before the strongest part of the storm hit but got drenched running back to the house. I found a kitten in the chicken boxes, made peanut butter and jelly sandwiches for dinner—since the power went out, and we were having fun playing with the kitten on the floor until Susie yelled at me, stalked off, and told me to stay out of her damn business."

Jamison's deep laughter rumbled over the phone. "Same shit, different day. Things seem to be going about normal."

"Yeah, it seems so. Since then, I've been sitting here on the floor, staring up at the ceiling and wondering about the mysteries and feelings of the female species."

"Wow, that's deep, especially for you. Let me know if you ever figure it out." His amusement was impossible to miss.

"What the hell's that supposed to mean?"

"It means I'm impressed that you're wondering about a woman's feelings instead of only what she's like in bed. Progress, my friend."

I laid my head on the couch. "Am I really that shallow and disrespectful?"

"Not always, but you could focus a little more on other people's feelings."

"So, you're saying I'm self-absorbed, narrow-minded, rude, and a sexist pig. Basically, I'm my old man."

Again, he chuckled. "No. You're nothing like him. He was married to his high school sweetheart, though he didn't love her, and treated her like crap throughout their entire marriage. You're a little better than that. You recognize you're not ready for commitment, which makes you still single at thirty-six."

"Fuck, I am a dick. She has me pegged."

"Well, at least you're not hiding your true self. Let Susie know Lilly was worried about her and be good."

The phone went dead.

I sighed heavily, pushed to my feet, and walked quietly to Susie's bedroom.

I knocked softly, my ear to the door.

She didn't tell me to enter, and there was no noise on the other side.

I laid my forehead against the wood. *Should I open it? Go in? Or should I give her space?* Walking away would probably be the best choice. *But when was the last time I chose correctly?*

I slowly turned the knob and cracked the door.

The room was dark except for the slight glow of her phone. "Hey. Can I come in?"

"Looks like you already are." She sat up tall.

I stepped inside. "Technically, now I'm in. Before I just had the door opened."

"Yeah, without permission."

"I knocked. You didn't say anything."

"Did you ever consider I didn't say anything because I wanted to be left alone?"

"I considered it but was worried about you."

She finally turned from her phone screen and looked at me. "Worried that I what? Snuck out my window into the downpour? Or worse?"

"Okay, when you put it like that, it sounds ridiculous." I pointed at the bed.

She sat up taller and nodded. The kitten was rolled up in a ball, purring away. I petted it. "He looks comfortable."

"Yeah, he fell asleep as soon as we got in here. I guess he's had a lot of excitement for one night." She petted him as well.

The cat was tiny, and our fingers touched. She flinched away and sat back again but not before a zing of electricity caused my heartbeat to pick up its pace.

Did she feel it too? Is that why she pulled away? I looked at her, yet she refused to meet my gaze. I sat tall and huffed out a breath. "Look, I don't know what I did, but I'm sorry I upset you."

That got her attention. She shot daggers in my direction. "Why do you think my mood has anything to do with you? Everything isn't always about you."

Her voice was so loud it woke the kitten. He stretched, turned, and lay back down.

I put my hands in the air. "I know. Trust me... I know." Her reaction irritated me. Hell, it pissed me off. I'd done nothing wrong, but she was treating me as if I had. "Look. I came in here because I just got off the phone with Jamison. Lilly was worried about you. She texted, but you didn't answer her."

Susie checked her phone. "I was ignoring them."

She sucked in the corner of her cheek like she was biting it, but she still wouldn't look at me.

There was so much I wanted to say and ask, but I thought better of it. If she wanted to talk to me, she would.

I stood to leave, yet hesitated. I'd give anything for her to talk to me and ask me to stay. I didn't want us to do anything. I just had a desire to keep her safe, to be a friend.

Damn, that was a first. "It's late, but I wanted to relay the message. As long as you're okay, I'm going to crash on the couch."

"Or you could just leave. I don't need a babysitter, and the road can't be in that bad of shape."

My head snapped toward her. This time, her gaze met mine, and it was filled with ice and hostility.

I ground my teeth together and shook my head. "Look, Susie." Irritation bubbled in my gut. "I don't know what I've done to make you not like me, but I think I've shown that my intentions are only good."

"Yep, you have, and I think I've shown that I don't need you around, and I don't want your help. You know your way out." Her words were short and laced with disdain.

Fuck. I raked my fingers through my hair, huffed out a breath, and stormed out of the room. *Why stay if she doesn't want me to? Move on.*

I stomped through the house, threw open the front door, and stepped out into the rain. I wasn't sure what was worse, the storm outside or the one churning inside my gut.

Hell, there was no contest. The one in my gut won hands down. The one outside was just a slow, steady rain. Inside me, rage churned like a hurricane destroying everything in its path.

The road better be open. There's no way in hell I'm staying here. I jumped into my truck and tore off down the driveway, spinning gravel under my tires, and turned right.

Dammit. Why does she bother me so much? If she doesn't want me around, why do I want to be around her?

I slammed on my brakes. Multiple trees—large ones—blocked the road. There was no way around them.

Shit. I banged my hand on the steering wheel and turned around on the small road.

About a mile past Kai's was where the road went over the river. Again, I came to an abrupt stop and hopped out of the cab. The water rushed over the road. I couldn't even see the top of the bridge. Squatting, I held my hands behind my neck and turned my head up toward the rain. *What the hell?* I wiped my hands over my face and stood with a slap to my thighs.

There was only one thing I could do.

I climbed into my truck and turned back toward Kora and Kai's. My gut churned and clawed with irritation as I approached the house. Ever since Susie had stepped foot in Orlinda Valley the previous October, she hadn't been far from my mind. I thought of her at random moments—during football practice or lying awake at night. Since she'd been back in town, it had gotten worse, and other women no longer existed.

Just when I thought I had my feelings under control, the storm hit, and we've been stuck in the house together. Watching her let her guard down and laugh around me instead of giving me that look filled with irritation caused my mind to be all muddled with irrational thoughts of relationships, and things I didn't want to face. Shit. I had no clue what the hell I was going to do.

But she's broken and needs time to put herself back together. I'd sworn I'd give her that time, but here I was, heading back to her—still needing her. Still fucking wanting her, and the shittiest part was that she was the only woman who wanted nothing to do with me.

I parked in the spot I had left no more than ten minutes ago and stared at the front door. *Just do it, Lance. You're not asking to be with her. You just need the couch.*

I took a deep breath, climbed out of the truck, walked up the sidewalk, and knocked on the door.

The door flew open before I finished knocking, making me jump back. The sight that filled my eyes made my pulse race.

Susie stood there in a pair of pink pajama bottoms and a skimpy tank top. The sliver of exposed skin at her midriff, along with her dark hair pulled back in a low ponytail, made my mouth go dry. And those eyes. *Damn those eyes.* I could have sworn they saw straight into my soul. And those lips, pouty with her anger, made me want to crash my mouth against hers and kiss her senseless.

I watched as her eyes slid down my body and back up. My heart skipped as her eyes met mine.

"What are you doing back here, and why are you soaked?" she asked. Her voice was a seductive whisper and caused my blood to flow south.

"The road is impassable in both directions. I got out of the truck to make sure there was no way around. I'm sorry. I tried." I stepped in the doorway before she threw me out again. "I'll just sleep on the couch, and I promise I'll leave you alone."

She closed the door and wrung her hands, staring at the floor for a long time.

She looked vulnerable and so damn desirable. *Get your thoughts out of the gutter, man. Don't think with your dick. Use your heart for once.*

Her eyes met mine. "I treated you so badly. I'm sorry."

The room smelled like her, flowers and vanilla. My heart melted, and my pulse quickened even more.

She took a step closer, and before I could react or register what she was doing, she cupped my face in her hands, and her lips were on mine.

My breath caught. I closed my eyes and took everything in—the softness of her lips, the taste of her tongue, the feel of her hands as they held my face. *This is unbelievable.*

Wait. I placed my hands on her arms and pushed her away slightly.

Her eyes fluttered open. Her lips were wet and swollen; her breath matched mine. I shook my head to remove the thoughts of my lips finding hers again and carrying her to her room. "Susie, what was that?"

"I'm sorry." Her eyes bored into mine.

I rubbed my knuckles across her cheeks and tilted her head up to see me better. "Did you want to kiss me?"

"No."

Fuck. I stepped back, and my arms fell to my sides. That wasn't the answer I had hoped for. "You kissed me but didn't want to?" Confusion etched onto my words, and heat climbed up my neck.

"Lance." She stepped closer.

I shook my head and stepped back. I wasn't going here with her. I couldn't. I wanted her too much to mess around with either of our feelings. "I don't know what kind of game you're playing, but this"—I gestured between us—"can't happen unless we both want it. I won't let it." *Damn, I don't know when things changed with me. I'm usually all about playing games. Having fun.*

But not with Susie. She's different. With her, I wanted more. I needed all of her or nothing.

"I know." She looked down, then our gazes locked. "I'm sorry I've messed this up. I've been fighting my feelings for you. I don't know when they started, but it doesn't matter. When you walked out, I realized how much I messed up and wanted you here."

Did I hear her right? A smile slowly filled my face. *She's been fighting her feelings for me?*

"I thought you were interested in me too, but if I was wrong, and you aren't..." Her gaze no longer held mine.

Lifting her chin, I forced her eyes to lock on mine. "Trust me." I leaned closer, my voice a raspy whisper. "There's no other woman I want more than you."

Her tongue traced her lower lip, catching my attention, and her lips parted slightly.

Damn. I stepped into her space, cupped her face in my hands, and kissed her. Soft. Careful. Like she would possibly come to her senses and disappear from my life.

Her mouth opened slightly, and our tongues met.

I held the back of her neck and tugged her closer. Her lips were soft as silk. Her taste was amazingly sweet, yet minty. This was so much more than I had imagined. Groaning, I pulled her closer. I needed to feel her body next to mine.

Susie answered with a moan of her own, which sent my need and desire skyrocketing and my blood pulsing throughout my body.

Pulling away, she put her hands under my soaked shirt, then pulled it up and over my head.

She trailed her hands down my cold, damp chest. They were warm against my chilled skin, and I sucked in a breath.

She scratched her nails across my stomach. I clenched my jaw and stared at her. The desire in her eyes made my body tense with need.

Then her warm mouth was on my skin.

I hissed out a breath and closed my eyes. "Susie," I said, my voice barely audible.

She said nothing but trailed her lips and tongue up my chest agonizingly slowly. Every nerve ending was firing, and the shock was almost too much.

She kissed a trail up my neck, and the shock blazed under my skin. Her kisses finally met my mouth again and became deeper, more intense. She curled her fingers in the back of my damp hair.

Heat seared through me at the touch of her hands and the taste of her lips. Desire and need burned within me. I couldn't remember ever feeling so much for a woman.

Hell, right now, I can't remember much of anything—except Susie.

CHAPTER 16

SUSIE

M y gaze locked on Lance's. I gave his hand a tug, pulling him to my bedroom, and closed the door behind us. My heart pounded as he filled my gaze. There was nothing I'd ever wanted more than this.

"Are you sure?" he asked. "Don't feel you need to do this. I don't want to pressure you into anything."

"Lance, I had no clue what I felt until you walked out. When I heard the door close, all the air left my lungs, and I couldn't breathe. You are a good one, and I let you walk away. The bad ones, I always seem to keep."

"What does that mean?" His brow furrowed as he pulled away.

I closed my eyes. *Really? I have to bring this up now?*

"Susie, talk to me."

I met his gaze. His eyes no longer held the heat and passion they had in the entry. They were determined. I shook my head.

He widened his eyes.

Looks like I have no choice. He's not dropping it. I sighed heavily. "The messages and phone calls. It's my ex, Michael."

Lance's eyes widened, and the muscle in his jaw twitched.

I brushed my finger against it. "See? This is why I didn't want to say anything. You're upset."

"Yeah. What the hell's he doing bothering you? He's your ex. If he's threatening you, I'll handle it."

I laughed and held Lance's face in my hands. His skin was rough with the day's stubble. His chin was strong, and God, he was handsome, especially when he was angry. "You know what? There's only been two men in my entire life willing to fight for me. And neither one was my father. It was always Kai and Sebastian." I lowered my hands and sat on my bed. "I've always been searching for someone to love me. Someone to see me as special. Someone who wasn't my brother, and I seemed to choose wrong every time. Michael was one of those wrong choices and the reason I left South Dakota."

"And I take it he's not happy about that."

I shrugged. "I hadn't heard from him until last week."

"Is he the one who gave you the flowers?" Lance asked as he sat next to me.

"Possibly. I don't really know. But if so, how?"

The muscle in Lance's jaw twitched again. I slid closer to him and brushed my fingers against it. "Your jaw twitches when you're upset. Just like Sebastian's."

"Yes, it does, and I am. He has no right to be frightening you." Lance closed his hands over mine. "He won't hurt you. I won't let him."

His gaze was determined, fierce, and warm.

He wasn't the egotistical ass I thought he was. He was caring, focused, and into me. I squeezed his hand like he was squeezing my heart and whispered, "You were right here all along, and I wasn't willing to see it."

"Susie" was all he said before his lips locked onto mine, and he pulled me close.

I wrapped my arms around his neck and kissed him back with all the need and desire that pulsed through my veins.

My body tingled from his touch, shivered from his kiss, and became electrified by his taste. Every nerve ending stood at attention, and I wanted more—more of his touch, his taste—of him.

I broke our connection and stood to pull my nightshirt over my head. I wasn't wearing a bra.

I could feel him take in my body, every curve, every mound.

The expression on his face sent flames into my heart.

He tenderly brushed his fingers across my skin and over one of my breasts.

I tried to suck in a breath, but it caught in my throat.

He pulled me toward him. A tingle shot through my body as his lips brushed against my skin, then he pulled my nipple into his mouth. The tingle turned into electricity, which heated me from my core.

He pushed me onto the mattress, stood, and pulled my pants off, slowly, one leg at a time. His warm, tender gaze traveled over my skin like he was memorizing every inch of me.

"Come here," I whispered.

"No, let me look at you first."

His eyes continued their slow caress up my body, took a break at my breasts, and finally locked on my eyes. "You are perfection."

I froze. No one had ever said that about me. No one had ever looked at me with that much desire before. No one had ever caused my body to react with just a look.

He stepped out of his jeans then joined me, caressing my cheek, and pulled my head toward him. "You are amazing. Do you know that?"

I looked away and shook my head.

He placed his hand lightly on my lips to stop my words. "I don't want to hear anything negative coming from these lips. Your body is flawless. Trust me. But that's not what I'm attracted to. I'm attracted to you. Your light fills a room when you enter. Your personality, your caring ways. You are the most amazing woman I've ever known. Since I first laid eyes on you at Kora and Kai's wedding, I haven't been able to think about anyone else."

My heart pounded in my chest. *Is he serious?* "Really? Since then?"

"Oh yeah. I was smitten with you when I first laid eyes on you, but after you took control of the situation between me and Rowan? I've wanted no one but you."

"You want me?"

He sat up and chuckled, rolling his eyes. "Hell yes. God. Susie. I want you so badly it hurts. But I'm willing to stop this right now if you're not one hundred percent sure. Because when I make love to you, I want you to want it just as badly as I do, and I want you to be sure it's what you want. Until you feel the same way, I'm willing to wait for you."

My heart swelled, and tears pricked my eyes. *He's giving me a choice. I could stop this, and it would be okay.* I sat up and gave him a long, lingering kiss.

He curled his fingers through my hair and held me close.

I didn't want the kiss to end. I needed to feel our bodies together. I lay back, my body on fire, and pulled him with me. I craved his touch, his lips—everywhere and all at once.

"Susie," he said against my lips. "Wait."

He pulled away again. I puffed out a breath, dejected.

"This...This will change things," he said.

"Yes. It will," I agreed.

He sighed heavily. "Trust me. There's nothing I want more than you. Than us. Than this." He pulled back, "but I don't think now is the time."

Tears filled my eyes, but I wiped them away, angry with myself. *Isn't this what I said I deserved? A man who cares enough about me to want something special between us? Sex that means something, not just lust? That was what Lance is saying. He wants me to be sure. He wants me. So why do I feel so unlovable?*

"Hey." His voice was sweet. "Don't do that." He wiped a tear that fell down my cheek and lay against the pillow. "Come here."

When I laid my head on his chest, he wrapped his arms around me and held me tight. "Let's just lie together tonight. Unless you want me on the couch. If so, I'll go."

I placed my hand flat on his chest. "No. Stay."

The corner of his mouth ticked up in that smirk he wore when I thought he wanted attention, but suddenly it had become the sweetest, most sincere smirk I'd ever seen.

Smiling back, I snuggled into him. My naked body was warm against his skin. For the first time in my life, I felt safe and wanted.

I closed my eyes and fell into a peaceful sleep.

⤜⤛

Sunlight was peeking in my window early the next morning when I opened my eyes. Lance's arm was tucked around me and held me close. My back was snug and cozy against his chest. The kitten cuddled against me. Warmth surrounded me, and I moaned gently when Lance's arm pulled me closer.

"Morning," he mumbled into my neck.

The warmth of his breath on my skin made me breathe deeply. I snuggled back into him and held his arm tight. It was relaxing and exactly what I needed.

I could feel what he needed pressed against my ass, and my gut became mush.

"Lance," I breathed. I brushed my fingers up his arm and moved his hand to my breast and waited. I wanted him like I had wanted no one before.

His hand moved ever so slightly.

I closed my eyes as he worked his finger over my nipple, and lightning shot down my body. I moaned and turned toward him.

His eyes were open and, if I wasn't mistaken, filled with the same desire I'd seen in them the previous night.

I held his gaze, then kissed him gently.

He brushed my hair from my face, and his lips left mine to travel down my body. Heat seared every place his lips touched, and his tongue tasted.

He blazed a trail to my breast, where he circled my nipple with his tongue, sending chills down my spine. His lips slowly closed over the tip.

I sucked in a breath.

My body melted under his touch, his kiss, and relaxed against him. Desire pulsed through my veins. While his mouth tasted, his hand traveled south.

I opened my legs, inviting him to touch me, and when his fingers met the tender spot between my legs, I was more than ready for him.

"God, Susie." He pulled away, and his eyes latched onto mine as he slowly pushed one finger into my wet, waiting core.

I moaned deeply, and my eyes closed.

"Look at me," he demanded as he massaged me tenderly, and moved his finger in and out, driving me close to climax faster than I'd thought possible.

I opened my eyes and moved gently with his rhythm.

"God, I love your sounds," as his lips kissed my neck.

The touch of his lips on my skin, and the movement of his fingers in my core caused me to moan his name as a shudder built from deep within my body.

"That's it. Come for me, Susie."

I moved against his fingers and reached for his cock. He was hard—so hard.

He hissed out a breath as I rubbed my hand against him.

His fingers moved faster, and so did I. I bit down on my lip as I came closer and closer to my release. His free hand held my face. "Look at me, and don't hold back, sweetness."

My eyes fluttered open, and I held his gaze as I finally reached the peak and my body shuddered again and again. "Lance," I said as his lips crashed onto mine.

He kneaded my breasts, and his mouth found them again.

I rocked against his hardness, which was pressed against me, and I wrapped my arms around him. I wanted him inside me. I needed to feel him. I squeezed his ass and led him toward my opening, but he pulled away.

What is he doing to me? I moaned his name as he kissed my chest and traveled south to my stomach, then lower still.

"God yes," I whispered and bucked beneath him as his tongue licked me and my core throbbed.

My body ached from everything he was doing to me. His tongue was magic. It felt better than I'd ever thought possible.

He picked up his pace, and soon, I was riding that wave of ecstasy again and again, until I was rubber, unable to move.

No man had ever made me feel like this. It had always been about them and sex, never me.

I needed an end to the madness and wrapped my hand around his cock. He was so hard and ready for me that I led him to my opening.

But he grabbed my hand.

I opened my eyes, my breathing coming in quick gasps. "I'm on the pill. It's okay." I kissed him again.

He shook his head. "Not now, Susie."

Pain once again coursed through my veins, and I pulled back. "Hey. Don't think it's you. Trust me. If you don't know how I feel about you now, I don't know what I need to do to convince you. I just want you to be sure, and I'm willing to wait until you are."

I took in his words. It was all about me. He was putting me—my feelings and my desires—first.

No man had ever put me first. It was always about them, about sex and nothing more. I used to see Lance as one of those men, but not anymore, not with me.

I brushed my hand up his side lightly, slowly, and I traced his jaw-line with my fingertips. This man, once egotistical and self-absorbed, was thinking of me and my feelings.

My heart soared and filled with something, but I had no clue what it was. "Thank you."

He again gave that smile I'd once thought was cocky but now saw as my smile, and I got lost in his gaze. For the first time, I was relaxed and secure with a man. I chuckled.

"What?" he asked.

"Nothing. Again, thank you."

"I should thank you," he said and kissed me lightly.

A soft meow broke our kiss. The kitten was standing on our arms, and it cuddled its little head under them.

We both laughed and petted the little bundle of fur.

"I guess we need to get up and see if we can get this little one some food today," Lance said as he picked up the cat and sat up.

I stared at the perfection of his torso and trailed my hand over his back.

"Watch out, woman. Your touch is toxic. Don't make me go back on my word."

I thought about that. A part of me wanted just that, to spend the rest of the day with Lance in bed, finding out what sex with him would be like.

But another part of me needed us to go slowly. I had to figure out what was going on with my ex and make sure that whatever I was feeling was real.

I'd been given a chance to have exactly what I'd always want-ed—time—and not to be forced into anything too quickly.

Chapter 17

Lance

The electricity wasn't back on yet, so I went and checked on the goats and chickens. Some branches were down in the goat pasture but nothing major. I fed all the animals, gave the goats new hay, and opened the garage doors. The goats bounded out, happy to be free.

My phone rang with a call from Patrick.

"Hey, what's up?""I heard you're at Kai's with Susie. I'm just making sure you're both okay. We have staff working on removing the trees. The other direction is still not passable."

"Yeah, I know it's bad. I saw it last night."

"How?"

"I tried to leave but quickly found out it was impossible. Hey, do me a favor. When you get through, bring kitten food, a litter box, and some litter with you, please. We found a kitten, and Susie has a new friend."

"Gotcha. Should be about an hour or so."

"Thanks." I walked around the house, checking for any other damage from the storm. I could hear the river raging. Thankfully,

Kai had been smart when he built far enough away from the river that he didn't have to worry about possible flooding. Everything was clear on the outside, so I walked inside.

I was starving. *What can I find for breakfast?* I dug through the cabinets. Peanut butter and apples, it is. I picked up some apples from the basket on the table and was slicing them when Susie walked in. She wore cotton shorts and an oversized shirt. Her hair fell against her shoulders, and even in the morning, she was breathtaking.

She leaned against me, the kitten in her arms. "What's for breakfast, Chef Boyardee?"

I chuckled, and my gaze halted on her. The scent of flowers and honey filled the air. "You smell good."

The smile she gave me, warm and relaxed, sent heat throughout my body. If she continued to look at me that way and we stayed stuck in this house, my promise to wait would be thrown out the window.

"That's what happens when you shower. Maybe you should try it," she joked.

"You saying I stink?"

"Maybe." She shrugged.

I nudged her with my shoulder and got back to slicing. "Grab the peanut butter."

"Again?" she asked as she placed the jar on the counter.

"You have something against the king of all snacks?"

"No." She chuckled again.

I loved that sound.

Our eyes locked, and my gaze dropped to her lips. Those red, luscious, sweet-tasting bits I longed for were suddenly on mine, and I was lost in a soft, sweet, lingering kiss.

I breathed her in and moaned.

"That was nice," I said as I opened my eyes slowly. I placed the knife on the counter and pulled her into my arms.

"Don't squish the kitty," she said.

"Don't worry. I'm always gentle with kitties."

"I remember," she said with a flirty grin. Her eyes darted to my lips.

That was all the invitation I needed. My mouth found hers again, and I pulled her to me to deepen the kiss.

"You drive me crazy, but..." I pulled away and took the plate of apples to the counter and pulled out two bottles of water. "We need to eat, then go for a walk. I talked to Patrick. They're working on moving the downed trees. As soon as they can get through, he'll be here with food for the kitten. Then they'll work on restoring the power."

We sat and ate the apples. Something about eating near this beautiful woman made even the simplest meal of apples, peanut butter, and water delicious.

CHAPTER 18

SUSIE

I didn't have the heart to tell him I wasn't a fan of apples, but with peanut butter, they weren't bad. I guessed everything was better with peanut butter.

We were going to get out and walk the property. I placed the kitten in my bathroom, not fully trusting him in the house alone. It was a big house, and he was so tiny.

The sun shone brightly when we stepped outside. "It always amazes me how the sun can shine after such a bad storm. Like nothing ever happened." I'd had the same thought when I was young.

"Hey, you good?" Lance asked as he wrapped his arm around my waist.

I leaned into him. I *was* good, and this felt so right. Nodding, I said, "I just had a flash of a memory from a long time ago." My chest clenched, and I breathed through my nose to calm myself.

"You don't have to tell me if it's personal."

"I know, but it's not like it's a secret. You know about my child-hood. Have you heard the story about the scar under Kai's eye?"

He shook his head.

The fresh air and having Lance beside me helped to make it easier to tell. "Sebastian and I were doing our homework at the kitchen table one night after dinner, and Kai was washing dishes. Our dad came in, drunk and stumbling and tripped over Sebastian's backpack. He went into a raging fit, which was normal for him, and went after Sebastian. Kai got in the way, like he always did, and punched him. They both ended up on the floor, and my dad on top of Kai. He threatened his life but cut him with a piece of a broken beer bottle instead."

Lance grabbed my hand, but I pulled away. I didn't need comfort. It was an old memory. "We spent that night locked in Kai's room, trying to get the cut to stop bleeding. It was awful. Dad yelled and threatened all of us not to tell anyone about what happened, then he passed out on the couch.

"The next morning, Sebastian and I walked to the bus stop. I wanted to skip school, but Kai insisted we go. His goal was to ensure we graduated no matter what. I remember it was a beautiful morning. The sun was shining, birds were singing, and a slight breeze was blowing. It was like there was no bad in the world." I shrugged. "Whenever I notice a day like today, I'm reminded of that morning and many mornings like it."

We walked in silence for a bit longer, and the sound of the river reached our ears. There was a line of mud on the ground.

"The water must have been up this high," Lance said. He grabbed my hand, and this time, I let him as we walked down the slight incline to the river.

The water was over the banks and up on the pebbled beach. It met the sandy area Kai had prepared and the firepit he'd built.

"I guess the water's receding," I said.

Lance wrapped his arms around my waist as he came up behind me. He kissed my neck, and I melted into him. I couldn't believe how good it felt, how right.

"I'm sorry Terry was like that. When you see him now, you'd have no clue. But he was a lot different last year when he first showed up in town."

I sighed. "I know. I have a hard time seeing him here. Kai thinks I need to forgive him but not forget. He says I'll feel better. But I don't know if I'm ready." I turned to face Lance. "Does that make me a horrible person?"

He brushed his fingers across my cheek and tucked a lock of hair behind my ears. "I think that would be impossible. There isn't a bad bone in your body."

His eyes traveled over my features, and my heart fluttered under his gaze. "You don't know me." My voice came out quiet. "Not really."

He grasped my shoulders. "You're right. I don't know you well. But I know you. I know Kai and Sebastian mean the world to you. I know you're tough and don't let things get to you. If you weren't, your past would have broken you."

Goosebumps formed on my flesh where he brushed his hand over my arms.

"You're caring, sweet, and forgiving," he said. "Hell, you're here with me." His smile was full, not the typical half-smirk.

I smiled back. "It's not like I had a choice. I did kick you out, but somehow, you found your way back."

"Were you disappointed that I came back?"

His gaze was serious.

I could lie and say yes. But that was impossible. "No. I didn't want you to go at all." I wrapped my arms around his neck and looked deep into his eyes. "But I didn't get what I wanted." My lips latched onto his, and I showed him how much I wanted him when my lips and my tongue tangled with his. I pulled him closer and took the kiss deeper. Desire burned deep in my gut.

"Maybe we should finish what we started earlier." Lance's voice was raspy.

A smile reached my eyes. "I totally agree."

He pulled me up the hill and toward the house. I stopped to arrange chairs around the patio table. "Hey, y'all."

I looked up to see Patrick standing there with his arms filled with bags. "How is everything?"

Shit. If I hadn't stopped to fix the chairs, he would have witnessed us holding hands and beelining for the kitchen door. My pulse picked up, and heat crawled up my neck. I hated how easily I wore my feelings, especially when embarrassed.

"It's all good," Lance said, and his eyes met mine. He raised his eyebrows.

I glanced away and sucked my lips between my teeth to hide the laugh that wanted to break free.

"We were just down by the river," Lance continued. "The water rose pretty high and is still higher than normal, but nothing was damaged."

"That's good," Patrick said. "The water's still over the road but should be down by tomorrow morning. The other direction's open, so I brought what you asked for."

"Great," I said and walked toward the door. "Let's go inside and get the kitten. I'm sure he's starving for actual food, and he needs a litter box."

CHAPTER 19

LANCE

I sighed heavily and followed them into the house. *Dammit, Patrick. Why couldn't you have kept us stranded for a couple more hours?*

Patrick placed the bags on the counter, and Susie went to get the kitten. I sat hard on a counter stool.

"You good, Lance? Looks like something's bothering you. I didn't interrupt anything, did I?"

I met his teasing gaze. *Should I ask him to place a large tree back on the road and tell him to get out of here and pretend he never saw us?* Probably not a good idea. Instead, I shook my head. "Nope, it's all good."

"I'm surprised you're still alive. You're not her favorite person, from what I've been told."

"Who's been talking about me? Trevor?" Patrick held up his hands. "Don't get me involved in y'all's little joust over the princess. I'm here performing my civic duty. Saving a kitten and checking on the safety of the locals. So, like I said, I'm glad to see you're still breathing."

Susie appeared with the kitten in her arms. "He was playing with the toilet paper. It's now all over the bathroom floor, and his makeshift litter box stinks."

As I petted the kitten, Susie's eyes met mine, and our gazes held. Something—I wasn't sure what—passed between us in those seconds, and she didn't move away from the slight touch of our shoulders.

Dammit. If Patrick hadn't interrupted us, I'd have this amazing woman in bed, and we'd be completing what I'd stopped the previous night. She wanted me, and the feelings were mutual. Hell, just looking at her, breathing in her space, made my body react.

The kitten meowed. "Hey, buddy. Are you hungry? Where's that food?" I asked Patrick, taking the kitten from Susie.

He looked between us.

"Dude, food?" I needed to keep him focused on the point of his visit. "Yep, here you go." He placed the box of kitten supplies on the floor and pulled out the bag of kitty kibble.

"Thank you so much for doing this," Susie said, as she got a small bowl from the cabinet and filled it.

The kitten ate enthusiastically, with a slight growl coming from its little body.

"Damn, he's a little dinosaur. Listen to him," Patrick said as he petted him. The kitten hesitated, gave him an evil look, and the growling got louder.

"I wouldn't bother him," I said with a laugh. "He might tap into his inner T-Rex and take off a finger." I picked up the litter box and kitty litter. "I'll take this into the bathroom and get his real litter box ready. I'm sure he'll need it when he's done."

"Thank you," Susie said.

I nodded and brushed against her shoulder as I passed.

A sewer smell slammed into my nose as soon as I entered her bedroom. She hadn't been kidding. That little cat had made a colossal mess of the bathroom. Good thing she'd thought about keeping him there and not in her bedroom. By the time I finished and got back into the kitchen, the kitten was done eating and Patrick was holding him.

"So, what's his name?" he asked.

Susie shook her head and pinched her lips together. "No clue. We haven't thought of one." *We.* I didn't miss that word and wondered if it meant she saw the kitten as ours.

"Don't say 'we,'" I said, taking the kitten from Patrick. "He's all yours. I only found him. I bet he's ready for his new litter box." I looked at the bowl, which was half empty. "Shit, guy. I bet you need to go now."

He looked at me with those golden eyes, meowed, and moved around in my arms.

"Oh, no you don't," I said and took off at a trot through the house to Susie's bathroom.

"Did he shit on you?" Patrick asked when I returned to the kitchen.

"No, thank God," I said, dusting off my shirt.

"So, do either of you know a vet I'd be able to get the kitten to?" Susie asked.

"There's one in town," Patrick replied. "He's older, but his daughter just started working for him, so he has help now. Dr. Walker."

"That old man's been a part of this town for decades," I said. "I didn't know Janet was back, though."

"She came back to help her father in the practice. He's planning on retiring soon and needs someone to take over."

"You seem to know a lot about everything," I commented.

"I'm Orlinda Valley's finest. It's my job." He walked to the front door. "And my job is calling. I think I've done my good deed here."

His smirk pissed me off.

"Susie, if this jackass bothers you, just give the station a call. We will gladly pick him up and haul him off to jail. It would give Orlinda Valley something to talk about."

"I'll keep that in mind," Susie said at the door. "Bye and thank you."

He waved, and Susie closed the door.

Her phone pinged, and she glanced at it. "Trevor wants to know if I can come into work at noon," she said as she texted back. "I need to get ready." She opened the door. "Thank you for being here and helping me."

Suddenly, she was cold and aloof. Her attitude made the temperature in the room drop thirty degrees. *That's all she has to say?* No way would I let her act like the previous night and that morning were nothing. I reached toward her arm, but she flinched away. It wasn't quick, but enough to tell me she was done with whatever this was.

Hell no. I had to try again. I wrapped my arms around her waist and pulled her toward me.

She didn't let go of the door but put her other hand on my arm.

I stood tall and looked into her eyes. "Is everything okay?"

"Of course," she said. "Why wouldn't it be? I just have to get ready and make sure the kitten is good before I leave." She gave me a hug. "Again, thank you, Lance. I appreciate everything."

She stepped away again.

My eyes brushed over her features, and my pulse ticked up. My gaze dropped to her lips, and I brushed my fingers against her cheek.

Damn, I wanted to taste those lips once more, but I wouldn't force myself on her. "Well, thank you for an amazing night." I held her gaze. Her eyes looked sad and watery. It broke my heart.

Suddenly, she leaned closer, and her lips brushed against mine in a barely there kiss. I savored that moment and breathed her in.

When she pulled away, her smile didn't meet her eyes. "Goodbye, Lance."

She wouldn't meet my gaze, and I brushed her arm as I walked past.

The finality of her words hit me hard.

CHAPTER 20

SUSIE

I let out a sigh as I closed the door and leaned heavily on it, covering my face in my hands. Emotions churned in my gut. I wanted him to stay, yet I needed him to go.

The previous night and that morning flashed in my mind. His kiss lit me on fire, his gentle touch made me shiver, and his smile—that damn smile—made my heart flutter. *How could something so wrong feel so right?*

My phone vibrated with a text from Trevor. I assured him I could make it in then scrolled to the text I had received earlier, and my blood ran cold.

> **You and Lance are getting close.**
> **I don't like it.**

How does Michael, if that's who this is, know this? Are we being watched?

Whatever was going on between Lance and me didn't matter. It couldn't happen again. There was no telling what Michael was capable of. It was for Lance's own good. My baggage wasn't worth it. I turned the lock on the front door and trudged to my room.

I took an unnecessarily long shower. The hot water beating on my body relaxed me and calmed my nerves. After wrapping a towel around me, I strolled into my bedroom. It was quiet and empty.

I collapsed onto the bed and traced the empty mattress beside me.

Did I do the right thing? Should I have let Lance stay? Should I have told him about the text?

I rolled over and stared at the empty pillow, imagining him lying there watching me. I closed my eyes, and my mind took over. His hand was in my hair, then it brushed down my cheek. A tingle started in my body.

"Fuck. What am I doing?" I buried my face in my pillow. Lance's scent surrounded me, and my heart rate sped up. "Stop. Get him out of your mind."

I sat up, put on jeans and a Jerry's Pub shirt, tore the sheets from my bed, and threw them into the wash. I'd never be able to forget the previous night if I smelled Lance everywhere. It was enough that I had the memories—the amazing memories.

The kitten looked up from its perch on the windowsill. "You have everything you need. Just be a good kitty and use the litter box." I gave him a scratch on his head and froze. Kai's truck was still in the shop. I couldn't take it to work.

I found Kora's keys hanging on the hook in the kitchen and left the house.

⚓

"Hey, Susie," Trevor called as I walked in. It was still early. The pub didn't open until noon, so it was quiet.

"Hi, Trev. I'll be out in a minute." I went into the small office, placed my purse in a drawer, tied on my apron, walked back out, and sat at the counter.

"Thanks for coming in. I'm sure it wasn't easy. I heard trees were down across your road."

I nodded. "They were, but it's all cleared now. Thanks for asking me to come in. I needed to get out of the house."

Trevor smiled. "I'm glad you did. I have a feeling we'll be busy today. Some of the town is still out of power, and there are a lot of people helping with cleanup, so many will want a quick meal and someone to fix it for them."

"I'm surprised you're here today. Shouldn't you be at the station?" I asked.

"I'm checking in when I'm finished here and will help with cleanup later." His smile was sweet.

My gaze traveled over his features. "Trevor, why are you still single? You are the perfect man." And he *was*. Hardworking, sweet, well-liked, and handsome. He would be a great catch—for someone.

He shrugged as he dried glasses, his eyes latched onto mine. "I'm waiting for the perfect woman."

"And he has yet to realize the perfect woman doesn't exist." I turned to see Rowan walking across the pub. "See, Susie? He's not as amazing as he seems. He lives in a fantasy land of perfection."

"What the hell are you doing in here? We aren't open yet," Trevor said.

"Yeah, well, one perk of being best friends with one of the owners is that I can do what I want."

"You're an ass," Trevor said, chuckling.

I laughed at their banter. There were so many things I liked about Orlinda Valley, but the close friendships of the residents was one of my favorites.

The door to the kitchen swung open, and a pain hit my gut.

My father walked toward us with a bag in his hand. His eyes met mine for a second, then flitted to Rowan. "Here you go, Rowan. One special for Summer and a buffalo burger for you."

"Thanks, Terry. At least your workers are respectful. They sure don't learn that from their boss, Trev," Rowan joked as he dropped money on the counter.

"You know my kitchen isn't open until eleven thirty," Trevor shot back.

"And you know I have Nico's direct phone number. We have a brotherhood connection you'll never understand."

"You veterans and your brotherhood," Trevor said with a smile. "Tell Summer hi."

"Roger that. Are you coming to my mother's Friday? She wanted to make sure you'd be there. You've skipped out for the past couple of weeks. You know she doesn't like that."

Trevor's gaze met mine.

I raised my eyebrows. "You should come. We always have fun."

"Maybe I can get Max to watch the bar, and I'll be there."

"Hell, get Max to manage for the weekend. You could use a break," Rowan said as he walked away.

"I'll see!" Trevor hollered.

I watched the door for a bit after Rowan left. "I love the relationship the two of you have."

Trevor leaned on the bar, his hands splayed flat on the top. "He was the brother I never had growing up. I loved going to his house.

It was always loud and chaotic. With three boys, it had to be. Mrs. Tonya is an awesome mom, and his dad, Carl, was amazing. He encouraged us in sports and was always there, cheering me on along with his boys." He shrugged, his eyes getting a faraway look before it disappeared. "Rowan and I were attached at the hip."

"I've never had a friend like that," I said.

"How about the one you went to South Dakota with?"

"Let's say sometimes bridges get burned, and it's almost impossible to repair the damage."

The door opened again, and Barb entered with a group of people behind her. "Hey there, sugars. Let's get this party started."

It was noon, and we were slammed as soon as the doors opened. Between businesses being closed to help with cleanup, families being without power, and townspeople helping their neighbors, people looked to us for food, fellowship, and fun. It was a good day and made me love Orlinda Valley even more.

Mrs. Carlisle came in with a group of ladies from the church. They had been driving around town, handing out water to workers.

I watched their table while I waited at the bar for their drinks, and my father delivered their food. He stood with his hand on the back of one of the ladies' chairs and laughed at something that was said. He looked relaxed, and they reacted to him as if he were a friend.

Even he has been changed by the magic of this town.

He looked up as I approached their table and smiled, though he seemed unsure and questioning. I reacted how I always did. I looked away and gave the women a smile. "I see you've gotten your appetizer. Your food should be ready shortly. Is there anything else you need?" I asked.

"No thank you, Susie. We're fine," Mrs. Carlisle said.

I smiled at the women, glanced at my dad, and checked on another table.

Kai would be home on Sunday, and we needed to talk. I didn't understand how he had forgiven Dad so easily. If anyone had a right to hold a grudge, he did.

"Hey, you're lost in thought," Trevor said, as he placed his hand lightly on my back.

I stood at the computer, entering an order, and glanced at him. "I know. It's just—" I waved my hand and continued typing in my newest order. "Doesn't matter."

"Is Susie Lawson here?"

My eyes jumped to a man carrying a bouquet.

Trevor stepped up. "Why?"

The man held up a hand. "Look, I just need to deliver these." He held out a bouquet of roses.

I froze.

Trevor stepped in front of me like a shield. "Who are they from?"

"I don't know, man. I went and picked them up and delivered them. Just doing my job." He placed them on the counter and left.

The roses were in a vase from the local flower shop, Budding Boutique.

"There's a card." Trevor took the card from the plastic claw clip and held it out. "Want me to read it?"

My heart thumped madly. I shook my head and rubbed my hands on my apron before I took the small envelope.

I felt Trevor's gaze fixed on me, and I took a deep breath. *Don't show him you're afraid. They could be from anyone. They could be from Lance.*

I pulled out the card, and fear tore through me. They weren't from Lance.

> ***You can't run from me.***
> ***I know where you are.***
> ***You and that cutie by the river—***
> ***what are you thinking?***

My body shook with fear, and I dropped the card on the counter.

"Susie?" I jumped when Trevor placed his hand on my back.

He picked up the card and led me to a stool, where I sat down heavily.

He read the card and looked at me. His eyes narrowed with anger. "Who is this?"

I shrugged. I didn't want to answer him.

"I'm calling Patrick."

My eyes bulged. "Don't, please," I squeaked out.

Trevor glared at me and leaned on the counter, his eyes in line with mine. "It's your ex-boyfriend, isn't it? I don't know what it means or who you were with, but if you were by the river with someone, he knows, and he's watching you." He took his phone from his pocket and dialed. "That's not okay."

I dropped my head into my hands. Michael told me I could never leave him, that he would never let me. My chest tightened. He was right. It was impossible. Panic clawed at me. Tears blurred my vision and soaked my hands.

I'd thought I was gone, safe. *How did he find me?*

Trevor's hand rested on my back and moved in slow circles.

Barb's hand slipped under my arm and pulled me up. Her motherly eyes searched mine. "Sugar, are you okay?"

I shook my head. That was all I could do. I was cold, voiceless, and hollow.

"Barb, can you take care of all this and Susie's tables? If you need help, grab Terry, and send Patrick to the office when he gets here."

"Not a problem. I've got this."

I heard the buzz of voices and the clanging of silverware on plates as Trevor guided me to his office. I followed in a trance, as if I were having an out-of-body experience. *How is Michael here?* I raked through my memory. *Did I tell him about Orlinda Valley?* When I'd come for the wedding, I told him I was going to my brother's. He knew I'd flown into Nashville, but I didn't tell him a town—I didn't think.

Fear gripped me tightly. *He must have done his homework and* known *more about me than he'd ever let on.*

"Hey." Trevor's voice was steady and coaxing when we made it into his office. He opened his arms, and I collapsed against him, my sobs finally breaking free.

He said nothing, just held me.

"What's going on?" Patrick asked as he walked through the door. "Susie?"

I pulled away from Trevor and gratefully took the tissues Patrick handed me from the box on the desk. I blotted my face and sat heavily on the overstuffed couch. Trevor sat next to me and handed Patrick the card.

As Patrick's eyes skimmed the words, the color drained from his face. His eyes snapped to me, sharp with concern. "Who is this?"

I cleared my throat and took a sip from the water bottle Trevor handed me. "I'm pretty sure it's my ex. He's been sending texts from different numbers, and the other bouquet, I'm pretty sure that was him too." My shoulders sagged, and the tears flowed again.

Trevor pulled me to him, and I gratefully leaned against him. My body was already heavy with exhaustion from the workday, and this didn't help. I buried my face in his chest as the tears fell.

"What's going on?" A gruff voice pulled me off of Trevor.

I looked up, and Lance's gaze, filled with concern and a tang of anger, met mine. My heart jumped.

"What are you doing here is the question," Trevor replied. He sat up straight but didn't leave my side.

"Patrick and I were at the school, dealing with some damage on the field, when he got your call." Lance's gaze ping-ponged between us then rested on Trevor's arm over my shoulders. "I was concerned."

Our eyes locked, and I pulled away from Trevor as Patrick passed the note to Lance.

I glued my gaze to him as he read the note.

He looked up slowly, his eyes wide. "He watched us this morning?" His voice was a harsh whisper.

Trevor's body stiffened beside me, then he stood. His gaze met mine briefly, and I saw hurt in his eyes. Then he turned to Lance. "You were the one he saw with her? What were you doing at her house?"

"It's none of your business."

"You're right. It's none of my business, but how could someone be watching you and you not know it?" Trevor's words dripped with venom.

They argued back and forth, their words becoming more and more heated by the moment.

They were arguing because of me. *This is crazy.* I was not in the mood to deal with either of them. Irritation bubbled like hot lava in my gut. "Stop! Both of you!"

They shut their mouths.

I wiped my eyes and took a deep breath. "Trevor, yes, Lance was at my house, but it's not a big deal."

Lance opened his mouth, but I put my hand up to shush him and shook my head. "It wasn't a big deal." I enunciated the words, looking hard in his direction.

The muscle in his jaw twitched, but he didn't argue.

I turned to Trevor and Patrick. "He came over to help with the animals and got stuck there when the storm hit and the road became blocked. That's it. Not that I need to explain my actions."

The reality of what was going on hit me like a ton of bricks. Michael, if it was him, was watching me—stalking me. My blood pressure rose. I'd moved to Orlinda Valley to get away from him, but his crazy-self followed me. "Patrick, I have no clue how he found me, but I know it's him. His name is Michael Lanyear. He works at Southern Middle School in South Dakota. I met him when I worked there. We started dating and eventually moved in together. He became an alcoholic and a demanding asshole, so I left him and came here. He swore I wouldn't be able to get away from him, and it looks like he's right."

"Susie, if you could stop by the station after your shift and give an official statement, that would be a great help. Until then, I'll put out a bulletin with his name and see what we can find."

"I'll do you one better," I said. "I'll go with you now." I took off my apron and dropped it on the couch. "Barb can finish my shift and take my tables. She won't mind. Are you okay with that?" I asked Trevor.

"Yeah, that sounds like a good idea. Call me when you're done. I'll come get you."

I nodded and walked out.

Lance grabbed my arm as I passed him.

My gaze snapped to his, and I lost my breath for a second. His eyes sucked me in, but I shook my head. "Not now," I whispered, and he let go of my arm.

CHAPTER 21

LANCE

Anger burned hot in my chest.

Dammit, I'd handled things all wrong, as usual. But when I'd seen Trevor's arm around her, jealousy clawed its way up, and I lost all control. I was gone, completely undone by Susie, and the urge to protect her drowned out everything else. I couldn't help myself. All common sense evaporated.

No fucking way was I was letting her walk past me like we were just friends, like nothing had happened between us. "Susie, wait." I caught up and grabbed her arm.

She turned, and the look on her face—*fear and is that shame?*—tore at my heart.

"What, Lance?" Her voice was flat, stripped of the spark she'd had the last two days.

"It's going to be okay. I promise."

Her eyes shimmered. "Yeah, okay," she whispered.

I wanted to pull her close and tell her he'd never touch her again. But I couldn't, not when he'd already gotten near her—with me right there. He'd been watching, there among the trees. *How did I miss it? I failed her.*

I stepped back and let her leave the pub with Patrick. He pulled open the door and nodded when our eyes met.

Patrick would keep her safe. He wouldn't let anything happen.

"Hey, asshole, what was all that about?" Trevor's voice brought me back to reality.

I shook my head. It wasn't a good time to start an argument with him. I scrubbed my hands over my face and walked away.

"You know she's too good for you." Trevor said quietly, but made sure I heard him.

I halted and ground my molars. *Don't take the bait. He's trying to get under your skin. Walk away, Lance.*

"She'll never be interested in you. You're wasting your time," he said, a slight edge to his voice.

I halted, a low, frustrated chuckle rumbling in my chest. "You don't know how wrong you are, little man," I said, not bothering to turn around. "I've had those sweet lips on mine. I've touched her soft skin. Can you say the same?"

I paused for a beat, let my words sink in, then walked off.

I ignored my name being called as I pushed out the door, and I didn't stop until I had climbed into my truck and pulled out of the parking lot.

"Shit, what the hell did you say that for?" I sucked in a breath and sighed. "Fuck. When he brings that conversation up to Susie, she's *really* not going to talk to me again."

I headed to the police station. She might think she didn't need anyone, but tough shit. I was going to be there for her anyway.

She'd have Kai if he were around. I should probably call him. *Yeah, right.* If I told him what was going on, he'd cut his vacation short to get home. Then, Susie would be pissed at me for making that happen.

I pulled into the station and walked in the door.

"Good morning, Lance," Ethel Landry, the records clerk, greeted me.

I smiled widely. "Good morning, Mrs. Landry. How's Charlie doing this summer?"

"Oh, you know him. He's fishing and enjoying his free time." Her husband was the basketball coach at the high school.

"Good to hear. Did Patrick come in here with Susie by any chance?"

"He sure did. Go ahead to his office."

I thanked her and walked down the hall.

My nerves ran wild. Susie could easily tell me to fuck off and force me to leave. I was probably the last person she wanted to see, but I had to let her know I cared and was here for her.

I glanced in the window of Patrick's office as I walked past. He was on the phone, and Susie was picking at her nails in a corner chair.

I knocked twice, then walked in. "Hey."

Susie glanced at me. Her shoulders rose and fell in a heavy sigh, but she gave me a small smile. It wasn't much, but I'd take it. On my short drive here, millions of scenarios had run through my mind about how she'd greet me. Yelling, cursing, and throwing me out for bothering her and not taking a hint were at the top of the list. A smile, no matter how small, was a good sign.

Patrick held up a finger, and I sat gingerly in the chair next to Susie and placed my hand on her thigh. "You okay?"

Her gaze traveled over my face, and she shrugged. "As good as I can be, since my crazy ex-boyfriend somehow found me in Orlinda Valley and is stalking me without anyone knowing."

"I'm sorry I let this happen."

"What?" She sat up straight. "How did you let this happen?"

"I've been with you for the past two days, and he was there. Watching. I should have known."

"How? With your superpowers? The amazing Lance Hartley. Keeper of safety over all residents of Orlinda Valley?"

I chuckled. "I guess that is ridiculous. But still." I held her hand, and she didn't pull away. I took that as good sign number two. "He was near you when I was there. I promise you, though. It won't happen again. Nothing will happen as long as I'm with you."

She stiffened next to me.

I fixed my gaze on hers. "I want to be with you. Is that okay?" Our eyes connected, and the pull I had felt the past two days was back.

Her smile almost met her eyes, and she nodded.

That was good sign number three. My heart relaxed.

"Patrick called Kai. They're coming home."

"Good. You need your brother."

Tears welled in her eyes, and I pulled her close. I held her and was thankful she let me.

Finally, she puffed out a breath and pulled away. "Sorry," she said as she wiped her eyes. "It's all been a lot."

"It's okay. I'm here for you." I brushed my hand lightly across her cheek, wiping away a lone tear.

"Sorry about that," Patrick said as he hung up the phone. "That last call was from Trevor. He said Terry heard what happened and was worried. I didn't think you'd want him here, so I told Trevor that you would get in touch with him when you're ready, but he could tell him you're doing fine. He's going to relay the message. I hope that's okay."

Susie nodded.

His gaze passed from one of us to the other. "We still have to get your statement, and if you have any pictures of Michael, they would be helpful," Patrick said.

"Can Lance stay?" Susie asked and turned to me. "Do you want to?"

"Of course. If I can."

Patrick nodded. "As long as you let her talk and don't get in the way."

I sat on the other side of the room as Patrick questioned Susie. Her body language was tense and tight. I had to bite the inside of my cheek to keep from throwing in my thoughts.

Finally, after what felt like hours, they finished, and Susie pushed herself from her chair as if the weight of the world had settled on her and held her down.

"Thank you, Susie," Patrick said. "I know that wasn't easy. We will make sure an officer drives past your house periodically, but don't go anywhere alone for a while. Kai should be home tomorrow, so you won't be alone long. Maybe you should stay with someone."

I stood next to her and wrapped my arm around her waist. "She won't be alone."

Patrick raised an eyebrow and bit back a smirk, then turned his attention back to her. "You have my number and the direct line to the station, but remember, if you find yourself in a questionable situation, don't hesitate to call 911."

She nodded. "Thank you."

Patrick walked us out.

I kept a protective hand on her lower back as we walked through the waiting area. Mrs. Landry was on the phone, so she couldn't send out information about us being together to the gossip line, though I was sure she'd already said something.

Once we were in my truck, Susie's shoulders slumped, and she laid her head against the window.

"Hey," I said and rubbed her thigh.

The corners of her lips tipped up slightly.

"How about I take you back to the house and we check on the goats and the kitten?"

She laid her head on the seat. "I could use a little kitten cuddle."

It didn't take long before we pulled into the driveway. She jumped out of the truck, and I ran ahead of her, grabbed the keys from her hand, and unlocked the door. Maybe I was being crazy, but I needed to go in first and check out everything. "Wait here. Let me make sure it's safe."

"Lance, you're being ridiculous."

She pushed past me and went directly into her room, while I did a quick sweep of both floors, checked the downstairs windows and doors, and went into the backyard.

Kai needed a security system. I would talk to him when he got home.

I walked around the yard and down the path to the river but didn't go far. There was no way a person could see the house from the river or on the opposite bank. But the bank where we'd stood earlier, absolutely.

Michael couldn't see inside the house if he stayed in the treeline. He would have to go up close, and he'd be crazy to do that.

I walked back inside and found Susie curled up in her bed with the cat cuddled next to her. They both looked so sweet and innocent.

I covered her with the throw blanket at the foot of the bed, grabbed her keys, and went out to check on the goats, locking the door behind me.

After giving them attention, I walked the pasture with them close on my heels, gathered eggs, and returned to the house.

When I looked in her room, she was sleeping peacefully.

Quietly, I slipped off my shoes and climbed into bed next to her. Her soft scent wrapped around me, steadying me and undoing me all at once.

She breathed lightly, her face calm. A loose strand of hair fell across her cheek. I tucked it behind her ear and let my fingers linger for a moment.

The kitten stirred, eyes slitting open, as he stretched and purred louder. I scratched his head as he nestled under her chin. "You've got the best place in the house, kitty," I whispered.

I left my arm resting lightly on hers as I studied her face, memorizing every line, every curve.

Though I'd been with more women than I cared to admit, none had ever made my heart melt like Susie did. I'd never experienced this overwhelming need to protect, this heart-clenching desire to make her happy. And I'd sure as *hell* never thought I would fall in love. But dammit, I had. I was head over heels, crazy in love with this woman.

Words crowded in my chest, but I swallowed them back.

She was asleep. It wasn't like she could read my mind. *But still. What if she did?*

It was too soon. I could lose her before I ever really had her. Some things were worth waiting for, and Susie was worth it.

I closed my eyes, my thoughts echoing through me as I placed the faintest kiss on her lips.

CHAPTER 22

SUSIE

When I woke up from my nap, Lance was gone, but he assured me I wouldn't be alone for long.

As I waited for whoever was pulling the first round of what I have coined "Guard Duty: Susie Edition", I sat outside on the patio, the sun warming my skin, soaking in some fresh air and vitamin D. I knew Lance cared, but he was being overbearing. *Making someone come hang out with me? I'm an adult. I can be alone and can take care of myself.*

I opened the book in my hand to the first chapter, read the first few pages, but had no clue what was going on. I sat it on the table next to me and laid my head back, sipped iced tea, and let the heat of the sun make my skin tingle.

The weight of the past days melted away, and my breathing became steady. The only times I'd felt so relaxed lately had been when Lance's lips were somewhere on my body. He had a way of working out the tension.

Suddenly, the crunching of tires on gravel caught my attention, and my pulse skipped. *So much for being relaxed.* I sat up and wondered if I should go see who it is and greet them, or go in the house and prepare to call Patrick in case it's someone without good intentions. *None of the above. I'm* overreacting.

"Hey!" Kristy said as she, Lilly, and Summer rounded the corner with bags in their hands, followed closely by Rowan and Trevor.

I placed my hand over my thumping heart. *See, you were overreacting.* Company wouldn't be such a bad idea after all. I stood. "What's all this?"

"Lance asked us to keep you company," Rowan said. "So, I went one better, and we're having a party."

"Yep," Kristy said. "And Trevor brought the food." She gave me a hug. "No need to be here under house arrest without having fun."

Trevor and Rowan walked into the kitchen.

"That's what it feels like," I said as the rest of us followed.

Trevor and Rowan pulled carton after carton of food from the bags, and Lilly grabbed plates and utensils from the drawer and cabinet.

"Trevor. There's enough here to feed two armies. Why? And who's at the pub?"

He shook his head. "I don't know why y'all think I live there. I am a *co*-owner. Which means more than one owner."

His gaze searched my face. He wore an expression I couldn't quite place. *Concern, maybe?*

"Here you go," Lilly said, handing me a bag.

I grabbed it quickly. "You shouldn't be carrying that. Damn, guys. Why did you let her carry anything?"

"I'm pregnant. Not useless," she said, sitting at the counter.

"Have you ever tried to tell her what to do?" Rowan asked. "It's impossible. She's stubborn."

I laughed. "Maybe, but if Jamison were here, there would be no way he'd let you carry anything," I said to her.

"Exactly. That's why I did it. Jamison smothers me, so I have a few hours of freedom. He and Lance are coming over after football practice."

Lance will be here again. My heart skipped a beat.

"Smothering their women seems to be a McKendry trait," Summer said with a roll of her eyes.

"Is that complaining I hear coming from your beautiful lips?" Rowan asked from across the room.

"If it is, are you going to shut them up?" Summer's voice was sultry.

"Maybe."

She pushed up from the stool she was sitting on. "Well, then, I wish I could spend more time alone. All your hovering is annoy—"

Rowan wrapped her in his arms, and his lips crashed against hers. She laced her arms around his neck and returned his affections.

"Come on, you two. Give it a rest," Trevor said. "I liked them better when they were fighting the sexual tension between them constantly."

"Yeah, well, there doesn't seem to be any of that left." I chuckled as they finally came up for breath.

"Trevor, it's not my fault your sorry ass can't find a girl," Summer said.

Trevor's eyes caught mine briefly, and I turned away. Guilt filled me. I knew he had feelings for me, and he was an amazing man, but my heart was occupied.

Just then, the kitten strolled into the kitchen with a tiny meow.

Thank God. Saved by a bundle of furry cuteness.

"Oh, my gosh. He's so adorable," Kristy said as she scooped him up. "Where did you find him?"

"He's so lovable," Lilly said as she scratched his head.

"Right before the storm hit, Lance and I went out to check on the animals. Lance found him in one of the chicken boxes, curled up. We brought him inside. Patrick brought him food and a litter box once the road opened."

"You're keeping him?" Summer asked.

I shrugged. "I guess. He's cute and friendly."

She nodded.

"Why?"

Rowan looked at her, then the cat, then me. "Kora's allergic."

My stomach fell. It had only been a couple of days, but the little guy had already purred its way into my heart. I'd never thought of anyone being allergic to cats.

"Oh, well." I hesitated. "When she gets home, we'll talk about it. Maybe if I keep him in my room, he won't bother her."

We ate at the table on the patio. They'd brought chicken fingers, buffalo wings, jalapeño poppers, fried green beans, and fries. The stress of the past few days melted away as laughter filled the air. It was exactly what I needed.

"Hey, all, you better have left us food," Lance said as he and Jamison entered the yard.

My heart fluttered at the sight of him.

He wore a T-shirt; the arms cut out at the shoulders, basketball shorts, and tennis shoes. His clothing choice showed every curve and bulge of his muscles in his chest, arms, and legs.

Jamison greeted Lilly with a kiss and took the seat by her.

Lance took the seat across from me, and our eyes met. He raised his eyebrows and gave me a sexy smile.

I smiled back and returned my attention to the conversation. It was hard to concentrate on the discussion with Lance so close. I could feel whenever his gaze cut to mine, and my body had an awareness of everything about him—his body, his voice, his lips. Heat crept up my back to my neck, and not because it was the end of June in Tennessee.

He and Jamison discussed the upcoming season. I enjoyed listening to him talk about the team. His excitement was contagious. He held everyone's attention, so it wasn't strange that I could watch him and hold on to his every word.

His closeness with Jamison was obvious when they ragged on each other. They made us all laugh with their stories of practices and their hopes for the upcoming season.

The sound of hooves on rocks got our attention, and Percy, Jackson, and Baby Goat joined us. "How did they get out?" I huffed and got up. Trevor held my arm. "Don't worry about them, Susie. They're fine. They always get out and hang out here when Kora's home."

"I know, but they also listen to her and follow her everywhere. They don't listen to me at all," I said as I fell back into my seat.

"Leave them. We'll put them away before we leave," Jamison said.

"Put them away?" Rowan asked. "You make them sound like clothing."

"Yeah," Summer said. "Unfortunately, it won't be that easy."

Rowan hovered close to her. "How about you, babe? Will you be easy?"

Summer smirked and raised an eyebrow.

Trevor rolled his eyes. "Here we go."

"Only for you, Row." Summer grabbed his neck and pulled him to her for a long kiss.

Lance whooped, and Jamison let out a whistle, which got the goats riled up. They hopped and pranced around.

"I think we're going to call it a night and get home," Rowan said. "I need a bit of good ole' Summer-time."

"I don't know if we'll make it home."

"There's always the goat house," Jamison said. "A little roll in the hay's always fun."

Lilly laughed and blushed.

I turned to Kristy.

She rolled her eyes. "You don't want to know," she said as she started clearing the table. I jumped up to help, and Lilly followed.

The lights were back on when we walked into the kitchen. *Thank God.*

It didn't take us long to clean up, as there wasn't much food left, so we headed outside.

The men were nowhere to be seen.

"Where'd they get to?" Kristy asked.

I shrugged, and we walked around the yard to the driveway and then up to the pasture. The men and Summer were closing the gate and deep in conversation.

"They look serious," Lilly said, "and Summer and Rowan didn't leave."

"I'm sure the goats got in their way when they tried, and they all worked together to get the devils back where they belong," I said. "Trust me—it's the truth. Those goats are stubborn."

They stopped talking when we joined them.

"What's going on?" Kristy asked. "Why the secrets?"

Lilly glanced at Jamison. "Yeah, what's going on?"

Jamison and Rowan both avoided my eyes. Lance shook his head, and the muscle in his jaw twitched. It only twitched when something was bothering him.

My gut clenched, and I turned to Trevor. "What's going on? You'll tell me." He was the most trustworthy.

"The goats didn't jump over the fence."

"Trevor, what the hell?" Lance scowled.

"Lance, hush. I asked him a question." I gestured to Trevor to go on.

He looked at Rowan, who tilted his head.

Jamison shook his.

"She deserves to know," Trevor said as he turned to me.

His honest eyes held concern. My stomach tied in a knot and twisted hard. Something was wrong. The air was full of tension.

"The gate was open," he said.

"Open?" I asked and turned to Lance. "We tied it shut this morning. I remember doing it myself, and you checked it."

Lance nodded. "I know."

My eyes widened, and my pulse raced. *Goats can't untie things. That meant someone else did.*

CHAPTER 23

LANCE

Fear darkened her face. It didn't take her long to realize what it meant. I crossed over to her and held her arms. "Hey." I pulled her chin up so our eyes met. "It's okay. I told you I won't let anyone hurt you, and I sure won't let him."

She averted her gaze and looked out across the pasture. "He was here. In the yard." She said and pulled away from me.

"Hey, you're good," Kristy said, placing her arm around her shoulders. "I'll stay with you tonight, or you can come to my place."

Susie laid her head on Kristy's shoulder and relaxed. I let out a heavy breath. The need to be the one she turned to consumed me. Damn, I wanted her head on my shoulder and my arms wrapped around her.

Susie stood up straight, crossed her arms tightly, and shook her head. "I can't go anywhere. I have the kitten."

I couldn't just stand there and watch as fear filled her features. I glanced around at the edge of the property, in the tree line. *I swear, if he's watching us, I'll kill him.*

I crossed over to Susie. "I'll stay again tonight if you want me to," I said and tucked a lock of hair behind her ear.

Her crystal eyes were red with unshed tears. Relief filled me when she nodded. I glanced up at Jamison.

He raised an eyebrow and clapped once. "That's settled. Call if you need anything, at any time."

"Absolutely," Rowan said. "And Susie, I'll be here for you in a heartbeat if you need anything."

"Thank you," she said. She gave Lilly and Kristy each a hug and said bye to Summer.

I watched Trevor and Susie talking as I said goodbye to Jamison. She shook her head and nodded but never smiled. She looked sad and almost broken. He hugged her, and a part of me wanted to tear his arms from her, but it was okay. She was with me.

This makes it clear to everyone, even Trevor.

"Take care of her," Trevor said as he passed me.

"Of course," I said as I placed a protective arm around her waist. Relief flooded me when she melted into my side.

Once everyone's vehicles were out of sight, I turned to her and held her face in my hands. "Hey, I promise you. I'm here. And nothing will happen."

Our eyes locked. Her sadness disappeared, and her eyes glittered. A small smile pulled at the corners of her lips. "And I'm grateful." She rubbed her palm in a circle on my chest.

The friction of her touch warmed me to my core, and I searched her face. I wanted—no, needed to memorize every inch of her perfect features, but those eyes held me transfixed.

Then her lips closed on mine, and my breath hitched.

She laced her fingers in the hair at the nape of my neck and pulled me closer. I did the same to her as our tongues met and danced together. The kiss differed from before. It wasn't as desperate. It was like we knew each other in a sacred way.

I melted into her and got lost in her until we finally came up for air. "Let's go inside and lock up," I whispered, then we laced our fingers together as we walked around the house and into the kitchen.

She took care of feeding the cat while I, once again, did a walk around the house, locking doors and checking windows, then entered her bedroom.

She was in a thin white T-shirt that fell just below her ass, and her long legs looked damn sexy. Her hair cascaded down to her shoulders.

"God, you're beautiful," I whispered. Those were the only words I could think of, but they weren't enough to describe her.

She walked toward me and placed her hands under my shirt, on my bare skin, and caressed my chest muscles.

I hissed in a breath as she pulled my shirt slowly over my head like she wanted to enjoy the appearance of every inch of my skin.

"You are amazing," she said as her eyes traveled with her hands down my chest.

She explored the ridges and valleys of my abs, then her lips were on my nipples.

"Fuck," I said under my breath.

"You like that."

It wasn't a question. She knew I did. But it wasn't the time, not after what had happened. I pulled her up and held her shoulders. "You don't have to. This isn't right," I said.

"What do you mean? I know I don't have to. And there's nothing else that's more right. You've shown me how you feel today more than once." Her gaze met mine as she took a small step away. "I know you won't force anything on me." She pulled her shirt over her head.

My pulse picked up.

"I need to be wanted and desired." She reached around her back, unhooked her bra, and dropped it to the ground.

My blood flooded south.

"I want you to tell me you want me, because I want you, Lance. I want your lips on me. I want your tongue—"

"Stop, woman." I couldn't hold back. I reached for her, but she shook her head and stepped back.

"Tell me you want me." Her voice was sultry. "Tell me you desire me."

"Fuck," I said through gritted teeth. I took a step forward. "Yes, I want you."

Her eyes filled with need.

I caught her around the waist and jerked her against me, feeling every one of her curves align with my body. My voice came out rougher than I had intended. "I want to make you come again and again until you're trembling and your body's rubber. I want to worship you all night, because you drive me crazy." My lips found hers—hungry, demanding. She kissed me back just as greedily, and the taste of her made my head spin.

I broke away enough to speak against her lips. "I've never wanted anyone the way I want you." I slid my hand up to cup her face; my thumb brushed her flushed cheek as I held her gaze. My other arm tightened around her and held her close. "But I need to know you want this too."

She sucked in her bottom lip and nodded.

"Not good enough. I need to hear you say it." My breathing was heavy, and my heart pounded.

Her breath hitched. For a moment she stared at me, lips parted, eyes dark with desire. Then, her fingers curled into my shirt.

"Yes, Lance," she whispered. "I want this. I want you."

I clutched her ass and lifted her as my lips met hers. This kiss was deep, seductive, and hot.

She wrapped her legs around my waist.

I pushed her against the wall and held her there as I kissed down her neck, toward her breasts. I sucked one nipple into my mouth, hard and deep.

The noise she made created flames under my skin, and I did the same to the other. The taste of her skin on my tongue and my lips turned me on unlike anyone ever had.

I carried her to the bed and nipped the tip of her nipple, and she breathed in heavily with a throaty sigh.

As soon as I laid her on the bed, I enjoyed the sight of her white lace bikini panties. I brushed my hand down them, and she arched her back.

Heat blazed in her eyes, and I wanted to give her everything I could. I wanted her to forget the past few days and drown in her desire for me—for what she wanted.

I held her arms above her head. "Don't move," I said, our eyes locked. "Don't. Move."

She nodded slowly and closed her eyes.

I kissed her mouth and then nibbled her lip.

She moaned in acceptance.

I trailed kisses down her sexy body. Her skin was soft and tasted as sweet as honey. Her breathing sped up.

I licked and teased her nipples, first one, then the other, tugging with my teeth.

Her moans were encouragement, cheering me on.

I licked down to her belly button, then got on my knees and pulled her to the edge of the bed. "Don't move. Keep those arms up there," I repeated.

She closed her eyes as I pulled her panties down and slowly caressed her legs.

Goosebumps appeared on her skin.

I kissed them away. Then kissed the inside of one thigh, near her knee, as my fingers inched toward her core until they finally found home. I caressed her sensitive spot as I trailed my kisses lazily toward her core, enjoying every moan that escaped from her.

When I was tantalizingly close, I paused for a brief second.

"Lance," she breathed.

Our eyes met as I spread her legs and my tongue made its way teasingly to its goal. The moan that escaped her encouraged me.

I brushed my finger and thumb over her, and she arched toward my hand. Her eyes were slits, and she sucked in her bottom lip.

"God, woman." Those were the last words I said before I licked and played with her. She tasted sweet, delicious, and her moans of ecstasy drove me to continue, and I pushed my fingers inside her while I tasted her. I reached my other hand up and played with her breasts.

"Lance, yes. Please," she said as she bucked against my tongue.

I held her hips down as she squirmed under me.

Her breathing quickened.

"Susie, yes," I said as her moans ended, and her body stilled.

"Lance," she pulled my head, and I crawled to her and our lips met. "Lance, I need you inside me. Now. Please."

My gaze held hers as I stood and dropped my shorts and boxers to the floor. "I don't have a condom."

"I told you I'm on the pill. Please don't make me wait anymore." The desperation in her voice and the desire in her eyes burned deep in my soul. I climbed onto the bed, and our lips met. The kiss was deep and sexy. We said so much without any words.

As I positioned myself at her opening, she spread her legs. Our eyes met as I slowly pushed into her.

I let out a sigh as she pulled in a breath.

She wrapped her legs around my waist, and I brushed her hair from her face. I searched every inch of her beautiful features. Her eyes, silver and filled with desire. Her lips, rosy and swollen. Her skin, soft as silk and kissed with color.

I once again claimed her mouth with mine. This woman, this goddess, was here with me. I pushed in deeper. My heart swelled with each thrust. Sex with Susie was like a heaven I'd never known before. I closed my eyes to ingrain this moment into my memory.

I picked up the rhythm, and she met every thrust. We moved effortlessly together, like we were made for each other. Heat rushed throughout my body. I was going to explode any minute. "Susie. Yes."

She pushed me into her harder and opened more until I couldn't hold on.

I felt her body shudder under me as her muscles tightened around my length. With one last thrust, I exploded inside her with the most earth-shattering orgasm in my living memory. We both moaned as we finished together.

Our eyes locked, and our lips brushed against each other.

I lay back on the pillow and turned toward her, breathless. "Thank you."

She laughed—her sweet, angelic laugh. "For what?"

"For allowing me the pleasure of getting to know you." I brushed my fingers over her arm, and she shivered at my touch. "All of you. You're an angel, and your laugh proves it."

She shook her head. "You are always surprising me, Lance Hartley. I never thought you had a sweet side to you, and I sure never thought this would happen."

Chuckling, I wrapped an arm around her waist. "Well, I promise you. I'm living my dream. I didn't think you'd ever look at me with anything but disdain, but I wanted so much more."

I leaned in and kissed her gently.

I needed her to know that whatever this was, meant more to me than just a one-night stand. She rolled on top of me, and it didn't take long until we were ready for round two—then round three.

CHAPTER 24

LANCE

The morning came early, and my body ached in all the right places. I rolled over, wrapped my arm around Susie, and pulled her to me.

She gave the most delicious moan.

I could easily kiss her, feel her, and yeah, well, I needed to stop before I had another hard-on I couldn't get rid of.

Quietly, I climbed out of bed and pulled on shorts. I stepped into the bathroom and grabbed a quick shower before heading to the kitchen. I was hungry and wanted to impress Susie with my culinary skills and show her I could do more than grill and make peanut butter and jelly sandwiches. Pancakes were my specialty, and I saw a box of mix in the cabinet and a pound of bacon in the freezer. The food in the freezer was still cold and mostly frozen, though the refrigerator needed to get cleaned out.

I whisked the pancake mix, then turned on the griddle.

Breakfast was my favorite meal. After my parents had divorced, my mother worked long hours at Shear Perfection and didn't have time left to cook dinner. Saturday mornings became our family meal day, and she made huge breakfasts for the three of us—well four, when Charles joined the family.

I'd wake up early to help her, and I enjoyed every second. Even when I was in high school and stayed out later than I should have Friday nights and was even a bit hungover, I was up and helping. We would talk about everything—mother-son bonding time.

She asked me about school, and if I was dating a girl, who Lilly often called the flavor of the week. My mom tried to make me see girls as people and not prizes or commodities. At the time, I rolled my eyes and ignored her, even when she played the big-brother card. "How would you feel if someone treated Lilly like something to throw away? What would you do?"

My answer was simple. I'd kick his butt and make him sorry he'd ever laid eyes on her.

I chuckled as I poured pancakes on the griddle. That was exactly why she and Jamison had kept their relationship secret years ago and again when they'd started seeing each other the previous year.

How many girls did I go out with last year? That answer was easy. Two, though Jayla had been the longest relationship I'd had by far.

Hell, the longest ever, eight months. "God, Lance, you are a jack-ass. No wonder Susie hated you."

I closed my eyes as flashes from the previous night invaded me—Susie on top of me, her hair over her shoulders, her head back, her eyes closed as she rocked and moved.

I placed my hands heavily on the counter. "Fuck." My boxers tightened uncomfortably.

"You okay?"

Her sweet voice, heavy with sleep, got my attention, and I turned.

She stood in the kitchen doorway in one of my shirts, which barely covered her ass. Her hair was messy, and her face was drowsy. Overall, she was beautiful.

My heart stuttered. "I'm fine, sweetness." I wrapped my arms around her and pulled her to me. "I was picturing you last night, on top of me, and the hard-on I ignored this morning came back with a vengeance."

She giggled, and I kissed it from her mouth. She tasted like mint toothpaste and pure perfection.

"Sweetness?" she asked.

I glanced down at her. She didn't like nicknames. "Shit, I'm sorry. It just came out."

"No," she said, shaking her head. "It surprised me." Her angelic eyes locked on mine. "I like it." A smile ticked at the corners of her lips.

"Can I ask you a question?"

She shrugged.

"Why don't you like nicknames?"

She stiffened in my arms, and I rubbed her back. "You don't have to tell me if you're not ready."

"Let's just say no one ever worth anything called me a nickname except Kai and Sebastian. Kai calls me Suz, and Sebastian calls me sis. No other man has been worth it. How're those pancakes coming along?"

"Shit." I turned back to the griddle and gave them a flip. "A little dark, but not bad." I placed them on a plate and poured more batter onto the griddle.

Susie got busy setting the table.

No other man who used a nickname for her was ever worth it. I hadn't planned to call her sweetness. It just came out, but it fit her perfectly, and she didn't mind. I flipped the pancakes as a smile filled my face.

I plated the pancakes, got the bacon from the oven, and took the food to the table. *Who would have ever thought I'd be making breakfast for a woman and enjoying myself?*

"I heard from Kai this morning," Susie said, pouring syrup on her pancakes. "They're already in Alabama and shouldn't be much longer."

"Do you work today?"

She shook her head. "No. I have the weekend off."

"That's probably a good thing. It'll give you time to catch Kai up on everything."

"Catch Kai up with what?" she asked as she continued to eat.

As I watched her methodical way of preparing her pancakes before each bite—the perfect squares, the stack of four she fit on her fork—a smile formed on my lips.

"What?" she asked.

I shook my head and took a bite of my breakfast. "You'll need to get Kai caught up with the stalker situation, for one. He'll keep an eye on things." She dropped her fork onto the plate and planted her hands on the table. "Look. I'm thankful that you and everyone are concerned and looking out for my safety. I am. But I will not stay under house arrest." Her voice was dripping with anger. "It's not like Michael's going to do anything to me. It's not in him. Texting, sending unwanted gifts, yes. But that's it. I know all this mess is why there's suddenly no space in the schedule for another server. Trevor's concerned. You're concerned. Now, Kora and my brother cut their vacation short. I will not be everyone's problem."

I reached across the table and squeezed her hand. "You're not a problem. We care. It's what friends and family do." I rubbed my thumb across her hand, and her shoulders relaxed. "Just so you know, I'm not going anywhere. I plan on spending my day with you."

"What about when Kai gets home?"

"What do you mean?"

"Don't you think they're going to wonder why you're here?"

And there it was. I wasn't backing away from us, no way in hell. "What if they do?" I held her gaze. "You don't want to be under house arrest, and I don't want us to be a secret."

Her eyes got that closed-off haze over them, and her body stiffened—her protective stance. She closed herself off from the world so she wouldn't get hurt, but that wasn't how it worked.

"Susie." I stood and pulled her to her feet. Fear that she might protest washed through me, but that didn't happen.

She stood, her arms slack at her sides, and her gaze fell behind me.

I moved so our eyes met. "I don't know if you've noticed, but what I'm doing here is caring for you. The first time I saw you last year, you took a piece of my heart. Then how you reacted when Rowan and I fought, and he broke my nose. That woman, the one who was angry and tough, God, she grabbed hold of more than a piece. It took me months to get over you when you went back to South Dakota. Then you showed up again, and that was it. You control my heart. Every bit of it is yours."

I tucked her hair behind her ears and tipped her chin up, so our eyes met. "You are an amazing woman. You're soft yet tough. You give, and you take. You're sweet and loving. You're beautiful and so fucking sexy."

She blushed and tried to look away, but I gripped her chin. "Don't hide from me. Susie. Ever."

Our gazes held.

Those crystal-clear eyes of hers sucked me in. I wished I could see deep into her soul and hold on to her.

She brushed her hand against my neck and tugged lightly.

Holding her head in my hands, I kissed her—gently, sweetly, totally.

She pulled away and leaned her forehead against mine. "Thank you. Those were the sweetest words any man has ever said to me," she whispered.

"I'm sorry. You should have been told those things so many times, but I'm glad you heard them from me."

She gave that sexy, crooked smile that made me helpless and under her control and wrapped her arms around my neck. "Breakfast was delicious. Thank you."

"You're welcome. What should we do next?"

"It's morning. We ate, and now I think we need to shower." Her voice was seductive and sexy as hell.

"I've already showered," I said.

She shrugged. "I haven't, and I think you should take another one."

"Together?" I asked with a smirk.

She chuckled and touched the tip of her finger to my lips. "Of course. We don't want to waste water. And do me a favor."

"Anything," I said against her finger.

Her smile turned wicked. "Never get rid of that smirk." She walked toward her bedroom, pulling me behind.

"I thought you hated my smirk. I think your words were something like, 'It's a self-righteous smirk.'"

"I lied to you. That smirk always got to me. It's damn sexy and turns me on."

I froze.

She pulled, but I didn't follow, so she turned.

"It turns you on?" I asked.

"Why the hell do you think I'm taking you to the shower? I need you to fuck me senseless."

My eyes widened, and my body throbbed with desire. "You are full of surprises."

She shrugged. "You bring out something in me I never knew existed."

I followed behind her and turned on the shower, and when I turned back, she had shucked off the shirt she was wearing.

My mouth watered as she stood in front of me. *How did I not know she was naked under my shirt?*

She pointed at me. "Your turn."

Chuckling, I pulled down my shorts and stepped out of them and into the shower.

Susie joined me and grabbed the soap. She lathered it in her palms and rubbed my chest and continued down my body. She kissed my lips as she pushed me under the spray of the shower and helped the water rinse the suds from my body. Her hands were soft, gentle, and so sure of what they wanted.

I reached for her breasts, but she grabbed my hands and pushed me against the wall, out of the spray of the water. "Don't move," she said as she kissed my lips, my neck, and continued her trail down my body, until she was on her knees.

"Jesus, are you sure?" I moaned.

Her eyes locked with mine. She nodded and slipped my length into her mouth.

I sucked in a breath and laid my head against the cold tile.

My cock throbbed.

Her lips were warm, moist, and perfect.

CHAPTER 25

LANCE

After feeding and tending to the animals, we walked around the goat pasture, our hands locked together.

She was talking about something the goats did one day when she and Kora had come out to tend to them.

I wasn't listening to a word she said because I was lost in her beauty. Her eyes gleamed as she retold the story. She sauntered through the field, as if the stress of the past days had never existed. Our fingers folded perfectly together.

"Are you listening to me?" she asked.

The smile she gave me made my pulse stutter, and I shook my head. "Not a word. I'm a bit distracted."

"Oh yeah? What's distracting you?"

"The most beautiful woman I've ever laid eyes on."

She laid her head back, and laughter shook her shoulders.

I stopped in my tracks and yanked on her arm.

Her face held surprise for a moment, then laughter once again.

"What the hell is so funny?" I asked.

It took her a moment to contain herself, and she covered her mouth, her eyes wide with humor. "I don't know," she gasped. "You're just so serious."

I pulled away and stalked off. "You know what? See if I'm a gentleman anymore. Seems as if you liked me better when I was an ass."

She ran to catch up. "Not true," she said as she grabbed my hand and pulled me to a stop. "Jackass Lance *was* hot, though."

I shook my head and laughed lightly. "You make no sense."

"Why?" she asked as she brushed her hand slowly up my chest.

I pursed my lips and placed my hand on hers. "You'd better watch out. You touch me like this, and I won't be responsible if I throw you onto the ground and take advantage of you right here in the grass, with the goats watching."

"Sounds like fun." The smile she gave me was pure wickedness and fucking sexy.

My cock totally agreed. "Ouch." Something had rammed into my thigh. I stumbled and lost my hold on Susie. "What the hell?" Jackson—I thought—had head-butted me and stood looking at me.

Susie's laugh rang out over the pasture like a bell. "Looks like they need attention."

I was head-butted again.

"Enough, stupid goat."

"Come on. He's not stupid. He just wants you to pet him."

The other two joined us, and Susie scratched the black goat on its head. "Come on, boys. Let's feed you some leaves."

She walked with the goats to the trees. They used the tree trunk for balance and stretched their necks to get the leaves. Susie pulled a branch low so they could all eat more.

I stood back and watched them, then combed the woods that lined the property with my gaze. My sense of awareness had kicked in. Someone might be watching. I listened intently and focused my attention, but nothing seemed off. The river went through the woods to the north, and across it were cornfields tall with stalks.

Even if I could see the river and the field, anyone could hide in them.

"Hey." Susie came up behind me and hugged my waist. "What's with the serious look?"

Damn good thing she can't read minds.

I shook my head and peered down at her. Her hair was silky in the sun; her skin, porcelain and smooth; those lips, luscious and needy. I pressed a quick kiss on them. "Nothing, sweetness. Just looking."

She narrowed her gaze and studied me. "I don't believe you."

I arched an eyebrow.

"But that's okay." She stood on her toes and answered my kiss with one just as soft.

I breathed in deeply. Her scent of flowers and strawberries floated on the breeze.

A branch snapped in the woods behind us, and my senses jumped into overdrive. I spun toward the wood line.

"Hey, it seems you're the skittish one now. You know there's wild animals in those hills, right?" She laughed and poked me in the stomach.

I twitched away and grabbed her hands. "Think you're all tough, do ya? You control me?"

She wiggled her eyebrows. "I did in the shower."

"Fuck yeah, you did."

She smiled. "Come on." She grabbed my hand and pulled me across the pasture toward the gate. Her laughter echoed in the air.

"Your laugh is beautiful. I could listen to it forever," I said as we exited the pasture.

"You're getting a little sweet. What would the townspeople think?"

I shrugged. "Don't know. Don't care. I'm not here to impress them."

"No, you're not. You've already done that with your football expertise."

Her joking around and flirting were the sexiest things I had ever witnessed. I pulled her to me and held her tightly, her hands behind her back. "Have I impressed you at all?"

She looked off into the distance and bit her bottom lip, then shook her head. "Nope. Nothing special about you."

"Really? If there's nothing special about me, why are we here?"

"Is the big man feeling uneasy?" She asked as she pulled from my grasp and wrapped her arms around my neck.

I searched her face. Unease gripped my heart and squeezed gently. *What if she didn't feel about me the way I feel about her? What if—Stop. Don't think about it.* I plastered a smile on my face. "Nope. Not at all."

She searched my face, and her smile faded. "You don't have to worry. I've been happier these past few days with you than I've been in a long time." She hesitated and took a deep breath.

My gaze held hers. I pushed her hair from her face and leaned in to place a kiss on her lips.

Gravel crunched as a car pulled up, and Susie pulled away quickly. "It's Kora and Kai."

I sighed as I watched her hurry toward the truck and greet Kora with a hug as soon as she got out, then went to her brother. I stuck my hands in my back pockets and followed her with slow steps.

Kai glanced at me and then hugged Susie.

This may get interesting.

"Hey, Kor." I gave her a hug.

"Hey, Lance," she said as she pulled away and held my arms. "I didn't expect to see you here."

The goats started making a ruckus at the gate.

"I think your children are calling you," Susie said.

"Yeah, they are, and I missed them."

Kora and Susie walked arm in arm to the goats.

That left me alone with Kai. *Wonderful.* I kicked at the gravel.

His gaze was glued to mine.

Be cool. You've done nothing wrong. "Hey, Kai. How was your drive? You made good time."

Kai's eyes narrowed.

I arched an eyebrow.

"And you're here. Why?" he asked.

I scratched the back of my head. "Taking care of your sister. She thinks it's her ex. She told you about him."

Kai nodded. "She did. She told you?"

I nodded. "She did."

"How much has she told you?" He leaned against his truck and crossed his arms over his chest.

The good thing was Kai and I were friends. The bad thing was he knew a lot about me. "Enough to know this guy might be dangerous. I've read her texts, and he mentioned seeing us near the river."

Kai's eyes widened. "You were at the river with Susie?"

I nodded.

"You were just in the pasture with Susie. You ate dinner here last night. She showed you her texts. You looked like you broke away from—something—when we pulled up."

Damn. It felt like I was back in high school and had gotten caught making out at the front door after a date. "Kai, it's all good."

"Lance, you're a friend. You're like a brother. But come on. Would you want to think someone like you was with Lilly?"

I chuckled, frustrated, and shook my head. "Damn, Kai. Someone like me *was* with my sister, and look how that turned out." I stopped. *Shit. That didn't help.*

Kai nodded. "Exactly."

How can I get him to see me differently? "I'm different with Susie. I can't explain it, but I'm not going to hurt her."

"Hey, what's going on?" Kora asked.

"Nothing," Kai said. "We'll finish this later," he said to me. "Right now, I'm glad you're here. You can help us unload. Do we have anything to eat in the house?"

"We do," Susie answered. "Everyone came by last night, and Trevor brought enough food from Jerry's Pub to feed an army. We have plenty of leftovers."

"Thank God. I'm starving. We can eat while we talk," Kai said.

Susie glanced at me and raised an eyebrow.

I shook my head.

She gave me a soft smile, squeezed my hand, and grabbed some bags.

It didn't take long for the car to be unloaded, then Kora and Kai went to their room to get cleaned up from their trip.

"Get the leftovers out, and let's see how we're going to warm them up," Susie said as she turned on the oven.

"We have chicken tenders, chicken wings, jalapeño poppers, and a large salad." I put everything on the counter.

Susie brought over trays, and we filled them with food.

"This works. A few minutes in the oven, they'll be as good as new," I said as she loaded the oven.

"I smell like a goat." Susie threw away the containers. "I need to change and check on the kitty." She gestured for me to follow.

The kitten was asleep in a ball on the bed, and toilet paper decorated the room.

"It looks like he got bored." I laughed.

Susie stood with her hands on her hips. "Yeah, I'd say so." She cleaned up the toilet paper and got a shirt from her drawer.

"Where are you going?" I asked as she walked toward the bathroom. "It's not like I haven't seen you."

She gestured with her head. "My brother is in the house now. It's bad enough you're in my room."

She was adorable when she was embarrassed and trying to hide. I couldn't keep away from her. I crossed the room in a few quick strides and wrapped my arms around her. "You are fucking adorable."

Her eyes were wide. "Lance, they might see."

"See what?" I asked with a wicked smile. "This?" I slid my hands around her and placed my lips on hers.

She moaned and opened her mouth for my tongue to dance with hers, then laced her arms around my neck.

A throat clearing got our attention. "Like I asked in the driveway, is there something I need to know?" Kai asked.

Kora chuckled.

Susie's eyes bulged, and she pulled away from me

I turned around. "Your sister and I—" I grabbed Susie's hand. *We what? We haven't named what this is.* "We like each other."

"We can see that," Kora said with laughter in her voice.

The corner of Kai's jaw twitched.

Susie tried to pull out of my grasp, but I held her tightly.

The kitten took that moment to stretch and yawn, a squeak coming from his mouth.

"What is that, and where did it come from?" Kai asked.

Susie pulled away from me and picked up the kitten as it meowed. "Lance found it in the chicken boxes the night of the storm. He's been staying with us. I know you're allergic, Kora, but he won't be a problem."

Kora walked over to Susie and petted the cat. "He's adorable. As long as I don't hold him close to my face and wash my hands after I touch him, it's all good. It looks like he's happy. What's his name?"

Susie shook her head. "We haven't given him one yet. We've been calling him Kitty."

I took the kitten from Susie. "He's really good and sweet and spends most of his time sleeping, except at night when we're in bed or when he's decorating the room with toilet paper."

"Except at night? When *we're* in bed?" Kai repeated while shooting daggers in my direction. He shook his head. "Fuck," he said under his breath as he combed his fingers through his hair.

Kora pulled her lips into her mouth to hide a laugh and pulled him from the room.

CHAPTER 26

SUSIE

I woke up Saturday morning with the kitten chewing on my hair. He lay on the pillow, taking Lance's place. Yes, the kitten was cute, warm, and cuddly but not quite the same as having Lance to wake up to.

The previous night, while we ate leftovers, Lance had filled Kora and Kai in on the details of the stalker. Kai and I argued about the choices I'd made in South Dakota, and Kai said I should have come home sooner.

I got angry and told him I wasn't a child anymore and that they should have finished their vacation. I didn't need them to come running home to me.

That pissed him off, and he yelled something about his choices that kept him away from me when I needed a male influence and adult guidance. He continued to say that if he had been there for me to talk with while I was in college, I would have been better acclimated to going off on my own. Then he blamed himself for encouraging me to leave and said we should have stayed together.

I sat up and brushed my hands over my face. It felt like I was still a kid.

Instead of being my brother, he'd become my father figure—again. Then Lance got a bit of his wrath because Kai said he was taking advantage of me.

That didn't go well. They both raised their voices. I tried to get Kai to see reason, and finally, Kora got them both to calm down.

In the end, Lance and I felt it was best for him to go home.

I sighed and hopped into the shower to wash away the dread and exhaustion that had seeped into my skin. Sleeping wasn't the same without Lance. Hell, the shower wasn't the same without Lance.

I turned off the water and wrapped a towel around my body. Everything about my room felt different—empty. It had only been two days since whatever we'd started, but I missed his warmth and company.

I plodded out to the kitchen. Coffee was brewing, so someone was up. *It better not be Kai.* I didn't know if I could deal with him this early.

"Good morning," Kora said as she walked through the back door.

"Morning." I looked around. If Kai were anywhere, he'd be near her.

"Don't worry. He's gone. He went into town. Kaye needed something fixed at the hair salon, then he was going to talk with Patrick."

I rolled my eyes and puffed out a breath.

"He promised me he'll be relaxed and in a better headspace when he meets us at Tonya's later."

I forgot Tonya was having the weekly get-together. "I really need to work."

"Yeah, that's a negative. I've talked to Trevor. He has your shifts covered throughout the weekend. You should be able to go back on Monday."

"Wonderful. I need money. Everyone needs to stop babying me." I fixed my coffee and sat at the table.

Kora grabbed a yogurt and strawberries from the refrigerator and joined me. She took her time pulling open the container and stirring it.

I could tell she wanted to say something and was thinking over her words carefully. I hadn't been in town long, but I'd learned Kora's mannerisms well.

"Have you thought about interviewing at the school? If you don't want to be a teacher right now, you could always be an assistant. Check it out. Do you really want to walk away?"

I shook my head. I didn't know. "The pub is good for me right now. It's low profile and fun, and I'm meeting a lot of people. Maybe sometime later."

"Well, think about subbing then. There's no commitment, and we always need subs."

That would be a good transition. I nodded. "I might."

She smiled and scraped the bottom of her yogurt container. "Good. Now, tell me about you and Lance."

I chuckled and took a drink of my coffee. *What can I tell her? I'm not even sure what's going on with us.* "I don't know. One day, I couldn't stand being around him. Then another, something clicked, and he went from an irritating ass to..." I wobbled my head as I thought of what words would describe him. "Sweet. Protective. I mean, it's not a lie to say he's attractive, and I can't deny that I like him." I glanced at her. "Do you think it's a mistake?"

Kora became pensive and licked her spoon. Finally, she shook her head. "I've known him my entire life. Yes, he loves himself and can be a bit of an ass. Yes, he has a history of being a playboy, but deep down, he really is a caring guy." She gave a small smile and put her spoon down. "Anyway, something changed with him. He looks at you differently."

"Differently?"

"Yeah. Like he actually sees you."

CHAPTER 27

LANCE

"Uncle Lance, can you come play with us?" Madeline asked.

I didn't have a chance to say no, not that I'd be able to. She pulled me toward the playhouse in the back corner of Tonya's yard, under the large oak tree. Lena, Darcie, and James sat at the picnic table, having a loud discussion.

"Uncle Lance is here. He will tell us who's right." Madeline plopped down on the bench next to James.

"You asked me to play. You said nothing about a disagreement," I said and looked at James. He had a scowl on his face and was resting his chin in his hands. "What's wrong, dude?" I asked, patting his back.

He shook his head, gestured toward the girls, opened his mouth, and closed it again, and placed his chin back in his hands. "Doesn't matter. They're so difficult. They never listen and are always bossy."

I nodded. *If he only knew half of it. Susie's yelling at me one day, with me the next, closed off the next, then back with me. Women will make your head spin.* "I feel ya, little dude. Unfortunately, it doesn't get any easier when they get older."

"Is that why you're still single?" Lena asked.

"He's still single because girls are annoying," James spat. "He's smart. He doesn't need a girl. I thought my uncle Rowan would be smart, but then he fell *in love.*" He rolled his eyes and his head in dramatic fashion then pretended to throw up.

I chuckled.

Darcie waved off James and stood in front of me, her hands on her hips. "Daddy says one day love'll bite you in the butt, but Lilly doesn't think so."

"Nope, she thinks you're selfish," Madeline added.

Wow, nothing like getting my hopes dashed by a bunch of soon-to-be first graders.

"Lance, why does someone want to get bitten in the butt?" Lena asked.

"I was wondering the same thing," Madeline said.

"It sounds like it would hurt," Darcie agreed. The girls looked at each other, nodded their agreement, then looked at me.

I looked back and forth between them then stared at the sky. *If they only knew.* "Didn't you ask me to come over here to play something? Can we get on with it?" Keeping up with this conversation was exhausting.

"Well, we need to play tag and have a prison, but James keeps cheating and guarding the prison so we can't get back to save anyone. We need you to help us. You play on our team." Darcie wrapped her arms around Lena and Madeline's shoulders."Not fair!" James yelled as he stood up. "Uncle Rowan, Uncle Jamison, Dad!"

"What's going on?" Bryson asked as he and the men joined us. The women trailed close behind.

"It looks like we need to have a massive game of tag. The table is the base," I explained. "No guarding base." I pointed at James, who gave me a mischievous grin. He was so much like Bryson, his father.

"Sounds good," Jamison said, clapping once. "I'll be 'it' first along with Madeline, Lena, and Darcie." He squatted to the height of his teammates. "Ready, girls?"

They nodded enthusiastically.

"We'll count to five. Y'all better run," he said.

They started counting, and everyone scattered. The backyard was chaotic as children and adults ran and scrambled.

The book club women and the grandpas cheered us on from the patio. It was hot, yet fun. The girls caught James first and dragged him across the yard by his feet, as he screamed for someone to save him.

"Don't worry, buddy, I've got you," Bryson yelled.

"And if your dad can't, don't worry. Momma won't let you down." Darlene hollered and sent Bryson a wink.

It had been a while since we all ran around like idiots together, and the yard buzzed with smack-talk and laughter.

"Hey, look, Aunt Kora and Uncle Kai," James yelled and left the game to beeline across the yard.

The girls followed. "You cheated. You were in prison," Darcie yelled, anger obvious in her voice.

James ignored her and flung himself in Kora's arms.

"Well, it looks like the game is over," Jamison said.

I agreed as I stood there catching my breath. I glanced across the yard, and my eyes locked on Susie. She hugged Darcie and laughed. Her face lit up, and my heart skittered.

"Are you going to say hi or stand there drooling?" Jamison asked with a smack on my back.

I shot him a narrowed gaze. "I'm not drooling."

He wiped at my chin and then smacked his finger against my shoulder. "Yeah, okay." He walked away with a hearty laugh.

Susie smiled at me across the yard and stole my breath. Her dark hair was in a messy bun on top of her head. The gray tank top she wore caused her eyes to pop, and her white shorts showed off her long sun-kissed legs. My pulse quickened.

Her gaze pulled at my gut, and I walked across the yard as if I were connected to her by an invisible string. The corners of my lips quirked up.

Kai laughed as he patted Jamison on the back in a hug, but his laugh disappeared when his eyes met mine.

My heart fell. It was pretty obvious he wasn't happy about the Susie-and-me thing. Well, he'd have to get over it at some point. "Hey, y'all," I said.

Kai raised his eyebrows, and if I wasn't mistaken, a low growl emanated from him. *That's it. So much for friendship.*

Kora nudged him in the side, then turned to me with a smile. "Hi, Lance," she said and wrapped me in a hug.

When I pulled away from Kora, my eyes met Susie's. Her face glowed.

"Hey," she said.

"Hi," I answered and gave her hand a squeeze.

She squeezed mine back.

Relief flooded through me. I wasn't sure what to expect from her with Kai acting the way he was. Damn, I wanted to kiss her. Those rosy lips screamed at me to taste them, but the daggers Kai shot from his eyes held me back. "Want a drink?" I asked her instead.

"Sure."

I tugged lightly on her hand, and she joined me.

I leaned close to her. "I don't think your brother is supportive of this." I gestured between us.

Her head tilted back with laughter, and her eyes gleamed. "You could say that, but I'm a big girl and can make my own decisions." She nudged me with her shoulder, and the smirk on her face sent my testosterone into overdrive. "What were y'all playing? It looked like complete chaos."

Thank God she'd changed the subject. My mind was playing scenes that my body wanted to act out, and this would not have been a good place for that. "James was being accused of cheating in a game of tag by the girls, so we all joined in to make it fairer. Then Kora and Kai appeared, and it wasn't important anymore." Those kids loved Kora and Kai.

I grabbed a Coke from the cooler for Susie and a bottle of beer for me.

"Watch how much you drink of that." Kai stood next to me, his arms crossed.

"Want one?" I offered him my beer and chose a Coke instead.

"Thanks," he said.

I stepped to the side with Susie.

She chuckled and tapped her can against mine.

"Hey, everyone!" Kai hollered above the noise.

Some listened, but there were a lot of people in the yard. Charles let out his high-pitched whistle, which worked every time.

"Thank you, Charles," Kai said.

"Anytime."

Kai wrapped his arm around Kora's waist and with a huge smile on his face, whispered something in her ear.

She grinned and nodded.

I asked Susie, "Do you know what this is about?"

She shook her head, her eyes wide, and grabbed my hand, but I did one better. I put my arm around her waist and pulled her close.

She smiled at me.

Kai scowled at us.

I shrugged, and Kora poked him in the side.

"Anyway..." He pulled his attention away from us and toward the crowd. "We want you all to know that even though our vacation was cut short..." He winked at Susie.

When she stiffened, I squeezed her closer.

"We had a good time, and I enjoyed getting to know Nigel."

"Of course you did. He's a great guy," Rowan said. "But what's this about?"

"We wanted him to be the first to know." Kai bit his lower lip, and a smile filled his face. "We're pregnant!" he hollered.

The screams and squeals that erupted throughout the yard were deafening. Susie left my side, sprinted to her brother, and wrapped her arms around him.

Kora and Kai had planned to start their family soon after the wedding, so everyone was ecstatic. I filed in line to hug the happy parents-to-be along with everyone else.

"Let me in." Tonya pushed her way through. "She's my niece." Her squeal was loud and long as she held them both in a hug.

"T, we all need to have a turn," my mother said.

The weekly backyard barbecue had turned into an enormous celebration. Eventually, the excitement died down, Lilly, Summer, and Darlene dragged Kora off to the back table under the oak tree, and I finally got to Kai.

"Congratulations. I know how badly you've wanted this."

We gave each other a guy-pat hug.

"I can't believe this," Susie said, wrapping herself around Kai again. "You'll be an amazing father. I don't know where you got this caring gene, but you were a natural with me and Sebastian."

Kai let out a heavy breath and wiped his hands on his jeans. "I've got to admit it's a little nerve-racking. You can't say I was amazing. I made stupid mistakes."

She shushed him. "You did what you did because it was necessary and out of love. You have the biggest heart ever." She hugged him again. "I love you, big bro."

"Love you back, Suz."

Susie grabbed my arm and pulled me away. "Can you believe that?" she gushed and started talking a mile a minute.

I heard only part of what she said because the glow of her face took my breath away. I couldn't fight it anymore, and I leaned in and silenced those talking lips. Her eyes widened, then she kissed me back, putting her hand on my chest before she pulled away.

My eyes didn't leave her face, but hers combed the yard. "Your mom and the ladies saw you do that," she whispered.

I chuckled. "Oh well. It'll give them something to talk about. I'm used to it."

Her eyes narrowed. "But I'm not."

"God, you're beautiful. Do you know that?"

"And you're crazy. I thought we were going to keep this quiet for now."

I shrugged. "We never really talked about what we were going to do, and anyway, I wasn't loud."

She punched me in the gut.

"Ouch," I said as I lurched forward.

"You deserved that."

I wrapped my arms around her, laughing. "You are more adorable when you're trying to be upset."

"I'm not trying."

"Then don't go to Hollywood."

"Kai's right. You are a jerk."

"And you love it."

She stared into my eyes.

My heart raced, and I smirked.

Then she kissed me.

"Okay, you two," Lilly said as she, Rose, and Kristy joined us. "Enough of the PDA. There are children watching."

"And we don't need them confused," Kristy said. "Just a few months ago, Lance was with Jayla. Now he's kissing you."

"Thanks for the reminder," Susie said as she pulled away.

"No way," I said, holding tight. "Don't even think about it."

Tom called us to eat, which was a perfect distraction.

I fell behind the women as Jamison and Kai came up to me.

"You like my sister," Kai said.

"I wanted to talk to you about it yesterday, but you sort of kicked me out."

He nodded. "Do me a favor."

"Of course."

"Treat her right. Whatever this dumbass is doing, I can tell it's bothering her."

"I agree, and I promise. She's my only priority."

"And another thing," Kai added, narrowing his eyes.

"You know we're friends, right?" I reminded him. "You look like you want to kill me."

"I thought about it, but Kora talked me out of it." Kai placed his hand on my shoulder. "Remember, Susie's my little sister. I don't want to see your hands all over her."

"I'll try my best. Trust me—I know how it feels to watch a friend with your sister," I said with a glance toward Jamison.

"I have nothing to do with this," Jamison said with a laugh and walked ahead of us toward Lilly.

My gaze fell on Susie as she walked across the yard, talking with Kristy. I'd love to know what they said, because she grinned and glanced at me. Her eyes held laughter. Then she pulled her phone from her pocket, her eyes bulged, and the color drained from her face. Her free hand came to her mouth as Kristy reached over her shoulder and grabbed the phone.

Susie's eyes met mine, and fear ripped through me as tears fell down her face. I sprinted toward her.

"What the fucking hell?" Kai said behind me. He pushed in front of me, got to Susie first, and wrapped his arms around her as her shoulders shook violently.

He grabbed her phone from Kristy's hand, and his eyes bulged. "What the fuck?"

"Kai, let me see it," I said.

Kristy shook her head, but there was no way I wasn't going to see what was on that phone.

"This is bullshit," Kai said, swiping through the pictures.

I took the phone. "Holy fuck." I scrolled through the pictures sent to Susie in a text—us in the goat pasture, kissing; on the patio, gazing at each other as I held her the night everyone had left the house after eating with us; us at the river, locked in an embrace. My heart pounded like a jackhammer in my chest.

It proved I hadn't been crazy when I thought we were being watched.

He'd been there, close by, watching everything.

I continued swiping through the pictures, and the last one made my skin crawl. I wanted to find him and kill him. It showed Susie in a bra and shorts, laughing. It was taken through the window of her bedroom. Shit. It was. We had just gotten out of the shower and were laughing at the kitten playing on the bed.

Michael had been there, watching through her window.

My gaze met Kai's, and the hate and anger on his face matched mine.

The text at the bottom read:

> *I watch you everywhere.*
> *There's no place safe for you to hide.*
> *I told you, you're mine.*
> *I'm a better man than Lance will ever be.*
> *Stop seeing him now.*

Chapter 28

Susie

I'm never going to get away from him. He knows everything I do. *He's watching me.*

A tremble started deep in my core and quickly took over my body. Kai pulled me tightly to him, then the sobs came. They were uncontrollable. I held on to Kai like he was my lifeline once again.

He rubbed my back and whispered that it would be okay, but that was far from the truth. This was nothing like when we were growing up and I would escape Dad's drunken rages by hiding in my room where I was safe from his wrath. This was different. This was bigger. Ominous.

"He won't get close to you again. I swear it," Kai said.

"You've got us both," Lance added.

That crazy man had been watching me, hunting me. There was nothing they could do. I looked up and stepped away from my brother, swiping my hands over my face.

I turned toward Lance. "This is the second time he's gotten near me. You can't keep him away from me. He threatened you. He knows your name."

"He didn't threaten me."

"That's what he meant. You need to stay away from me." My pulse was beating erratically. He knew where I was. He had come up to the house. "How does he know your name?" God, I hated crying. But the tears fell anyway. I swiped them angrily from my face and stared at the sky, blinking.

"Susie, relax," Kai said as he led me to a seat.

Kora sat next to me. "Breathe slowly." She held my gaze, and I matched my breaths to hers as she rubbed her hand in a circle on my back.

"Hey, I just got off the phone with Patrick," Jamison interrupted. "He said to get to the station and bring the phone."

Kai nodded. "Susie, we've got to go. Are you okay?"

Closing my eyes, I sucked in a deep breath. My pulse slowed, and I felt more in control. I nodded.

Kora gave me a hug. "It'll be okay." Her smile was calming.

She hugged Kai. "Relax and be careful," she said to him before she gave him a quick kiss goodbye.

Lance jogged after us and opened his truck door.

"Where are you going?" Kai asked.

"To the station. I'll follow you down. I care about her, and I'm not staying behind."

The feelings swirling inside me were strangling me. I was so confused. I pulled my gaze from his and climbed into Kai's truck.

"Suz." Kai squeezed my hand. "We're going to find him."

I smiled. "I'm glad you're here. Thank you."

Lance opened my door as soon as Kai parked at the police station and pulled me into a hug. "Are you good?" he whispered.

I nodded. "As good as can be expected with a crazy ex-boyfriend watching my every move."

He placed a gentle and quick peck on my lips and laced his fingers through mine. "You've got this."

I smiled, and we walked into the station.

We were escorted immediately to Patrick's office, and he held out his hand. I gave him my phone and pulled back my shoulders. The initial shock was over. I could do this.

He scanned the pictures and passed my phone to another officer. "We need to download them."

I nodded. "Do whatever you need to."

"We did some searching and found out that Michael no longer lives at the address you gave us. He moved out about a month ago. We finally heard from your friend Diana. She's the one who told him you might be here. It seems he said he owed you money and wanted to get it to you."

I closed my eyes and let that bit of information settle in my gut.

"Do you have any clue where he's staying?" Kai asked.

"What now?" Lance asked.

Patrick looked between the both of them, scrutinizing them. "Guys, I'm glad you're both here, and I know you're concerned, but let us do our jobs. He's been in town and knows who you are, Lance. That means he's been talking to people. We have his picture, and we're sure someone will identify him. For now, go on with life as usual, and Susie..." He turned his attention to me. "Don't go anywhere alone. Stay with people. There is safety in numbers."

I nodded, and he continued. "We will find him. If any of you have any more contact with him—or unexpected gifts—let us know immediately."

"We will. Thank you, Patrick," Kai said.

"Of course. Just doing my job."

He shook Kai and Lance's hands and walked us out.

"Let's get you home," Kai said.

"You go back to Tonya's and let everyone know what happened," Lance said. "I'll take her home."

Kai started, "She's—"

But I stepped between them. "Kai, I'm safe with Lance. Go back to the barbecue and celebrate your news. Let everyone know what Patrick said. Lance can take me home. I'm tired and want to lie down. I'll be fine."

A muscle in Kai's jaw twitched. "Fine." He hugged me, then pointed at Lance. "Don't leave her alone."

"Not in my plans."

Lance led me to his truck, and I climbed in.

I was quiet during the short drive to the house and stared out the window. Michael was out there somewhere. He probably saw us leave the police station and knew I was with Lance.

A shiver ran through my body, and Lance squeezed my hand. "Hey, you okay?"

I gave him a smile and a nod. "As long as you're with me." I held his hand tightly. The smile he gave me relaxed me, and I laid my head against the back of the seat and stared out the window until he pulled into Kai's driveway.

I climbed out of the truck, walked to the front door, and unlocked it, then I went directly to my room and fell onto the bed.

The kitten was in a ball at the foot. I grabbed him and cuddled him close to me. He purred and stretched without a care in the world.

Lance sat on the edge of the bed. "Do you need anything? Water? A snack?"

I shook my head and closed my eyes. "Just to rest. I'm exhausted."

"Can I lie with you?"

I opened my eyes, and the look of complete concern that shrouded his face sent my heart soaring. "Of course."

He lay next to me and smoothed the hair from my face. Our gazes latched onto each other.

I felt safe—content. "Thank you for being here."

He answered by putting his lips gently on mine. The kiss was tender, sweet, and filled with emotion. "There's no place else I'd rather be. Close your eyes and let me hold you."

I nodded and rolled over, tucked the cat against my chest, and snuggled into Lance. He laced his arm around my waist, held me tight, and pressed a kiss on my head.

My stomach twisted with everything I couldn't process. It had been a roller coaster of a day, and exhaustion took over as the adrenaline that fueled my last couple of hours left my cells, and I fell into a comfortable sleep.

It seemed like I had just closed my eyes when noises from the kitchen floated into my room. The kitten was no longer cuddled with me. I rolled over, and Lance was no longer there either, but I was covered with a blanket.

The curtain was closed tight at the window, but the sun filtered in through a small crack.

I stretched and slowly got out of bed. The smell of fresh coffee pulled me toward the kitchen. The kitten was in the window over the sink, and Kai and some men I didn't know were working outside. I walked to the coffeepot, which displayed ten o'clock on it.

"Good morning," Kora said as she joined me. "Morning?" I asked. We'd been at Tonya's and gotten home around five. *Now it's ten.* "Oh my God. I slept all night?"

Kora nodded. "Yes, Lance stayed with you. He didn't have the heart to move you under the comforter, so I gave him a blanket. You must have needed the sleep. Your body always knows what it needs."

I agreed. With Lance and me being busy the past few nights, and then the adrenaline of my crazy ex keeping me freaked out, I guessed I needed rest. "What's Kai up to?"

"His company is putting up security cameras around the property. He's been meaning to do that but hasn't gotten around to it. There's a camera at each door and the garage, and there will be one out at the goat pasture."

"That's crazy. He didn't have to do this."

Kora grabbed my arms. "Like I said, it's something he's been wanting to do. Your brother is very protective of those he loves."

I laughed. I couldn't argue with her. That was a part of Kai, and he wouldn't get rid of it.

"Okay. I have a shift today."

Kora shook her head.

"No," I said, pointing at her. "Trevor is not taking that from me. I can't stay around here. Even if it's only a four-to-nine shift, I need to get out and do something. It's the only way to keep my mind off the crazy. You can drive me if you want to, and Lance will pick me up. I won't be alone at all. Trust me. I'm sure Trevor will hover."

Kora chuckled. "I heard he likes you."

"I wish he didn't. I feel bad. He's so sweet."

"Because you like Lance."

I shrugged. "I tried not to. I tried really hard. But he never went away, and I finally stopped fighting it."

"Lance has that effect on people. Don't let his past make you insecure. I see the way he looks at you. He respects you." She chuckled. "I hate to say this, but I don't think he's ever truly respected a girl he's dated before. He's just dated them."

I nodded. "Summer and Kristy said the same thing." I petted the kitten, who arched his back and gave a tiny meow in greeting. "Are you okay with him?" I asked, looking at the kitten.

Kora nodded. "He's adorable, and as long as I don't hug him, which is very difficult, I'll be fine. But he needs a name."

"I don't know. I sort of like Kitty. We could call him Mr. Kitty. That's a name."

"I agree. Welcome to the family, Mr. Kitty."

CHAPTER 29

SUSIE

Kora dropped me off at Jerry's Pub at four on the dot. I was so ready to get out of the house and back to some sort of normal that I practically leaped from her car.

Patrick called and filled me in on the latest news about Michael. They tracked him to a rental car and were on the lookout for a silver Toyota, but none had been seen in town. I also talked to Lance, and he promised to be here directly after football practice in time to take me home. Seeing Lance later put an extra bounce in my step.

"Hi, Trevor," I said happily as I walked to the back.

"What are you doing here?"

Yep, I knew he wouldn't be happy to see me and prepared for his onslaught of questions. "Look. I'm here because I was going crazy in lockdown. I couldn't even go out to the goats. Kora drove me, and Lance will pick me up after football. So, unless you call someone to take me home now, you're stuck with me."

I wrapped my apron around my waist and cocked my head. "What else do you have to say, Trevor? Out with it." I gestured with my hand.

He sighed heavily, and his cheeks puffed out. "Nothing. Just be careful. If anyone makes you uneasy, say something. And whatever you do, do not walk out of the pub alone. I'm putting Shannon out on the patio tonight. You're inside only." He pointed at me. "I don't want anything to happen to you and have to face the wrath of Kai."

I put up my hands in surrender. "I gotcha, boss. Stay inside. Be good." I clicked my tongue and walked out.

Work was exactly what I needed. The townspeople were friendly and caring. I'd been here long enough that people knew who I was, and I found myself a part of many conversations.

Since it was a Monday night, there was a lull in the crowd after the dinner rush was over. Only a few couples filled the tables, and two men sat at the bar. One was talking with my father, eating a burger and drinking a Coke. I'd seen him there before and thought he was one of my dad's Alcoholics Anonymous buddies.

My gaze kept drifting to my father as I worked. I'd hardly talked to him since I started working at the pub. When we did talk, it had mostly been small talk as he handed my customers their food. He'd always seemed distant.

But that night, there was a lightness in him I didn't recognize as he laughed with the man at the counter. Laughter and a smile looked good on him.

My heart splintered a little. I'd grown up with the man, but I didn't think I'd ever seen him smile, let alone laugh. *How sad is that?* All I'd ever heard him do was yell, usually at Kai or Sebastian. But he never yelled at me. With me, it was always silence and a glare.

After his friend left, he wiped down the bar. The usual hard edges of his face seemed softer.

I placed the last ketchup bottle I needed to fill on my tray and walked toward him. "Was that a friend from AA? I've noticed he's here a lot."

He looked at me, his eyes wide, and the laughter in his eyes seemed to cloud over.

"Sorry." The air between us became thick and awkward. "I guess it's none of my business. You just seem to get along." I turned around. What was I thinking? I'd given him the cold shoulder even when all he'd tried to do was to be helpful since I'd been back. Why would he talk to me now?

"Susie, wait." His voice stopped me in my tracks, and I turned back toward him. "He is. We started the program at the same time. His name's Thomas. He's a good man."

I nodded. "It's good you have a friend."

The uncomfortable silence grew again.

"How are you?" he asked. "When I heard about everything, I was worried."

I stepped back, and a brick lodged in my gut. "Why would you be worried about me now? You've never been before." I closed my eyes. *That was harsh.* "I..."

He raised his hand to stop me and pursed his lips. "It's sad. You're my only daughter, and we're like strangers. Since you've been back, I've spent a lot of time thinking about your childhood." He shook his head and fidgeted with the towel in his hands. "You needed me, and I failed you terribly. A girl needs her father, and I was selfish. I thank God every day for giving you two brothers who protected you fiercely. Sebastian's loyalty to you was unbreakable, and Kai had the biggest heart, and the biggest drive to do whatever was necessary to keep you kids together and fed. I know his mistakes were my doing, and I've asked his forgiveness. Our relationship isn't perfect, but we've come a long way. Heck, *I've* come a long way."

Part of me wanted to walk away. Another part needed to hear whatever he was willing to say. I swallowed down the rock that had lodged itself in my throat. "Why are you telling me this now?" Feelings churned inside me. So many feelings.

He shook his head, and his eyes became watery.

God, I don't want to watch him cry. I don't want to feel sorry for him. But I couldn't tear myself away.

"I should have treated you better," he continued. "But you reminded me so much of her. All three of you have her eyes, but you are the spitting image of her, and after she left, I couldn't stand to look at you."

I took a step back. He didn't mean that how it sounded, but what a slap to the gut. *He blamed me for looking like her? That was the reason he never talked to me and treated me like I was invisible.* The feelings I couldn't pin down a minute ago rose to the surface with rage.

"You do realize I wondered what was wrong with me all throughout my school years, don't you? I listened to girls talk about how wonderful their fathers were. How much their fathers loved them. But you? You never talked to me. Hell, you hardly ever looked at me, and when you did, I remember thinking you wished *I* was gone instead of her." I chuckled and lifted my eyes toward the ceiling. "Maybe I wasn't too far off. That was probably exactly what you were thinking."

"Susie, I—" he started, but I put my hand up and shook my head.

There was no way he was going to talk his way out of this. "No. You listen to what I have to say. You started this. All I ever wanted was to be loved by my father. Just like those girls. But I never had that. But we do agree on something. I'm also glad God gave Kai a big heart, and I'm glad he made me a twin. Because of that, I had Kai and Sabastian always beside me. Kai was an amazing male role model even when he went to prison. He always put us first. And Sebastian kept me safe when you couldn't. The man who was supposed to love me, take care of me, and protect me failed in his job because he loved alcohol more than he loved his children."

I stopped speaking as hot tears filled my eyes.

My dad reached across the counter and touched my hand, but I flinched and pulled away. I shook my head and looked up into his old, worn face. Wrinkled skin and gray hair from years of bodily abuse made him look so much older than he actually was.

My heart felt as if a sword had gone through it.

"You're right." His voice was quiet, defeated. "Everything you said was spot on. I was selfish. I wronged you kids in so many ways. I hurt the boys physically, but I also hurt you by ignoring you. And now I can see I was so wrong. You're nothing like your mother. She was self-centered. You are kind, thoughtful, and caring. So much like Kai. Everyone loves you."

I swallowed the lump in my throat.

"Susie?" Lance said, and I felt his hand on my back.

Terry smiled and nodded to Lance.

"Terry. How are you?"

"Doing well," he said to Lance then turned back to me. "Thank you for talking, Susie." He walked away.

I rubbed my hands over my face and huffed.

"You good?" Lance asked.

"Yeah," I said and cleared the itch in my throat.

Trevor came over to us. "Everything okay? You and your dad were pretty intense."

I chuckled. "Years of built-up emotions. That's all."

Trevor's gaze searched my face, then he glanced at Lance, then turned back to me. "You can go. It's slow, and I think Barb can close on her own."

"Sure can, sugar," Barb said as she came up behind us. "You closed down most of the tables anyway."

I looked around to make sure it wasn't too busy. I didn't want to leave Barb with too much to do. Some people were still eating, and one man was at the bar, but the patio was closed.

"Okay, then." I turned to Lance. "I guess you're here to take me home?"

"Of course. Your chariot awaits." Lance said with a swoop of his arms. I laughed, and my heart swooned.

"Thank you. Let me go get my things." I walked to the back of the room, and when I came out, the man at the bar was gone, and the couples at the tables were finishing up. "Looks like everyone is clearing out anyway. I hope a big crowd doesn't show up at the last minute."

"On a Monday night, it's doubtful," Trevor said.

"Have a nice night, you two," Barb said.

Lance and I walked out of the pub.

The night was warm, and the sun was low on the horizon. Lance held open the truck door for me as I climbed in, then he did the same. "So, do you want to go home or stop for ice cream?"

Ice cream sounded perfect. "I'll text Kai so he doesn't get worried."

We ended up staying at the ice cream shop longer than we'd planned. A man Lance coached with, and his wife were there, so we stayed and talked.

The porch light was on when we got to the house.

Lance walked me to the door and pulled me toward him. "I've been wanting to do this ever since I saw you," he said as he kissed my lips. It was a quick kiss, but when he pulled away, I wanted more.

"Not so fast." I grabbed his shirt and pulled him back, threading my arms around his neck. I opened my mouth to his, and our tongues met.

A moan escaped him as he pulled me closer.

"Stay with me tonight," I whispered.

I felt a smile on his lips and cracked open my eyes.

"You sure?" Lance asked. "What will Kai think?"

"I'm a big girl. I don't care what he thinks. And anyway, I'm not the one he'll use as a punching bag," I said with a smile.

"I think it may be worth it."

I unlocked the door, and we slipped quietly into my room. The kitten meowed and stretched from where he slept on my pillows. "I almost forgot. Lance, say hi to Mr. Kitty."

He arched an eyebrow. "Is that the most creative name you could come up with?"

"Yep," I said, picking up the kitten and placing him at the foot of the bed. "Kora liked it. So, unless you come up with something better, Mr. Kitty sticks."

"I'll think of something, but I have other things on my mind right now." Our eyes locked.

"Oh yeah? What?" I tried to sound sexy, but my voice came out in a whisper as his gaze traveled across my face and down my body.

He pulled my shirt over my head, his hands caressed my skin.

A shiver ran up my spine and caused goose bumps to prickle.

Slowly, I peeled his shirt from his torso and dropped it to the floor. The ripples of his muscles contracted under my touch. I sucked in my lips and shook my head. "You're hot."

"Really?" he asked with a smirk.

I nodded and kissed that smirk right off his mouth.

"Fuck, woman." His voice was throaty with desire.

"Whenever you're ready," I said as I stepped out of my shorts.

His eyes traveled slowly down my body and took their time on their way back up. Finally, our eyes met again.

"Lie down," he commanded.

I held his gaze and did what he asked.

His eyes moved over my body. I could feel the heat of his gaze, and my body ignited with desire.

He trailed his hand across my thigh and so close to the tender area between my legs where he teased for a second before brushing his hand up my side. I sucked in a breath, and my eyes closed.

He kneaded my breasts and pinched my nipple between his thumb and finger, causing a fire to blaze deep within me. I arched my back and moaned deeply.

His eyes still weren't on mine but trailed over my body. I could feel the heat of his gaze deep in my core.

Finally, his mouth found one of my breasts, and he sucked and nibbled there before traveling south.

I squirmed beneath him as my heart pounded. I loved his touch as he brushed his fingers lightly against my skin, and the feel of the heat from his gaze, but I longed for something more.

Finally, he placed his palm on my stomach and held me still as he spread my legs apart.

"Please, Lance," I whispered.

He peered up from between my legs. "Do you want this?" He asked as he licked me slowly.

A tingle shot through my core, and I throbbed with need. I bit on my bottom lip. "Yes," I answered as I rocked against his mouth until he sucked exactly where I needed him to. The warmth of his lips and the gentleness of his tongue relaxed my body and made me feel things I didn't think were possible.

He continued tasting me while I rode a high, I didn't want to end. Finally, I exploded, but he didn't stop as wave after wave of ecstasy flowed through my body again and again until my breaths were heavy, and I moaned his name.

He traveled kisses slowly up my body, worshipping every bit of skin his lips touched.

I guided him to my opening, and he entered my wet and writhing core.

The pressure of him against the numbness of my body made me feel more alive, more wanted, and more desired than ever before.

As he thrust into me, I latched my legs around his waist and pushed him deeper. I matched his rhythm until his breaths came quickly.

He thrust harder and moaned my name as I shattered around him and bit down on his shoulder to keep the scream from exiting my throat.

For a moment, I forgot all the negative things happening in my life—the discussion with my father and the fear my ex had caused.

Lance was a perfect distraction.

CHAPTER 30

LANCE

I collapsed next to Susie and pulled her to me. The scent and the feel of her were intoxicating. I couldn't get enough. I kissed the top of her head; my lips lingered. One hand held her head on my chest. The other touched the skin of her back.

I'd never felt so satisfied with a woman.

Usually, sex was just fun.

This, though, was more, and I couldn't get enough. It wasn't just sex with Susie, and that thought frightened me.

"Thank you," she said and kissed my chest.

Warmth from her lips seeped into my skin and made my heart miss a beat. "You have nothing to thank me for. I should thank you."

She pushed off my chest and stared deep into my eyes. Those crystal mirrors of hers burned into my soul. I brushed my fingers across her cheek and tangled them in the hair at the side of her head.

I need this woman.

"What are you thinking?" she asked. "You look serious."

Do I tell her what I'm thinking? That I'm living a dream? She's perfect and fills me completely. Do I tell her I've never felt this way for a woman before, and I want to protect her forever? Or will those thoughts scare her off, make her uneasy?

I decided I'd keep it simple. "Nothing important," I said as my gaze trailed over her. Her cheeks were chiseled and rosy with an after-sex glow. I placed a kiss on each of them. "I'm glad I'm here with you." I placed a kiss on her perfect nose.

"I don't believe you," she said.

I brought my lips to hers. "It's just—" I shook my head.

"What is it?" She traced the outline of my face with her nails, and a smile pulled at one corner of her mouth. "Talk to me."

"I don't know if I can. I doubt you want to hear it."

"Try me." Her eyes held mine.

I sucked in a deep breath and blew it out slowly, and my heart calmed. "You are so important to me. Being with you feels—different. I care more about you than I thought possible."

Her gaze held mine, and a shadow crossed over her eyes. She laid her head on my chest and kissed me softly.

Maybe that was too much. I combed hair from her forehead and brushed my lips gently against her skin.

She kissed my chest one more time, rolled over, and snuggled close to my side. I tucked my arm around her. It didn't take long until her breath became a soft rhythm and mine soon followed.

⟞⟋

Light filtered in through the corners of the curtains, and Susie's gaze was on me. "Good morning," I said, my voice groggy.

"Morning." Her voice seemed focused and not at all like she had just woken up. Her gaze held mine, and fear crept under my skin.

All sleepiness evaporated, and I leaned my head on my arm. "It looks like you've been awake for a while. What's up?"

Her breathing halted for a second and then started again. "Can I tell you a story?"

"Of course."

She adjusted the pillows, sat up in bed, and tucked the sheets around her, covering her body. "When I was a teenager, maybe thirteen, I escaped into books. I kept a pile from the school library on my bedside table. I read mostly fantasy books of knights and fairies trying to come together in different worlds. This one book had a fairy princess who fell in love with a rogue knight. A human. They were from two different worlds but would give it all up for their love. It was a series, and they fought evil, fought their families, and ended up together in the end. I loved those books, and as I hid from my father's wrath, I wished I could have a knight in shining armor whisk me away into a better life."

She fell silent for a moment and lost herself in thought.

"As I got older," she continued, "I dreamed often of those books, but my thoughts of a knight changed. I no longer wanted a knight to save me. I wanted to save myself. But I did desire the love I read about. Love that would change the world around me. I still wanted a knight not because I needed him but because we made each other better. Together, we would fight the negatives of the world and find never-ending love."

She gave me a crooked smile that took my breath away.

"Unfortunately, I always attracted the black knights. The ones that said all the right things but did all the wrong things." She looked away. "When I left South Dakota, on my flight here, I did a lot of thinking. I promised myself I'd throw away the promise of a knight in shining armor and focus on myself. No one could save me but me. My childhood fairy tales were just that—fairy tales. I needed to save myself. Only then would I be able to face Michael and get him to leave me alone."

She climbed out of bed and slipped on a pair of shorts and a tank top, then went to her dresser.

My gut clenched. I slipped out of bed and pulled on my shorts. My heart hammered—not from want, but from dread. I didn't think I wanted to hear where this story was going.

"I love what's growing between us, but I've got to take care of myself, Lance," Susie continued softly. "Being with you has been amazing, and you've let me see a different side of men. But I think we need to take a break. I need time to figure out myself and deal with Michael."

A vise squeezed my heart. It was a new feeling, and one I sure as hell didn't like. "Susie?"

She turned. "I'm sorry. I need you to go before this becomes too much for the both of us." She stepped away from my touch. "I'm taking a shower. Please be gone when I come out."

She searched my face and touched my cheek gently.

I closed my eyes and didn't open them until I heard the bathroom door close and the lock click. My eyes burned with unshed emotions, and I leaned heavily on her dresser.

I wanted to fight, holler at her to not walk away, but that was what she was already dealing with.

I had to leave to give her the space she wanted and the time to figure out her emotions.

I scratched Mr. Kitty's head as he slept on her dresser. *Has it only been a week since I found him in the chicken box and Susie wanted nothing to do with me?*

So much had happened in so short a time.

I found my shirt and pulled it over my head and slipped into my shoes, then I grabbed my keys from the dresser. If she needed space, I'd give her that space. If she needed time, I'd give her that time.

If she wanted a knight who would show her that love was worth it and be willing to fight for her and with her, I'd show her knights could do that. They could fight alongside the women they loved and want nothing but the best for them, not because they were women and needed men but because the men couldn't be knights in shining armor without strong women who loved them by their sides.

I froze as my hand touched the doorknob that would take me from her life until she decided she wanted me back.

In my thoughts, I used the word love. *Do I love her? Is this why I'm willing to walk away?*

I sighed heavily. I had no clue. I had never loved a woman before. I opened the door and stepped into the hall. Thankfully, it was early, and the house was still quiet.

After letting myself out, I climbed into my truck. The goats were already hopping around the pasture as the sun peeked over the trees.

Everywhere I looked, I remembered times when Susie and I had been together. "Give her the space she needs. Give her the time she needs."

I swiped at a tear that slipped down my face and pulled out of the driveway.

CHAPTER 31

SUSIE

When I stepped from the bathroom and saw Lance's things gone, a slice of regret shot through my body, but he'd done what I'd asked.

It was up to me to take care of my past—all of it.

I would never move on until I could come to terms with my father and Michael. I realized Michael symbolized every man I'd dated, though there hadn't been many. They had all been manipulating and overbearing. I needed to face him. He was about control, but he couldn't control me anymore.

I also had to face my father and figure out how to be more like Kai and forgive, though I would never be able to forget. I couldn't go backward, but I might move forward. It wasn't like I was repairing anything we ever had. We'd never had a relationship, so we just had to get to know each other. At least I could try. Then and only then, would I be able to move on with any kind of relationship with a man.

I walked into the kitchen to fix a cup of coffee and a bagel, then leaned heavily on the counter as I waited for my bagel to toast. *Another day of work, and no way to get there. I really need my own car.* Kai's truck was out of the shop, but he was at work. Luckily, Kora was on summer break, so I could borrow hers.

I pulled into the parking lot of Jerry's Pub. Trevor's truck wasn't there, as it was his day at the fire hall, but Dakota was there instead. She was a co-owner but stayed in the background. She worked the books and focused on the inventory, so she often worked at home or early in the mornings.

Before I stepped out of the truck, I searched my phone for the number I was sure was Michael's and sent a text.

> **Michael. We know it's you.**
> **The police are searching for you.**
> **Please leave me alone.**
> **If you want to talk, I will.**
> **But please understand. We are finished.**
> **I'm not going back to South Dakota.**
> **And it has nothing to do with Lance,**
> **and everything to do with family.**

I pressed send, placed my phone in my purse, and walked through the door.

Dakota was behind the bar, completing an inventory of the liquor. She had brown hair that was straight and fell just below her shoulders. She was thick-boned with a weathered face and wore little makeup, mostly mascara only, and had a harsh look to her, like she'd be better suited as a bouncer than a bar owner. But I could see her as a firefighter.

"Good morning, Susie," she said.

"Morning." I nodded.

I placed my things in the back room, then tapped my employee number on the computer. Shannon was working with me that day and signed in right after.

"Okay, ladies," Dakota said. "We will keep the patio doors closed today. The weather's going to be rainy, so our goal is to keep everyone inside. It's just you two until around four when Barb comes in."

The door opened, and our first customers entered and sat in Shannon's area.

"Susie, are you okay?" Dakota asked.

I snickered. I shouldn't have been surprised that she was up-to-date on the happenings with Michael, but it still amazed me how things got around in this small town. No one had seemed so concerned about my family life when I was a child.

I nodded. "I'm fine." I was. Even though I wasn't with Lance anymore, I was secure, strong, and prepared for anything.

The afternoon was slow, which was good. I needed time to talk with my father. Whenever he ran food to tables, I watched him. The butterflies that churned in my stomach almost made me sick. I was more nervous about dealing with him than Lance and Michael combined. I didn't know how to start a conversation with a man I didn't know. *What should I say?*

But it turned out I didn't have to worry about it. Although it wasn't crazy busy, it was steady, and with Dakota managing, we always had side jobs to complete, which filled any lull.

I was talking to a family I'd gotten to know and cleared their table.

"Susie, can you grab his order?" Dakota asked and pointed at a man at the end of the bar.

I nodded and glanced his way. He looked vaguely familiar, though I couldn't place how or why. He sat at the bar, wearing a blue baseball hat backward, with his back to me.

I put a smile on my face and approached him.

I didn't get far before I froze, and the smile melted from my face. *I do know him.*

He glanced up from the menu, a chilling sneer creeping up his lips. "Hello, Suz."

My mouth went dry.

I swallowed hard, gained control, and continued toward him.

"Hello, Michael." My voice was void of emotion.

"I got your text. I answered you but didn't get a reply, so I thought I'd see if you were at work. I like the food here, so even if you weren't, it wouldn't hurt to grab a bite."

He liked the food. He'd been here before. I glanced around, wondering if anyone realized who he was. It didn't seem so. Shannon was laughing with the customers. Terry delivered food to one of her tables. Dakota was still in the office.

Be calm. Be brave. Don't give him the satisfaction of thinking his presence here has thrown you off. "What can I get you to drink?"

"I'll have a beer. Surprise me with your most popular IPA, and I'm ready to order."

I took his order, and Terry walked toward the kitchen and raised his eyebrows. I didn't give him any response, just tapped the order into the computer, and filled a glass with beer from the tap.

Ignoring the clenching of my gut, I looked into Michael's dark eyes and at the handsome, chiseled features of his face. "What made you come all the way to Tennessee?" I asked as I placed his beer on the counter.

He shrugged. "Had to make sure you were safe. You left without a goodbye and with no explanation of where you went. I was worried."

I chuckled slightly. *Worried, my ass.* He had never worried about me. He'd never thought about me in a caring manner except maybe to care that I serviced him appropriately in bed. "Don't you think if I wanted you to know where I was, I would have told you?" Irritation oozed off my words. Courage fueled me. "I hope you realize I didn't want you to know. I don't care about you."

I couldn't feel the usual pull that made me listen to him. He no longer had a hold on me. My shoulders relaxed, and I stood tall as confidence filled me, and I continued. "This is my home. My place. My security, and I have people here who are on my side. You have no clue what you're getting into, Michael."

"Oh yeah, that's right. You've already tried to replace me with...What's his name? Lance? How does the town feel about you fucking their football coach?"

I took a step back. "How dare you?" I said through clenched teeth, keeping my voice under control. I took a deep breath. "What I'm doing with my life is not your concern anymore. All I have to do is get Dakota over here and call the police, and you're going to jail. You realize stalking me and watching me through my windows is against the law. You're on private property and watching me." I leaned on the counter and toward him. "Why don't you just leave now?"

His eyes were void of emotion, and a smug grin filled his face. He said nothing and took a large gulp of his beer.

The calm that took over his features chilled me to the bone.

My father stepped out of the kitchen and placed Michael's burger in front of him. "Everything good here?" he asked, glancing between the two of us.

I nodded but didn't take my gaze from Michael's. "Yeah, yeah, it's all good."

He glared at me, and I turned toward him and didn't flinch. He tilted his head and walked away. When he reached the kitchen door, he turned and looked again.

I glanced back at Michael as he spread mustard on his burger. "Just so you know," he said nonchalantly, "your boy toy has nothing over me. Remember, I know all of your peaks and valleys. I created the person you are in bed. Does he know he's only your second? I was your first. I took your innocence." He took a bite of his burger, wiped his mouth on his napkin, and chewed.

I froze in place, struggling to get my breathing under control. *Stay calm. Don't show him any weakness.* I'd sworn to myself that I'd wait for the perfect man, my knight in shining armor. I'd been so worried I'd never fall in love that I fell in love with the wrong person.

He swallowed, and a creepy sneer filled his face. "I will always have that, Suz."

My heart clenched, and I stepped back, gritting my teeth. "I have other customers. If you'll excuse me." I continued my job, then took a quick dip into the bathroom to breathe.

Relax. Gain control. Breathe. I leaned heavily against the sink.

Dakota entered the bathroom. "Susie, is everything okay?"

I shook my head and breathed deeply. *In for two, out for two.*

My pulse relaxed. I had things under control. Now, *to keep the tears away.* I blinked rapidly.

"Patrick's here," Dakota said.

I looked up. "What do you mean, 'Patrick's here'? What's he doing here?" Panic crept into my bones. *What would Michael do if he thought I had called the police?* "My father called him, didn't he?" *Damn him.*

"Is it the guy at the bar?"

I bit my tongue. I didn't want her to get involved.

"Look, Patrick's right outside. If you don't tell him about the man at the bar, I will."

I opened my mouth, but she raised a finger. "Don't ask me not to. This is important. Again, if you don't tell him, I will."

"Fine." I huffed and stomped out.

"Susie, is there a problem?" Patrick asked.

"Yeah, there is," I said with my arms crossed. "A woman can't go to the bathroom without getting bothered by the police."

He tipped his head as Lance ran up.

"Seriously? You called him?" I said to Patrick, then turned to Lance. "What are you doing here?" *God, this is ridiculous. No one listens to me.*

"Patrick told me that there's something going on. I'm just here to check on you."

Dammit. All this attention is unnecessary, but now that Lance is here, there's no way he's going to leave. His determination was unwavering. "Fine. Whatever." I threw my hands up. "Michael's at the bar."

Patrick shook his head. "That's what Terry thought, but by the time I got here, he had left."

I pushed past the two of them and to the empty spot where Michael had been. He'd left a half-eaten burger and cash on the counter.

I gathered the cash and closed his bill. He'd left me a one-dollar tip. "He hasn't changed. He's still a cheap ass," I said as I pocketed the tip.

Lance chuckled, and our eyes met. My heart fluttered, but I tore my gaze away. It was not the time to get lost in him.

"Do you want to go to the office to talk?" Patrick asked.

"Nope," I said. "Anything I have to say can be said here. Everyone's going to find out anyway. It's not like there're any secrets in this town." I crossed my arms and leaned against the wall.

Patrick looked at Lance and shrugged. "Fine. Did he say where he was staying? Why he's here?"

I laughed. "He's here to affect me, to make me uncomfortable and my life hell until I go back to South Dakota with him."

Lance's eyes got big, and he opened his mouth, but I shushed him. "He will not hurt me. Physically, at least, but he knows a lot about you."

"What does he know?" he asked.

"He knows you coach football. He knows we've been together. He doesn't like you."

"Okay," Patrick said. "I'm going to pull the video feed from the security cameras so we can get a good picture of him from the cameras in the lot. Maybe we can find out what he's driving."

He walked away and talked to Dakota. She nodded, and he followed her to the office.

Lance started, "Susie—"

"I've gotta get back to work. I have customers." I turned away, but he grabbed my arm. I stopped and turned slowly.

His eyes held so many feelings, so many questions.

I shook my head. "Please. Lance. I'm okay." I glanced at his hand, then looked back into his eyes. "Let me go," I pleaded, my voice soft.

CHAPTER 32

LANCE

I did as she asked and let her go.

Without saying a word, she walked away. God, I hoped it wasn't a vision of what was to come—Susie walking out of my life.

A void filled my heart. *This is bullshit. Michael has the balls to come here, in our space, and mock her. Intimidate her. Who the fuck does he think he is?* I stalked into the office. She might not want me around, but I would find that asswipe.

Sure, Susie hadn't acted like his being there bothered her, but I could tell it did. She was stiff and anxious. He'd gotten into her business and followed her. She might think he wasn't dangerous, but a sane person didn't drive across the country to stalk an ex-girlfriend.

I barged through the office door. "What did you find out?"

"What the hell, Lance?" Patrick asked as he watched the video. "This has nothing to do with you."

"Bullshit." I walked behind Patrick, and before he could close the picture, I glimpsed the car he was watching.

"Hell," I whispered. "That car was leaving when I pulled in."

Patrick's gaze held mine. "Did you notice the driver?"

I should tell him about the guy. My adrenaline rose. "No."

"You sure?" His gaze held mine.

"Yep." I stared right back. If I told him yes, I'd seen a man with a baseball hat in the driver's seat, he'd keep me away from the investigation, and like hell would that happen. I turned and stalked out of the office and out of the pub.

Before I left, I glanced at Susie. She was taking a family's order, her back to me.

I hopped into my car and turned left out of the lot, just like the other car. I had only been inside the pub for about ten minutes, but there was no telling where he could have gone in that amount of time. If he were smart, he would have gone straight to the interstate and driven in either direction. But I hoped he wasn't smart, and if that was the case, he could still be in town. It wouldn't take long for Patrick to put out an APB on the car. If he were in any of the nearby towns, the cops would find him.

If I were going to find him first, I had to be quick.

I cruised the town and searched the parking lots of the stores but found nothing. My phone rang with a call from Jamison. "Dude, what are you doing?" he asked as soon as I picked up. "Patrick texted me. Asked me to check on you."

I filled him in on what had happened.

"Don't tell me you're getting involved."

"Fine. Then don't ask."

"I thought you told me Susie wanted you to give her space."

"Yeah, she did. And I'm not around her. I'm just trying to find the dick who's stalking her."

"Let the police take care of him."

"Would you ignore it if Lilly's ex-husband showed up in town, stalked her, scared the shit out of her, then showed up at her work?"

Jamison huffed into the phone.

I knew he'd be on my side. He loved Lilly. Hell, he'd loved her forever. No way would he let her ex come into town and do that. "Exactly. So, you know I have to..." I passed by the shitty hotel by the interstate, and there was the car. "Fuck."

"Lance? What?" Jamison asked. "Where are you?"

"I've gotta go." I hung up before he tried to talk me out of what I had to do.

I pulled into the parking lot and stopped at the edge of the motel. Adrenaline pumped through my veins, and I tapped a rhythm on the steering wheel. *What if he's in one of the rooms, getting the freaky on with some skank? What if they're going to be long? How long am I willing to sit here?*

Shit, that was easy. I'd stay here as long as it takes.

I turned off the truck and rolled the windows partially down. It was not the type of hotel I wanted to expose myself to.

I sat and waited.

A questionable couple came out of one room and climbed into a car. They both looked like they had seen better days, like their car. *God, this is boring.* I glanced at the time on my phone. *No way. Have I really just been here for fifteen minutes? How do cops handle stakeouts? This is more boring than a parent meeting about the concession stand's rules and regulations.* And damn, those were boring—and I had to get one scheduled soon. *Shit.*

Another door opened, and I sat up straight. *Damn, I'm pretty sure that's him.*

Yep.

He walked to the car and put his phone to his ear.

Shit. What would I do if he pulled out? Follow? He talked on the phone, cursed, and went back into the room.

Hell yes. My chance. I exited my truck and took long strides toward the car.

He came back out the door.

"Hey, dick!" I yelled.

He turned, raised his eyebrows, and looked around. "You talking to me?"

Who the hell does this asshole think he is? An Italian mobster? "Yeah. I am."

I could tell when recognition dawned on his face because his eyes widened. "Well, look who it is. Lance. The one fucking my woman."

"She's not your woman," I said as anger fueled me.

"Oh, she's mine. Trust me." The grin he plastered on his face made my gut churn. I gritted my teeth and sped up my steps.

"Did she suck your cock?" he asked. "Fuck, she's good at that."

"Shut up," I said, my voice calmer than I felt. "I'll beat the shit out of you."

"It looks like Mr. Football wants a fight."

I reached him and stopped. "Leave Susie alone and leave town, and we can forget any of this ever happened."

He chuckled. "That's not going to happen. Not yet. Not until she sees reason and goes with me, though I have no problem with forcing the issue."

"What the fuck? Are you crazy? She wants nothing to do with you." Blood pounded in my ears, and my pulse sped like a racehorse. *This dumbass is insane.*

He spat on the ground and cackled. "Did she tell you I was her first? I popped her cherry, as they say—and what a fine cherry it was. Sweet and perfect. Everything she did with you—to you—she learned here first." He pointed at his chest. "That little bitch is amazing in bed."

The thought of that shitbag touching her made my skin crawl. My anger exploded, and I swung my fist, connecting with his chin.

"You fucking bastard!" he bellowed and was quick to throw a punch, which landed square in my gut.

I doubled over and took deep breaths. *Damn, that fucker can land a punch.*

I answered it with one to his stomach.

We exchanged blows. He connected with my cheek, and I connected with a jab to his jaw. A woman screamed, and a door slammed. He answered with a punch that landed on my nose.

"Fuck!" I yelled and clutched my face. I pulled my hand away, and blood covered it.

Just then, sirens filled the air, and I attacked. I wrapped the asshole up, swiped his feet, and took him to the ground.

Tires squealed to a stop.

I punched his face once, twice, three times.

"What the fuck, Lance?" Patrick pulled me off the asshole, and another officer picked him up from the ground. He cursed and flailed his arms until they could get him handcuffed.

Patrick held on to me, and I tried to pull away. "We've got him. You relax, and I'll let you go."

I stilled and held up one hand. The other covered my nose.

"Good." Patrick released his hold. "Lance, I've gotta take you in, but maybe we should get that nose looked at first."

"No, I'm fine," I said. "Just take me wherever you need to."

Just then, an ambulance pulled up.

"After we get you checked out," Patrick demanded.

❧

I sat in Patrick's office at the police station with an ice pack on my nose and a jackhammer in my head. The blood from my nose had stopped flowing, Michael was in jail, and my head pounded. I really needed a handful of ibuprofen.

"Hey, dumbass."

I looked up and snickered as pain shot through my face. "Hey, Jamison." I spoke through gritted teeth as I stood gingerly. Every move made pain shoot from either my face or my head. "Thanks for picking me up."

"Of course. That's what friends are for." He whacked me on the shoulder, which sent another shot of pain searing through my face.

"Fuck." I winced carefully. Every move of a facial muscle hurt like hell.

"Sorry, man. I hope it was worth it."

I made eye contact with Jamison and smirked as best as I could. "Oh yeah. One hundred percent."

He chuckled, and just then, Patrick came out of the back.

"Is he free to go?" Jamison asked.

Patrick nodded. "Yep. Next time, though, don't take matters into your own hands."

"Whatever," I said. "What's happening with him?" My voice sounded as if it were in a tunnel, muffled and nasally.

"Susie and Kai are on their way. It's all up to Susie. If she wants to press charges, she will. But she asked for you to be gone before she gets here."

I did this for her, and she still doesn't want to see me. "Fine." I threw the ice pack at Patrick and trudged toward the door.

"Hell no," Jamison said. He caught up with me and handed me the ice pack. "You keep that on your face. No way in hell am I letting you bleed all over my truck."

I climbed into the passenger side. "Who got my truck?"

"Rowan. He's taking it to my house so you can go home later. Lilly's making dinner."

"Great. I'm starving."

When we pulled in at Jamison's house, there were more than Lilly and the girls here. Rowan and Charles's cars sat in the driveway also. *Damn, I hope that's all.*

We walked inside, and the noise coming from the kitchen made my head pound. *This is going to suck.*

In addition to Rowan and Charles, Summer, my mother, and Tonya were also there. *Of course.*

"Hey." My mother came rushing over and took the ice pack from me. "Oh my God, honey." She searched my face and pulled me to the sink. "You look like you smeared a gallon of red paint all over your face." She wet a paper towel and wiped at the blood.

"Ouch, Mom. Be careful."

"Sorry," she said and wiped more softly.

"Look at that nose. Looks like my handiwork has been destroyed." Rowan laughed. "I liked it better crooked. He straightened it."

"Fucker."

"Uncle Lance," Madeline said as she entered the kitchen.

"Seriously?"

"You know the rules," she continued.

"Ew," Darcie commented. "He does, but he's yucky. He needs to get cleaned up first." She pulled Madeline away, then stopped and pointed at me. "But don't you dare leave without paying up. Like Madeline said, you know the rules."

I closed my eyes and shook my head gently as I listened for their feet to disappear. "Mom, I'm fine. I need more ice."

"Go. Sit, and I'll get it."

I did as she commanded. I knew better than to argue with my mother when she was in that mode and sat between Tonya and Charles at the table.

"Damn, Lance. You look like a raccoon auditioning for a horror flick," Tonya said. "I thought you beat up the other guy."

Charles chuckled. "She's right, buddy. You look like shit."

Are these two seriously giving me shit right now?

I shook my head, and the kitchen spun, so I laid my head in my hands. "I can't. Can y'all hush and someone turn out the light?"

My mom gave me a glass of water. "I think you have a concussion. Maybe you should go get checked out."

My head pounded, and my face throbbed. I wished I had something stronger than ibuprofen. "I already did. The paramedics looked at me and told me what signs to watch for. I'll be fine. I just need to go home and sleep."

Tonya and Charles kept coming up with stupid metaphors for how I looked, and it didn't take long before Rowan joined in.

The noise was killing my head. "Look, can y'all just be quiet? I've got a splitting headache."

"Well, I should think so," Charles said.

My mom placed a plate of spaghetti in front of me. "I don't know if you can eat, but I'm sure you haven't had dinner. Try to eat something. And you three, be nice."

"Where's the fun if we can't rag on him?" Rowan asked.

I wanted to say something to Rowan, but just the thought of talking made my head pound harder and my stomach churn. Instead, I glared.

He laughed.

I looked at my mom. "Thank you." I ate a few bites before my stomach had had enough—of the food and the commentary. "Why are y'all here, anyway?"

"Why are we here?" Tonya asked. "We were invited for dinner and were visiting with our granddaughters."

"And I was being helpful and brought you your truck," Rowan said.

"That's right. My truck is here. Good. I want to go home and crash."

The girls skipped into the kitchen. "Well, you can't leave before you pay us for the bad word you said," Madeline told me.

I shook my head lightly and pulled out a dollar bill.

They both glared at it and then turned to each other, shook their heads, and looked at me.

"What's wrong? It's money," I said.

Madeline held up her hands. "Yeah, but it's only one dollar. What are we supposed to do with that?"

"Yeah, there's two of us," Darcie added. "What? It's always been one curse, one dollar." Madeline tsked and placed her hands on her hips. "Yeah, when it was just Darcie. Now there's two of us. One plus one is two." She held up one finger at a time to prove her point.

I bit the inside of my cheek and reached into my pocket to pull out my wallet to get another bill. "It's a damn good thing the two of you are cute." I gave them each a dollar.

They pocketed it and held their hands back out.

Chuckles and snickers went around the room.

"I think you do have a concussion," Rowan said. "You don't realize you just cursed again."

I placed my hand on my head to stop the thumping at my temples. "Here." I handed them my wallet. "Just take what you want and let me go."

Darcie pulled out two one-dollar bills and handed me back my wallet.

"There," Madeline said. "Uncle Lance, you just need to learn not to use potty words. You're out of money."

I looked at my niece, whom I loved with my entire heart, and shook my head. "What happened to the sweet and quiet little girl who showed up in town a year ago?"

Darcie placed her arm around her shoulders. "She's right here. She's just not quiet anymore. I taught her everything I know."

I loved Darcie just as much as I loved Madeline. She was my best friend's daughter, and they were both a pain in my ass.

I hugged them. "Okay. Don't spend all your money in one place." I messed up their hair. "Lilly, thank you for dinner. Someone drive me home. I don't think I should be behind the wheel."

"You're welcome," Lilly said as she kissed my cheek gently.

I hugged my mom.

"Charles will drive your truck, and I'll follow. We should get going anyway," Mom said as she put her hand out, and I gave her my keys. I knew better than to argue, and I didn't have the energy anyway.

"You'll go home and get some sleep. Do you have any ibuprofen there?"

"Yes, I do."

I hugged Tonya and then pointed at her. "Be quiet."

"I didn't say anything," she said with a smirk.

"It's not what came out of your mouth but what's in your thoughts."

"T, are you coming with us?" my mother asked.

"Nope. Jamison will take me home later."

I gave Jamison a handshake. "Thanks for picking me up."

He patted my shoulder. "Of course. You do look like shit, by the way."

"Thanks." I grinned. I put my middle finger up at Rowan once I'd checked to make sure two little girls were no longer in the room.

I heard his chuckle as I left the house.

I struggled to stay awake on the short drive to my place. I thanked Charles as he climbed into the car with my mom.

Once I'd entered my house, I grabbed some ibuprofen, undressed as I walked into my room, and crashed onto the bed. I hoped everything would turn out okay with Susie at the station.

My fingers itched to call her. My heart needed to make sure she was okay, but she wanted her space, and I needed to give her that. Plus, I could have sworn there were people in my head, smashing hammers against my skull. The thought of talking still made my stomach churn.

I closed my eyes and willed sleep to come and take away the pain.

CHAPTER 33

SUSIE

The sun shone brightly, and there wasn't a cloud in the sky, so I grabbed a book and headed to the river to sit, read, and reflect over the past few days.

I was in another calm after the storm. The pattern had become all too familiar. I settled in a chair, hoping that the gentle sound of the water would quiet my mind long enough for me to lose myself in a story. But it didn't work. The words on the page blurred together as my thoughts drifted to Lance.

I hadn't seen him since the incident with Michael. He'd called and sent texts, and I'd ignored him. I told myself I needed space and time to think, but sitting with the rush of the river filling the silence, I couldn't lie to myself anymore.

I missed him.

I should have answered his calls or at least his texts. He'd gotten a broken nose and a concussion because of me. Maybe chivalry wasn't dead after all.

"Kora and Kai said I could find you down here."

My eyes widened, and I jumped. It was my father. He was another person I had been avoiding. After our last talk, I wasn't sure what to think, or better yet, feel.

"I didn't mean to startle you. Do you mind if I join you?" He asked.

I shook my head, my lips locked tight, and I motioned for him to sit.

We sat in silence. The singing of the birds and the running of the river were the only noises.

"What brings you by?" I asked, finally breaking the awkward silence.

"You've been quiet and by yourself lately. I haven't seen you at work. Just thought I should check on you."

It had been five days since I dropped all charges against Michael. He didn't have a criminal record, so as long as he promised to leave Orlinda Valley, stay out of the state of Tennessee, and never contact me again, he wouldn't serve any jail time. Kai thought I should have held him accountable for the stress and anxiety he'd caused me, but I wanted him gone and out of my life. I wanted it to be over.

Since then, I'd spent time by myself, as I had a lot I needed to sort out. I hadn't been to work or anywhere. Instead, I'd been by the river or cuddled in bed with Mr. Kitty.

It was a cruel bit of irony. The previous week, no one let me leave, and it pissed me off. Now, no one was making me stay, and I didn't want to leave.

I'd been reading, thinking, and trying to figure out what to do about my future, my father, and Lance.

I glanced at my father out of the corner of my eye. His hands repeatedly grasped and let go of the arms of the chair.

What should I say to him? He's never checked on me or worried about me before. But of course, that had been when all he cared about was drinking.

He wasn't the same person I'd grown up with. He was sober and kind. He smiled a lot and was becoming part of a community. "Thank you," I said without looking at him, my attention on a squirrel chattering on a tree branch near the river.

"Are you okay?" He squirmed and wiped his hands on his jeans.

I could tell that he was nervous, which made sense. It was the most he'd ever talked to me except for that day at Jerry's Pub.

"No," I said. "I'm not okay. It's been a lot, and...yeah." I couldn't put my feelings into words, and being here with him made it more difficult.

"I'm sorry," he said. Those two words held so much emotion.

"Why are you sorry?" I asked and shook my head. Frustration bubbled over. "Why now?" Irritation dripped from my words. I leaned on my knees and rested my face in my hands and breathed.

He sighed heavily. The years of alcohol and drug abuse were apparent in his ragged breaths. "I know there's nothing I can say to give you back a childhood. I know I was a lousy father. And I know that because of me you're struggling with positive relationships, friendships, all of it. I can't go back and change anything, but we can start over."

I lifted my face from my hands, and he looked at me, his eyes watery. "What do you think?"

Though it was a simple question, I had no simple answer. I shrugged. "I don't know. I...I'd like to, but I don't know where to start."

"How about at the beginning?" He put his hand out toward me. "I'm Terry Lawson. I used to love to read and camp until I started drinking. I have three amazing adult kids I hardly know, and I've made so many mistakes I can't even count them, but I'd like to get to know you and maybe be a friend."

I looked at his hand, then studied his face.

When Michael had left town, it felt like I had a new start. My past was over. I could leave it behind.

Being in Orlinda Valley with a new family and, for the first time, friends, was a new beginning. Maybe a relationship with my father could be a part of that. If Kai could put the past behind him, I had no excuse. It was worth a shot.

I placed my hand in his, which was surprisingly strong, warm, and steady. This was the first time I could remember holding my father's hand.

A lump lodged in my throat, and I cleared it before I could speak. "Hi. I'm Susie Lawson. I went to college to be a teacher but am now working at Jerry's Pub as a server. I have a twin brother I don't see enough. I'm living with my amazing brother Kai and his wife and am going to be an aunt." Just saying it filled me with excitement. "If Kai could move on and find happiness, I think there's hope for all of us."

The corners of my father's mouth curled up.

"But I don't want any more friends," I continued.

His smile faltered.

"I have all the friends I need." I added my other hand to hold his, and my heart thumped hard. "But I could really use a father." Emotion filled my eyes.

"And I could use a daughter," he said, smiling as his eyes brimmed with tears. Silence built between us as we looked at each other, but this time it wasn't awkward.

I gave him a smile and stood. I took a deep breath of fresh air and stretched. My body seemed lighter, like the last bit of weight had lifted from my shoulders, and peace seeped into my muscles.

I turned to my dad. "I'm sure Kora and Kai have dinner prepared." I could smell pork chops grilling. "What do you say we eat?"

"Sounds great." He stood, and we walked back toward the house. My steps were lighter, and a smile filled my face.

My dad turned to me. "Thank you for giving me a chance."

"Thank you for asking."

"Just in time," Kora said as she placed a salad on the patio table. "It's a perfect night. We thought we'd eat out here."

I helped Kora bring drinks out, and we settled around the table. Kai set a platter of grilled pork chops in the center.

We helped ourselves, and I glanced around.

Kai filled his plate and leaned over and gave Kora a peck on her cheek. He was always happy, and he seemed even happier since he was going to be a dad.

Terry laughed at something Kora said and glanced at me with an unsure smile. I smiled back.

"How are you doing, Suz?" Kai asked.

I nodded. "I'm good. I'm at peace with things." I squeezed his hand. "You are going to make an amazing dad. You really are. And the baby is going to grow up surrounded by family and love." I shrugged. "I knew families like this existed in books, but I never thought it would be possible for me to experience it. I was so wrong."

We ate in silence filled only by the sound of goats playing and a rooster crowing.

When we finished, my dad left for his place, and I kicked Kora and Kai out of the kitchen. I wanted to clean up and do something for them for once.

Lance popped into my mind as I finished wiping down the counter. *Does he miss me?* I leaned on the counter and watched the cat sleep in the middle of the kitchen floor. Mr. Kitty had changed so much in such a brief span of time.

I chuckled. *Almost like me.*

A month ago, Lance had irritated me so badly. He never left me alone and constantly annoyed me. *Now he's doing exactly what I asked him to do. He's giving me time and space, and I miss him like crazy.*

But what if he's tired of waiting for me? What if he's fed up with my drama?

"Hey," Kristy said as she entered the kitchen. "Kora told me you were in here." She gave me a hug, and I leaned in, not wanting to get my wet hands on her. She picked up the kitten and got comfortable on the stool. "How you doing?" She asked.

I laughed.

"What?"

"Everyone's asking me that. What did y'all think? I was going to fall apart and become a quivering mess of a woman because I had to face my ex?"

"No. I just haven't seen you since all that happened. I hoped you'd reach out, but…"

"I know." I dried the sink, threw away the paper towel, and leaned my elbows on the counter across from Kristy. "I've been doing a lot of thinking."

She raised her eyebrows. "About?"

"My life. How much things have changed over the past year." I traced a line in the wood. "I always thought love wasn't something I was worthy of, so in South Dakota, I was determined to just be alone. We can see how well that worked out. As soon as a man showed interest, I latched on desperately. But when I came here for the wedding last year and saw how happy and adjusted to this place Kai was, I realized life could be more, and I deserved to be happy. When I went back to South Dakota, I put the steps in place to leave Michael but quickly realized I couldn't just break up with him. I needed to get away from him. I loved my brief visit here last year, and Kai and Kora were excited to have me stay with them."

"I'm glad you came back. I hope you stay."

I smiled widely at Kristy. She was so pretty, down-to-earth, and my friend. "I'm not going anywhere. This place is the home I was always looking for. And you, Lilly, and Rose are my first real friends."

She placed the kitten on the floor and grasped my hands. "Good. We love you. I love you."

I smiled and felt peace wash over my body.

Home, check.

Family, check.

Friendship, check.

"Now, what are you going to do about Lance?"

Relationship, no check.

I sighed. "Did you have to go there?" I covered my face with my hands and breathed deeply, then stared at the ceiling. "I don't know.

That's the one thing I haven't figured out. He got involved in my life when I asked him not to. He's a lot to deal with."

"Correction. He *was* a lot. There's something different about him."

"What does that mean?"

"We were all at Kaye and Charles's on Sunday. He was quiet and wasn't part of the banter. He ignored Rowan's jabs about his nose. All the teasing. It was weird."

"Weird how?"

Kristy's stare held mine. "I've known Lance forever. He's always been loud, turning every conversation back around to himself or Jamison. Egotistical and top-rate annoying. He wasn't like that on Sunday, and it's because of you."

I puffed out a heavy breath. "That's ridiculous. It has nothing to do with me. I'm sure he got his ego handed to him when Michael gave him a hard fight, but what do I have to do with anything?"

"I think he misses you."

I glanced away and pursed my lips. "I need air."

I walked out the kitchen door and took a seat on the patio, shaking my head. "Maybe he misses me, but I asked him to stay out of things. Give me space. He didn't listen. He needed to be in charge and to take care of everything. I didn't want him to do that. I asked him *not* to do that."

Kristy sat next to me. "He's used to being the alpha male and having women fall all over him. Giving a woman space and waiting on them is unfamiliar territory for him."

"Well, he needs to get over it. I just got away from one alpha-male asshole. I'm not going into another relationship with the same type of person. I want someone to see me as an equal."

"I get it. I do. I'm still single too. But in my case, I need a man to give me a challenge. Not fall at my feet."

I laughed. "What you're saying is, you're the female version of Lance." She could be. She was pretty enough and had the attitude to fit the bill.

Kristy shrugged. "Don't know. Just waiting for the perfect man and haven't found him yet."

"Maybe the perfect man doesn't exist, and we have our sights set too high."

"Maybe," she said, tucking her arm through mine.

Just then, rustling came from the trees near the path from the house.

"Baby goat, what are you doing?" I asked as the black-and-white goat came out of the weeds and nudged my thigh with its head. I scratched his ears, and he looked up at me with his blue eyes. "You are so sweet."

"Well, maybe one perfect male does exist," Kristy said.

I laughed and stood.

We walked on the path to the pasture, and the goat followed.

"I know you want to avoid people," Kristy said, "but Jamison and Lilly are having a get-together at their house tonight. Lilly asked if you'd come."

A get-together meant everyone, including the extended family, and Lance would be there. "I don't know."

"You can't avoid him forever. This is Orlinda Valley. Not a huge metropolis."

"I know," I said. "But I was hoping I could try."

CHAPTER 34

LANCE

Saturday afternoon, I pulled into my mother and Charles's driveway.

Charles and Tom were heading out. I waved to them both, glad they wouldn't be here. They usually found a useless job or two for me to do with them and today I wasn't in the mood. I needed to talk with my mom. *An adult male looking for one-on-one time with his mother. How pitiful am I?*

I went inside then looked out at the pool deck and found out quickly that mother-and-son time wasn't possible. Tonya, Diane, and Ruth were out there with my mother, drinking wine and laughing.

I could leave. They wouldn't know I was ever here. But I'd told my mom I was coming over. I sighed. *She should have warned me the book club would be here.* I grabbed a beer from the fridge. *You got this.* I opened the door and stepped outside.

"Well, look who it is," Diane said. She was refilling everyone's glasses with wine. One bottle sat empty on the table.

Wonderful—the book club—already one bottle in.

This should be fun.

She gave me a hug. "Here, sit." She led me to the only seat available, and I got comfortable with her on the loveseat. I popped open one beer and set the other on the ground.

"Hello, ladies. What book are you discussing today?" Surprisingly, there was an actual book on the table next to Ruth. It had a couple embracing on the cover. "Maybe I don't want to know."

"Come on, honey. It's just a romance," my mother said.

"That's right. With spicy scenes that would make your toes curl," Tonya added. "Mmm, it was a good one."

I rolled my eyes.

"You don't have anything against romance and love, do you, Lance?" Tonya asked.

I shook my head and sipped my beer. "Nope. Nothing against either of them. I just don't think I believe in them."

"Oh, that's a lie," my mother replied. "You want someone to love, but sometimes, you just have to be willing to fight for it."

"And be able to put someone else's needs over your own," Ruth added.

"And listen when you're told to give someone space," Diane said.

"And if all that fails, you may need to go down on your knees, ask for forgiveness, and satisfy your woman." Tonya wiggled her eyebrows, and the book club hooted with laughter.

"Oh, good God," I whispered and massaged my forehead. *Why did I think I could get any decent help out of these women?* I turned up my beer. Then started to stand up, but Diane held my shoulder. "Seriously, Lance, give her the time she asked for. She has so many things she needs to figure out."

I stared at my beer and sucked in a heavy breath. *Give her time. Give her space.* I'd heard that a billion times in the last week. That was what everyone told me, and when Kristy had showed up without her at Jamison's and Lilly's, my heart shattered. I thought we had something together, something different.

My leg bounced, and I shook my head. "I've given her time and space. I got my nose broken, and she never even called or sent a text to check on me."

"Hey, look at me," my mother insisted.

I turned toward her. She was blurry. *Fuck, don't cry.* I blinked the tears away.

"I'm sorry you're hurting. But see it as a good thing."

"A good thing?" I stood quickly and took a few steps. She followed. "How can I see it as that?"

"Lance," she said, her voice stern, and grasped my hands.

I gritted my teeth, seething. I was a grown man being talked to like a child by my mother.

"I've never seen you upset or willing to fight for a woman and a relationship. You've always been so much like your father that I've been afraid you'd be alone forever or worse—deserve to be." She took a step back. "So yes. I am thankful." She put her hands together in a praying gesture. "This shows me you want an actual relationship and love. You're willing to fight for it. That's huge."

Her voice became softer, and she placed a hand on my cheek. "I'm your mother. I love you more than anything, and I want you to find love. If Susie's the one, she'll see it. She has so many skeletons she's dealing with right now. It might take a day, a week, a month. But I know she'll figure it out. You might end up together. You might not.

Have faith. It will work out for the best, and when she gives a little, be willing to prove yourself to her—if you still want to."

I met my mother's gaze and swallowed hard. "I can't picture wanting anyone more."

A smile filled her face, and she pulled me in for a hug.

As tears slipped from my eyes, I held her close.

"That is music to my heart," she whispered. "You might just give me grandchildren yet."

I leaned back and glared at her.

"What?" She shrugged. "You'd make adorable babies."

I puffed out a breath as the sliding door opened. *Thank God, a distraction.*

"Uncle Lance!" Darcie and Madeline's voices reached levels I hadn't even known existed.

I wiped at my face and turned with a smile to catch them both in a hug. "Well, little princesses, what brings you both here?"

They rolled their eyes at each other.

"We're here to swim. Duh," Darcie said.

"Yeah. Lena will be here any minute," Madeline added.

"Well, this is my cue to leave. I've got to get going." I finished my beer and placed it on the table next to the empty wine bottle. "Ladies, thank you for your encouragement." I gave Ruth and Diane each a hug.

"And helpful tips," I said to Tonya.

"Of course." She patted my cheek. "I'm always here to help. You know that."

I chuckled, then hugged my mom hard. "I love you, Mom."

"Love you too, baby."

"Goodbye, princesses. Be good."

"We're always good, Uncle Lance," Madeline said.

"Yep," Darcie added. "But I am a little disappointed in you."

A six-year-old is disappointed in me. I've got to hear this. I arched an eyebrow. "Why?"

"I need more money, and you didn't say any bad words."

I chuckled. "Well then, I am sorry to disappoint you, but I'm broke." I messed with her hair, waved, and shook Charles and Tom's hands when I passed them at the door.

As I drove down the road, my mom's words echoed in my mind. Then I thought back to what relationships I'd had. They were always all about me, mostly. If I had something to do, we did it. *Shit. Is that really how I've been? Demanding? Selfish?* My relationship with Jayla, the woman I'd dated before Susie, was all about fun—in the bedroom, mostly, but there weren't any genuine feelings.

Then Susie showed up, and she was all I saw from day one.

"Well, Lance, it's time to grow up. You don't want to hit forty and still be single or let this one get away."

⋙

That night, we had another successful practice. The team was really shaping up and showing promise.

"This might be the year we make a run at state," I said to Jamison.

He laughed. "You say that every year, but I agree. They have possibilities. Why don't you come to the pub and grab a drink with us?"

The coaches were standing at the exit, waiting for an answer. I hadn't been to Jerry's Pub in weeks. I shrugged. "I don't know. I need to give her space."

"Are you giving her space or avoiding all contact?"

"Does it matter? She's been avoiding me."

Jamison chuckled. "She's been trying to wrap her head around the craziness she had to deal with. She's not avoiding you."

It seemed like it. "She asked me to give her space. I didn't. She wasn't happy with me and asked me to give her time. That's what I'm doing."

"You need to live, and you can't stay away from Jerry's Pub forever."

"Sure, I can. It's not the only place to eat in town."

"Maybe not, but it is the only place for good beer."

He had me there.

The guys hollered for us to join them.

I sighed heavily. "Fine. Let's go."

CHAPTER 35

SUSIE

I was thankful we were busy at work. My mind needed the distraction. After taking a break, which I spent talking with my father, I checked on tables and went to the bar to refill drinks.

"Looks like you and Terry are getting along," Trevor said as he filled a pitcher with beer.

I nodded. "We are. It won't be perfect overnight, but one step at a time."

He glanced over my shoulder as he put more glasses on my tray. "You're right. One step at a time. That works for everything." He tapped the bar twice and walked away to help customers.

I balanced the glasses on my tray. One step at a time seemed to work. I hadn't heard from Michael since he left town, and Terry and I were making amends. Things were looking up.

I smiled. My heart was lighter, as I turned with the tray in my hands, then stopped short.

Lance, Jamison, and a couple of other football coaches were sitting at a table in my section.

My gaze locked immediately on Lance, and my heart skipped a beat.

I hadn't seen him since he left the pub the night he hunted down Michael. From this distance, I could make out yellowing on his cheeks. I'd heard about his broken nose and how awful he'd looked. Rowan hadn't hesitated to joke about it.

I'd never even sent him a text to see for myself that he was okay. *God, I'm awful.* My eyes continued their scroll of rediscovery. His hair looked wet and tousled, probably from just finishing practice. My fingers itched to comb through it. He had a slight shadow of stubble on his face, and my hands yearned to brush over it. My heart swooned when his smirk covered his face. *Damn, I missed that smirk.*

"I can have Shannon take that table." Trevor's voice surprised me.

Shaking my head, I replied, "I can't avoid him forever. Like everyone keeps reminding me, it's a small town." I pushed my shoulders back and went to deliver the drinks to my other two tables.

I ignored the weight of Lance's gaze, which I felt on my back. Once my tray was empty, I placed a smile on my face and willed my heart and pulse to relax their psychotic rhythm.

"Hey, guys," I said, placing coasters on the table in front of each of them. "Just finish practice?"

"We did," Kent said. He sold insurance in town with his father. "It's going to be our year. The jamboree's coming up."

"Jamboree?" I asked.

"Yeah, it's when we host short games with local teams. It's a fun kickoff to the season. First Saturday in August," he added.

"You'll go," Jamison said. "It's a tradition. Just about the entire town does, and the girls will cheer."

I nodded. "Well, then, I guess I'll be there." I smiled. My first Orlinda Valley tradition. "What can I get y'all to drink? It's still happy hour. Two-for-one drafts."

They placed their food and drink orders. Lance's gaze was on me the entire time. Then it was his turn to order, and there was no avoiding him. My breath caught as our gazes locked.

"I'll just take my usual."

I nodded. "Got it." I smiled at him. "The Jerry's burger with everything, add jalapenos."

"Yep." His smile didn't quite meet his eyes and held something I couldn't quite place.

"I'll put the food order in and come right back with your beers."

Puffing out a breath, I walked away. *Round one successful.*

I typed in their order and waited on another table while I waited for their drinks.

"Here you go, guys," I said as I placed their beers on the table. "Your food will be a little bit."

"Great." Jamison grabbed his beer and stood. "Let's play a quick game of cornhole."

I turned to go.

"Susie, wait." Lance's voice sounded desperate.

I chewed on my lip and turned. "I'm busy, Lance."

"I know. I can see that. But give me a minute. Please?"

His sadness and desperation tugged at my heart. I nodded, placed my tray on the table, and took a seat.

"How've you been?" he asked.

I forced a smile onto my face. "I've been good."

He nodded, and the quiet between us became stifling and uncomfortable.

"Lance..."

"Susie..." he said at the same time.

We laughed.

"I'm sorry," he said quickly.

He seemed so serious, and my heart clenched. As my gaze lingered on his, I longed to reach out and grab his hand, brush my palm over the scruff on his face, and comb my fingers through his hair, but I wasn't ready. "I know, and I accept your apology."

His face lit up. "I miss you," he admitted.

"It's only been a few weeks." Damn, this was hard. I missed him so much it hurt, but I didn't want him to know that yet.

"I know, and I'm willing to wait, Susie. I just want you to know that."

I stood and picked the tray up from the table. "Thank you." I smiled and walked away to check on my other customers.

The rest of the night went slowly because I kept watching their table. Every once in a while, our eyes met, and my heart stuttered. When they left, I kept my eyes on Lance until the door closed behind them.

"You know, I never thought I'd see it, but he really cares about you," Trevor said as I wrapped silverware at the end of the night.

I didn't respond, just kept wrapping.

"Can I tell you something?"

I froze. His expression was serious and controlled. I nodded.

"I saw him flirting with you when you first got back in May. He was with Jayla then, and it really bothered me. Why would he flirt with you when he was already dating someone? I wasn't going to let him treat you like he had every other woman in this town. I liked you. I don't know if you knew that."

I chuckled and shrugged one shoulder. "I sort of did. Summer said something about it."

His cheeks reddened. "Of course." He put the tray of clean glasses away, then leaned on the bar. "Watching you talk with Lance grated on my nerves. I thought you were too good for him, and I was jealous. I'll admit it." He finished putting the glasses away and planted his hands on the counter. "I also admit when I'm wrong."

He stood up straight. "And I was wrong about Lance. He might have always been a womanizing royal pain in the ass, but he's been different since he's been with you. You've brought out the good side of him he had hidden away. Deep inside. Deep. Deep inside."

I laughed at his enunciation of the words. It was exactly what I'd thought of Lance the previous year.

He continued, "I know you're trying to figure stuff out, but once you do, maybe you should give Lance a second chance."

I reached across the bar and grabbed his hand. "Thank you. You're amazing."

"I know." He winked, tapped the bar twice, and walked into the kitchen.

CHAPTER 36

SUSIE

L ife went on as it always did.

We had a picnic on the Fourth of July at Tonya's and watched the fireworks in town. Lance wasn't there. He and Jamison had gone camping for the weekend. I was sure it was to avoid me, and I didn't blame him. Kristy, Rose, Kora, Darlene, Summer, and I entered a sand volleyball competition at Jerry's Pub. We didn't win but had a blast competing.

I was enjoying my life, getting to know my father, and loving my friends. It was the life I had always dreamed of—family, extended family, friends, and a town that wrapped their arms around me and accepted me. Everything about me—crappy past and all—and I loved every minute of it.

I also got to know Kora better as we spent time together. We kayaked on the river, cared for the goats, and enjoyed the newly hatched chickens. Mr. Kitty followed me wherever I went around the farm. He loved hanging out with the other animals.

Life was good, and I was in a good place.

"I was at the school yesterday, as you know," Kora said as we returned from tending the goats one afternoon. "We have an assistant position open this coming year. It's not great pay, but you'll get all the benefits, get your foot in the door without the responsibility, and see if maybe you want to step back into teaching one day."

I glanced at Kora and turned away. An assistant position might be perfect.

"What do you think? If you're interested, I can let the principal know. I'm sure he'll get you in for an interview."

"Yeah, okay. I think I'd like that." I could still work part time at Jerry's a couple nights a week and on the weekends.

"Great." Kora's face lit up as she sent a text. "There. He knows."

I laughed. "You have the principal's number on your phone?" That wouldn't be something that happened in South Dakota.

"Yes, I've known him most of my life. He graduated with Jamison and Lance. His wife teaches fifth grade."

"Only in a small town would everyone know each other, and husbands and wives work together."

"Maybe," Kora said. "But I wouldn't know how it is anywhere else. I've only lived here."

"I know. And this is exactly what I picture whenever I read a small-town romance book." I placed my arm around Kora's shoulders as we crossed the yard. "I'm glad Kai found Orlinda Valley and met you. It has changed the trajectory of our lives, and now with me being an aunt soon, life can't be much better."

Kora laced her arm around my waist as Mr. Kitty ran to us and plopped in front of me. I stooped and picked him up.

"I know someone who wishes he could be a part of your amazing new life," Kora said.

I raised my eyes to her and followed her gaze. Kai and Lance were emptying lumber from the back of Kai's truck.

My heart fluttered as I watched Lance lift stacks of wood from the truck and place them in a pile on the ground.

Don't show Kora you care that he's here. "What's Kai building now?" *Good distraction question.*

"He's been wanting an extra storage shed for the lawnmower and whatever else so we can use the garage for actual cars. I guess that's what he's building."

"Hey, ladies," Kai said as he dropped the last load of lumber on the ground. Then he came to Kora and kissed her.

A smile filled my face as I watched them. They were made for each other, and he was made for life in a town with friends and family. It was as if our past had never existed.

He and I had walked the property a few weeks ago, and I asked him how he'd moved on and put the past behind him. His words came back to me.

"I didn't put it behind me, but I came to terms with it." He also said, "Because of the struggles we went through and the choices I made, I knew what kind of life I wanted. I swore to myself when I left Atlanta that I wouldn't go down that road again. I would change my life. I know I was led to Orlinda Valley and to Kora. She and her family accepted me even with my flaws and my past, and they loved me despite them. She made me a better person."

Mr. Kitty meowed at Lance. He reached down and petted him. "He's gotten so big."

I smiled but had no clue what to say.

"Hey, y'all, we'd love to stay and chat, but we have to get ready for Susie's party tonight. See you later, Lance," Kora said.

Mr. Kitty bounded after Kora and Kai toward the house.

Lance and I laughed as we watched him. I kept my attention on the kitten until he was out of sight.

"I'll be right back." Lance walked to his truck, opened the door, and pulled out a pot with beautiful blue irises.

"Happy birthday." He held out the pot to me.

"Who told you it was my birthday?" I asked.

He shrugged. "Don't know. I'm sure it was either Lilly or Kai."

"These are beautiful, Lance."

His blue eyes were so welcoming. They pulled me in, and my pulse picked up.

"It's not much," he said and placed the pot on the ground. "I wanted to give you something that would last. You can plant these, and they'll come back every year. I wanted something that represented you, and irises symbolize courage, wisdom, and hope. And that's you. The courage to face your past, the wisdom to find what you're looking for, and the hope for the future you desire."

Irises have always been my favorite flowers. They symbolized exactly what he said, and I always thought that was beautiful. My heart skipped many beats. "Do you want to stay for dinner? Kora and Kai are making a big deal of my birthday."

He gave me his sexy smirk, and my pulse raced. "Kai already asked me," he said

My gaze traveled over him and took in his features. He was so handsome, and the look in his eyes was sincere. My heart swooned. He was here. He was being respectful, and he'd brought me a gift, but so much more needed to be said.

I smiled shyly and shoved my hands into my pockets when he walked toward me. My stomach was all muddled up, and my pulse raced. I sucked my bottom lip and took a deep breath. "Lance, I..."

My words faltered. I didn't know what to say to him. *How can I put these feelings into words?*

When I looked up, his gaze held mine. The emotions I saw there made my heart leap.

He grabbed my hands. "Susie, I know I told you I'd give you space and time. If you still need it, you've got it. I just wanted to see you and say happy birthday. The flowers aren't much, but I hope that maybe I could make good on that date I talked about, and we could go to dinner one day soon."

He paused, searching my eyes. His gaze left heat everywhere it touched.

He squeezed my hands. "Look, I know going after Michael was stupid. Fighting him was uncalled for. I know it's not what you wanted, but I..." He shook his head and puffed out a breath. "This is so hard," he said as he looked behind me.

I'd never seen him have a hard time with anything. Lance was always so sure of himself and everything. He wore confidence like a badge of honor.

He continued, and his gaze met my eyes. "I've never needed or wanted to be with a woman as much as I want to be with you. I miss you. I miss us. I miss what I am when I'm with you. You make me want to be a better person." He released my hands and combed his fingers through his hair. "I don't know how else to say this." He cupped my face in his hands.

His gaze became serious, and my heart skipped a beat.

He rubbed his thumbs across my cheeks. "I love you, Susie."

My eyes widened, and my breath ceased for a moment.

He laughed, dropped his hands, and looked at the sky. "I'm sorry. That's not how I wanted it to come out," he said, stepping forward.

My throat went dry. My pulse raced so fast it was like I had just finished a marathon. *He loved me.* The only people I'd ever told I loved them were Kai and Sebastian, and that was totally different.

But this kind of love? I'd never considered it before.

"Susie, I don't want to make this more awkward than it already is. I don't expect you to say anything." He shook his head. "I just need you to know that what I see happening between us is different from what I've ever had with another woman. No woman has ever made me feel like this. You make me a better person. You make me care for people more than I care for myself." He laughed. "That sounds crazy and egotistical. But I've been called an egotistical ass quite a few times in my life."

I laughed. "I think those words came out of my mouth a few times over the past few months." I squeezed his hand. "But I was wrong. Lance, you're not an egotistical ass," I said, stepping closer. "I don't know what I feel, but I feel something for you. And until I'm sure of what it is, until I know without a doubt, I hope you can be okay with the fact that I really like you. And I miss you."

He stepped closer and brushed a hand across my cheek. "You miss me?" His smile lit up his face.

I nodded as a shiver shot down my spine at his touch. My pulse calmed, my heart slowed, and my body warmed. *I miss this.*

I missed how his touch made me feel needed, wanted, desired, safe. I'd never had that before.

"Susie, I've got to ask you something, and if it's no, it's okay. So please only answer yes if you truly want to agree to it."

I tilted my head, confused. "What is it, Lance?"

"Can I kiss you?"

All he wants is to kiss me?

My eyes darted to his lips, and memories of having those lips on mine, on my body, the warmth, the tingling, and the sensations it caused filled my mind. My heart stuttered, and I chuckled. "No one has ever asked for permission to kiss me. But it's all I want. I've missed your lips on mine. I've missed your warmth. So yes, please. Kiss me."

His smile grew and met his eyes. He grasped my neck and pulled my face toward him.

We were millimeters apart. I could smell him. His scent was outdoorsy, masculine, Lance.

I licked my lips, and our lips finally met.

All the air escaped from my lungs as his taste filled my senses. His tongue asked for entrance, and I readily obliged. I wrapped my arms around his neck and held him tightly to me.

This kiss. Wow.

I hadn't realized until that moment how much I really missed him. My heart swooned, and warmth slipped deep into my bones. When we broke apart, I kept my eyes tightly shut, wanting to remember that feeling and his taste long after he left me.

When my eyes fluttered open, he stared deep into them. "Thank you," he whispered. "Thank you for not walking away from me."

"Lance, I can't walk away from you." I laced my fingers through his. "Will you stay and be my date for the party tonight?"

The corners of his eyes wrinkled. "I wasn't planning on coming, since I wasn't talking with the birthday girl, but since she asked so nicely..." He kissed my lips gently. "I think I will."

I got lost again in Lance as our lips danced together. I took a deep breath when we broke apart to calm my erratic heart.

"The flowers and an invitation to dinner seem like a pretty small gift for such an amazing woman."

"Be a good boy, and I'm sure she could come up with something else you can give her." I held his gaze.

"How long will this party last? I hope it's not too long."

"Hopefully not."

"Let me run home and get cleaned up. I'll be back in a little over an hour," he said, then gave me another quick kiss.

I waved as he pulled out of the driveway and carried the pot of irises to the backyard. My heart soared. Lance and I were together again. *This is the perfect birthday present.*

CHAPTER 37

SUSIE

"I can never get over how crazy this town is for football," I said as Kristy and I climbed out of her car. We had parked at the Orlinda Valley Methodist Church across the street from the high school since the parking lot was already full an hour before kickoff.

"Friday night lights are a real thing. Just wait until you see how sad things are once the season is over. Basketball is fun, but it's not quite the same."

"Hey, Susie," Nancy, a teacher I worked with at the elementary school, waved as she, her husband, and her young son walked across the lot.

I waved back.

"So, did you decide to take the interim position when Nancy goes on maternity leave?" Kristy asked me.

Nancy was due at the beginning of December and was planning on taking the rest of the year off. I nodded. "They offered, and I said yes." I enjoyed being a teacher's assistant but was ready to get back into the classroom. The interim job was a perfect steppingstone.

"I heard she may not go back after the baby," Kristy said.

We made it to the gate, paid the admission, and walked toward the home stands. "I heard the same. We'll see." I wasn't going to get my hopes up, though I would love her job.

We found Lilly, Rose, Kora, Darlene, and Summer sitting with the book club women. Nolan, Bryson, and Rowan were with the boys and the grandfathers, playing football.

I waved at Madeline, Lena, and Darcie, who were on the field with the mini cheerleaders. They did small cheers and one dance at halftime. They always looked so cute in their mini-cheer uniforms.

It seemed the entire town showed up every week, and that year, the team had been undefeated in their first few games. I tried not to talk too much about it with Lance, as he was very superstitious when it came to football season.

I made eye contact with him when they came on the field, and as usual, he winked, and I blew him a kiss.

"God, you two are disgusting," Summer said.

Kora laughed. "And you and Rowan aren't? Please. You two are stuck together like Velcro."

"That's the truth. You need to get married already," Darlene said. "Pick a date. What are you waiting for?"

"If you must know," Summer said, "we did."

"What?" we all said in unison. Summer and Rowan had gotten engaged back in May, but as far as we all knew, they hadn't decided on when or where.

She turned toward Tonya. "You really kept a secret?"

"Of course not. These ladies know. I just didn't make it public knowledge."

"Now we can say congratulations," Kaye said. "A spring wedding in Tonya's backyard will be perfect."

"Spring?" I asked. "That's such a perfect time of year. What month?"

"March. My grandmother's birthday, to be exact."

We all congratulated her as the game got started.

After four exciting quarters, the Orlinda Valley Tigers came out with another win.

"Thank you, God," I said. I hadn't yet had the experience of dealing with Lance after a loss, but the Lance I got after a win was fun and exciting. Our celebration after our dinner at Jerry's Pub was always memorable.

⋰

We were at Jerry's Pub, had finished our meal and our celebratory drinks, and were on the dance floor. This ritual was another thing I hadn't thought was real. Every Friday night after the team got a victory, the town celebrated at Jerry's Pub. I could no longer be in the background and invisible while dating the head football coach.

I stared up into Lance's eyes and leaned in for a kiss. It was sweet and lingering. I pulled away with a smile on my lips. "I love watching you out there doing your thing. You're so relaxed and excited. You're like a kid on Christmas morning." I combed my fingers through his hair.

"I *feel* like a kid on Christmas morning. I'm living my dream. Coaching at the school I attended, a beautiful woman in my arms. I love everything about my life."

My gaze trailed over his face. I was calm and sure of myself in Lance's arms. I looked over his shoulder. Kai held Kora tightly as they swayed to the music, a look of peace filled his face.

We'd both finally found a family.

Lance brushed his knuckles over my cheek, and the now familiar flutters filled my stomach. My eyes met his, and I knew without a doubt I was home. "Thank you, Lance."

He raised his eyebrows but didn't respond.

That was so much like him. His patience with me was epic. Once, I'd asked him how he could be so patient, and he said, "I have faith that you will always be honest with me."

But I hadn't been.

I hadn't told him everything he needed to know. I'd let my insecurities keep one little wedge between us without a reason. "Thank you for being so understanding and giving me the time I've needed to sort out the chaos that is my life."

"You're not chaos," he said. "You're the calm before the storm."

"See? You always say the sweetest things. You always encourage me. Help me see what I can really do. You once said I make you a better person, but you do the same to me. I was nothing before I opened my heart to you. I was just getting through the days and didn't think I deserved anything wonderful. But you proved me wrong."

I looked deep into his eyes, my heart thumping wildly. "Lance, you help me believe in myself, and you make me believe in family. You encourage me to see joy in the small things. You made me believe in forever, and I love you."

We stopped moving, and a smile slowly filled his face.

My heart skipped a beat.

"What did you say?" he asked, blinking rapidly.

I tilted my head back and laughed. "You grabbed hold of my heart and didn't let go. No matter what I gave you, what I asked, you never gave up on me, or us. You've loved me through everything, and I love you." I said it with confidence, which Lance brought out of me.

He held my face in his hands, and his eyes traveled across my features. "God, that sounds perfect." He kissed me, a smile pressing against my lips. "I don't think I'll ever tire of hearing those words from you."

He kissed me again. Everything about this was perfect. Warmth spread through my body, and my heartbeat sped up.

When he pulled away, his face lit up. He laughed as he picked me up and spun me in a circle.

Couples stopped dancing.

"She loves me," he yelled to everyone who could hear over the music.

Heat covered my face, and I pulled his arm. "Lance, quiet."

"What? Everyone needs to know." He turned back to the crowd. "Did everyone hear? She loves me!" Laughter and cheers filled the room. He held my face in his hands. "It's okay. I love you. You love me. Life is perfect."

We kissed. He was right. Life was perfect, and my heart was full in a way I'd never thought possible.

EPILOGUE

THREE MONTHS
LATER-DECEMBER

"There, that should do it." I jumped off the table I'd been standing on to reach the top of the balloon arch.

"Perfect," Kora said.

Kristy and Lilly stood back, admiring their work on the second arch. We were decorating the field for the celebration that was going to take place later that afternoon.

"Lance and Jamison are more excited about this than the rest of the team," Lilly said with a smile as she rubbed her enormous belly. "It's a good thing the boys waited until after the game."

"True. If you'd gone into labor during the playoffs or the championships, you would have had the twins on your own," Kristy said.

"No, the book club would have stood in for Jamison," Kora added.

"Good lord. That would have been a show," Lilly said with a laugh.

"No kidding," Kora said.

I stood back and looked around the stadium. Balloon arches in blue and gold were at the field entrance, and a small stage was set up in the center. The town had planned a parade for the team, scheduled for around two, when the team should get back.

The entire town came out to celebrate the Orlinda Valley Tigers' state championship game win, the first one since Jamison and Lance's senior year. To say they were ecstatic was an understatement.

The parade would wind through town, ending at the stadium. The band was going to play, and the cheerleaders were going to cheer—including the minis. Darcie, Madeline, and Lena were so excited.

"Let's grab food at the pharmacy and get ready for the parade," Kora said as she rubbed her protruding belly. "My little buddy and I are starving."

"That sounds good," Lilly answered. "But my feet are killing me. I need to stay here. I brought water and snacks. I'm not walking anywhere."

"Yeah, well, we told you we didn't need your help, and your mom said she'd bring you once the girls passed in the parade," Kristy said.

"There was no way I was going to miss decorating. You don't know how excited my husband is."

"No kidding," I piped in. "He and Lance have been talking about this for months, and now it's here."

The team had an amazing undefeated season. Lance said I was his good-luck charm, and I told him he was crazy. I enjoyed the roller coaster ride that was his emotions every game day. His excitement about the game of football was contagious. I had never really watched any sports before, but they had become part of my life.

Kristy stayed at the field to keep Lilly company, and Kora and I walked to Orlinda Valley Pharmacy, where a grill had been set up outside, and food was being sold to the people waiting to be a part of the festivities. Then we joined everyone in front of Shear Perfection. Tom and Charles had set up a tent, and they were all sitting under it. Yes, it was December, but it was sunny and sixty, a perfect day.

"Rose sent me a text," Ruth said. "The parade is ready to start."

We heard the sirens of the fire trucks before we saw the parade. "I hope there's no emergency today," I said to Kora over the noise. I could have sworn every firetruck and police car was in the parade.

"No kidding."

The mini-cheerleaders led the procession. Madeline, Darcie, and Lena waved enthusiastically when they saw us.

Then the alderman and mayor walked by, waving, and the mayor beamed with pride. You'd think it was his victory.

The Pee Wee football league was next. James stood tall, with his hands behind his back. Just the previous night, he'd been bragging about how he was going to be the next big thing on the high school team, like both his uncles. Bryson wasn't happy about it and tried to get him to run for class officer instead.

James wanted nothing to do with it. According to him, it was the Heisman Trophy or nothing.

It's good to have big dreams.

The band marched behind the Pee Wee teams and finally came the football team. My face lit up when Lance's gaze met mine. He winked, and I blew him a kiss.

Those of us who could walk were to file behind the team and make our way to the field.

The air was electric with excitement, and Lance grabbed my arm. "Walk with me."

I laughed and let him pull me into the parade.

Growing up, I'd been okay with being invisible and blending into the background, but being with Lance made that impossible. I now found myself front and center of all the attention. Everyone in town loved Lance. There was nowhere we could go without someone stopping him to talk.

The walk to the field was short. When we separated, I kissed him and went to the stands.

The mayor gave a quick welcome speech and introduced the team. The crowd roared with excitement.

I looked around the stands. School spirit and town pride were everywhere. The stands were filled with the same blue and gold as the balloon arch on the field. Orlinda Valley Tiger shirts were everywhere. The air was electric with excitement, and I was a part of it all. A thrill swept through my body.

Lance and Jamison walked to the center of the stage to award the MVP trophies. Lance was in his element, and I swelled with pride.

"All right, everyone." Lance raised a hand to get the sizable crowd's attention.

I didn't know how he stood there, in charge of all those people, and wasn't a nervous wreck. He amazed me in so many ways.

"We need the wives, parents, and girlfriends of the coaches and team members to join us, please."

Lilly and I looked at each other. *What is he doing?* That would be a lot of people. "You good?" I asked her.

She nodded, and I walked at a slow pace with her toward the stage.

The parents stood in front of the stage with the team, and the coaches' wives and girlfriends climbed the stairs to join the men. Jamison helped Lilly, and Lance pulled me next to him, wrapping an arm around my waist. I was front and center and very exposed.

I searched the crowd until I found Kai and Kora together. Terry stood with them. They both smiled at me.

"We asked the families up here because football is a team sport, and we couldn't be such a successful team this year without all of you willing to give us your time and make sure the boys...and the men...could be at every practice. We thank you so much for your dedication."

He turned to the wives on the stage. "Wives, girlfriends..." He winked at me, which made my heart turn to mush. "It's not easy loving a football coach. This job takes time away from you and your families, but without the support of these coaches, these young men would not have reached their goals, and we wouldn't be state champs!" He yelled the last two words, and the crowd went crazy, the band played the fight song, and he and Jamison held up the trophy.

The excitement on his face was contagious, and it infected everyone.

As the cheering died down, Lance got the crowd's attention again. "Okay, everyone. This was a successful year, but next year can be even better." A cheer went up again, but he silenced it quickly with a hand in the air.

A look passed between him and Jamison, who gave him a nod, then stepped up and took the microphone from the stand and held it in front of Lance.

I looked at Jamison through narrowed eyes, but he ignored me. I turned to Lance, who wiped his hands on his pants and puffed out a breath. His eyes locked on mine, and butterflies took flight in my gut. His smile wavered as he reached into his pocket.

"Susie," he started. A hush fell over the crowd.

I looked around. No one moved. Not even the breeze stirred. The only sounds were birds chirping in a tree somewhere and a baby crying quietly.

"I love you, Susie. You've made my life complete. You're exactly what I was always looking for yet didn't know it. You bring out the best in me, and I hope you'll stay with me for the rest of our lives."

I glanced at Lilly. She had her hand over her mouth. When I looked back at Lance, he was kneeling on the ground in front of me.

An audible gasp came from the crowd. *Or was it me?* I had no clue.

"Make me the happiest man ever and say you'll marry me," he said, and held up a ring.

Marriage? We'd talked about spending our lives together. I loved him with every bit of my soul. *But marriage?*

I stood there, staring at him. My heart pounded out of my chest. Nerves shook me to the core. I glanced around. All eyes were on us.

"Sweetness, it's just me," Lance said as he stood again. "It's okay." He held my chin and tipped my eyes to his. "Look at me. Focus. On. Me."

And I did. My attention locked onto Lance, and my universe fell into place. He was my rock. He was my support. He was my life, and he held my heart.

Tears filled my eyes, and I tried to clear my throat to find my voice, but I couldn't. Instead, I nodded, slowly at first. I knew when he understood, because he smiled.

"Is that a yes?" he asked.

I held his gaze as a tear fell down my cheek. "Yes," I whispered as I nodded vigorously.

He let out a yell. "You said yes?"

I laughed. "Yes," I said more loudly. "Absolutely yes."

He slipped the ring onto my finger. It was a round diamond that sparkled under the lights. I glanced at Lance, my heart full.

He pulled me to him, and our lips met in a restrained kiss the entire town was a witness to, then he wrapped me in his strong arms. "Damn, you scared the shit out of me," he whispered in my ear.

I chuckled. "You scared the shit out of *me*."

He chuckled and squeezed me tightly. Then pulled away. "I love you forever and a day, sweetness," he said with a hand on my waist and another on my cheek.

"I love you forever and a day plus one," I answered.

The cheer of the crowd was deafening, but it disappeared when Lance's lips met mine again, and I became lost in him.

When we broke apart, I peered into his eyes, and it was there that I found love, I found joy, and I found home.

***

Thank you for reading No Heart But Yours. Check out my website for all future releases, to join my newsletter, and everything else about my writing journey. **www.donnarmadden.com**

ACKNOWLEDGEMENTS

The journey from No One But You to No Heart But Yours has been so much fun. When I started this self-publishing journey four years ago, I had no idea where it would lead, but it has led me to meeting so many wonderful new friends.

Thank you to everyone who has shown me support on social media—especially TikTok. Your support and dedication to my romance novels are appreciated more than you will ever know.

To my marketing guru and cover designer, Emily Hensley from Small Fry Marketing—I appreciate you so much, and even though I can be difficult to work with at times, keep on pushing me.

To my friend and proofreader, Melissa Weisner, thank you for all your help. I couldn't have done this without your support.

Then, of course, is my family. Tonia—keep forcing me to write and letting me know when things aren't working, and when they are. You are the best beta reader around.

Sean, I know I spend a lot of my free time writing. Thank you for supporting me. One day it will all be worth it.

About the Author

Donna R. Madden has been happily married to her husband for over 30 years—proof that true love exists. Together they've raised three amazing boys, and they did something right because they all made it to adulthood.

When Donna's not dealing with the chaos that is her life, she is dreaming up stories which are possibly inspired by real-life situations (remember the chaos discussed above).

She also enjoys sitting beachside, poolside, or on her front porch swing with a drink in one hand and a book in the other.

Drop her a line. She loves to hear from her readers: author@donnarmadden.com

www.ingramcontent.com/pod-product-compliance
Lightning Source LLC
Chambersburg PA
CBHW050025120726
47903CB00006B/1910